Joseph Henry Hilts

Experiences of a Backwoods Preacher

Joseph Henry Hilts

Experiences of a Backwoods Preacher

ISBN/EAN: 9783337338404

Printed in Europe, USA, Canada, Australia, Japan

Cover: Foto ©Andreas Hilbeck / pixelio.de

More available books at **www.hansebooks.com**

EXPERIENCES

OF A

BACKWOODS PREACHER

OR,

FACTS AND INCIDENTS

CULLED FROM

THIRTY YEARS OF MINISTERIAL LIFE.

BY

REV. JOSEPH H. HILTS,

A Member of the Guelph Conference of the Methodist Church.

SECOND EDITION.

TORONTO:

METHODIST MISSION ROOMS,

WESLEY BUILDINGS.

1892.

DEDICATION.

—•—

TO THE HONEST TOILERS

WHO HAVE CARRIED THE BURDENS, ENDURED THE HARDSHIPS, AND
SUFFERED THE PRIVATIONS, OF PIONEER LIFE,

This Book is respectfully Dedicated,

AS A SLIGHT TOKEN OF REGARD FOR THE COURAGE AND ENERGY
THAT HAVE CHANGED THE WILDERNESS INTO BEAUTIFUL
FARMS AND HOMESTEADS; AND FOUNDED CITIES,
TOWNS AND VILLAGES UPON THE WASTE
PLACES OF OUR COUNTRY.

TO THE READER.

To WALK together in harmony two must be agreed. This is Bible sentiment, and it is as applicable to going through a book as it is to walking along a country road or a city street.

But no two independent thinkers can reasonably expect to see exactly alike in every particular. The best thing that they can do is to agree to differ without alienation or contention.

In writing the following pages I have stated many facts and incidents. For the substantial truthfulness of every line I can vouch without any misgivings. But I have also given my opinions on a variety of things. Of the correctness of these you must judge for yourself.

You will find some things that will not suit you ; and you will say things that would not suit me, if I could hear them. So that in the matter of fault-finding we will come out about even.

But, on the other hand, you will find some things that you will like, and you will say some things that I would like, if I could hear them. So that in the matter of appreciation and approval we may reckon ourselves to be about even also.

Now, with this understanding at the start, you may safely commence the perusal of the book, and I hope that in going through it you will have a pleasant time, and that we will be no less friends when we part at the conclusion of your task than we were at the beginning of it.

The book has been written almost entirely from memory, and in calling upon that faculty to furnish the materials that fill the following pages, I have found some difficulty in determining what to select and what to exclude, as I could not find room for all the matter presented by that faithful recorder of passing events.

I have made no effort to produce a sensational volume ; nor have I attempted anything like fine writing. I simply tried to write so as to avoid dulness on the one hand and frivolity on the other. How far I have succeeded in doing this you must decide, and for that decision I wait with some solicitude.

J. H. H.

CONTENTS.

Experiences of a Backwoods Preacher

CHAPTER I.

PRELIMINARY.

ONLY a few biographies are worth the time spent in either writing or reading them. To make that kind of literature a success it requires an extraordinary subject to write about, and a first-class genius to do the writing. When one of these factors is wanting, any attempt to produce a work of that sort will almost certainly end in disappointment and vexation. The cartloads of "biographies," partly fiction and partly something worse, that are thrown upon the market and read by both old and young, are useful only as indicators. The fact that they find readers goes to prove that people are fond of facts and incidents.

But much of this kind of writing is like garments made without any measurement. They can be made to *hang* on almost any one, but they will really *fit* nobody. Just so the descriptions of life given in many of these books are mere distortions as compared with the real, active, every-day doings of living humanity. To magnify or minify either the virtues or vices of men and women is not to give correct views of individual or social life.

But while all this is true, there are many incidents in almost any lengthened life that are of sufficient importance to deserve a record.

In this chapter I propose to relate a few incidents in my own life before I commence to give the experiences that I have had as a minister in the backwoods.

I was born in the township of Clinton, in the county of Lincoln, Upper Canada, May fourth, eighteen hundred and nineteen. My parents were both children of U. E. Loyalists, so that on both sides I claim descent from those whose loyalty cost them something, and whose attachment to Britain and her institutions led them to leave good homes in the States and come into the wilderness of Canada to make new homes for themselves, where, under the protection of the British flag, they might be safe, and under the shade of the maple leaf they might be contented.

My father did military duty during the LAST year of the war of eighteen hundred and twelve, and at the close of the war he was granted land in what was then called the *new purchase,* on the north of Lake Ontario.

When I was a few weeks past three years old my parents moved to their home in the wilderness, it being on the last lot in the ninth concession of the township of Esquesing, in the county of Halton. The home consisted of a log shanty that my father had put up

the summer previous, and about an acre of clearing
that had been done at the same time.

Among the first things that I can remember is looking at the shanty the day that we arrived. It seemed
to me that it was a strange-looking house, with its

PIONEERS AT WORK.

bark roof and stick chimney and floor of hewed logs,
and its door of split cedar, and its one light of glass
for a window. But that little unpretentious building
was our home for several years. At that time I had a
little younger sister and a baby brother two months
old. They have both gone over to the great company

on the other side of the river. The sister went more than fifty years ago, and brother within the last few months. My father had a brother who had settled the year before on an adjoining lot, and another brother came in the following year and settled near by, so that his life in the new country was not so lonesome as it otherwise would have been.

Not long after we had got settled in our new home, one evening about sundown we were treated to an impromptu chorus by some of the denizens of the forest, which was, in hunter's language, *the howling of a pack of wolves.* To describe the peculiar music made by "a pack of wolves" would be too much for the genius of a Dickens or the poetic power of a Scott.

To one who never heard the sound before, the impression would likely be that the noise came out of the ground. At first he hears a plaintive tone, as if low down on the minor scale. Then it seems to ascend step by step until the highest major notes are reached. And, what seems most strange of all, is that the lower tones do not cease as the higher are produced ; but they continue right on until the listeners hear sounds that represent every note on the musical scale, from the lowest minor to the highest major, including all the transpositions.

My father was a blacksmith by trade, and he had brought some of his tools with him, and among the rest an anvil. When the wolves commenced to make the woods vocal with their musical efforts, father thought that he would give them as much of a surprise as they had given us. So he loaded up the anvil with

a heavy charge of powder, and set it off with a coal
that he held with a pair of tongs. The noise produced
by the firing of that anvil was, perhaps, the most
startling sound that had ever awakened the echoes of
these forest wilds. When the anvil went off, at first
the report seemed to pass away, but as the sound
struck the wall of the tall forest trees that surrounded
the little clearing it seemed to be broken into fragments
which came back to us like a thousand distinct echoes.
But the wolves seemed frightened, and we heard no
more of them for that time. It was not long, however,
before they made their presence known in a more tan-
gible way than by making a noise. My father brought
some cattle with him. One was a nice heifer two
years old. One morning just outside of the clearing
the bones of the heifer were found picked by the
wolves. The first settlers often lost their cows and
young cattle in this way. And for some years the life
of a sheep was worth nothing, unless kept in an
inclosure with a fence so high that a wolf could not
get over it.

And the black bears were by no means scarce in the
locality, as more than one empty pig-pen bore its testimony in the early days of the settlement. I might
relate almost any number of " bear stories " if it would
be desirable to do so, but I will relate one at all events.
One of my uncles had left the place that he first
located on, and had gone on a lot a mile and a half
away from any house right into the solid bush. One
morning about the break of day the loud squealing of
a pig awakened him. He had two nice pigs in a pen

near his house, and it was one of these that was making the noise. He ran out in a hurry to see what was the matter. He saw a large black bear clambering out of the pen and dragging one of the pigs after it. He picked up a handspike and began to belabour the bear with such force that it dropped the pig which was almost dead, and ran off towards the woods. My uncle put the pig upon a shed, and started to get help to catch the bear. By nine o'clock he returned with a lot of men, and dogs, and guns, which belonged to a sort of Club that had been formed for hunting bear and wolves. When they came they found that bruin had returned and carried away the pig from off the shed. They set the dogs on the trail, and started in pursuit of the depredator. They had gone about a half a mile in the woods, when they came to the place where his bearship had made a hasty breakfast off the stolen pork. He left the remains for more voracious and less fastidious eaters than himself, while he went on to find a safe retreat where undisturbed he might enjoy his noonday snooze without molestation. But the dogs soon stirred him up, and started him off at a rapid rate, while by their barking they gave notice to the hunters that they had found the bear.

The chase now became very lively, and from the fact that the bear did not take to a tree, the inference was that he was a very large one, which proved to be true. After a run of three or four miles, the hunters came up to the dogs, and found the bear in a small pond. Part of the dogs were in the water, and the bear apparently was trying to drown them by dipping them under the water with his paws. The men were afraid to shoot, lest they should kill the dogs, which refused to leave the bear, and he as stubbornly refused to come out of the water. At length, one of the men took a gun loaded with two bullets, and he waded into where he could place the muzzle of the gun to the bear's ear and fired the whole charge into its head. In a minute it was lying dead in the water. The men pulled it out and found it to be a very large and fat one. In skinning the carcase they found traces of old bullet wounds. By following the tracks they found no less than six balls, all of one size, with the flesh grown up around them. It was quite evident that at some time the poor brute had formed a very painful acquaintance with lead, but whether it belonged to white men or Indians no one could tell. But I must leave the bears and wolves to themselves, and write about something of more importance.

Our First Pastoral Visit.

The first minister to visit our home in the bush was a Methodist by the name of Heyland. Though it was more than sixty years ago, it seems as fresh in my mind as if it was but a few months since. In front of our shanty there was a good-sized creek, over which had been made a temporary footbridge of poles to walk on. One day my mother was standing in the door, and seeing a man trying to feel his way over the creek, she called father to go and see who it was, and if he needed help. When father got to him, he found that the man was near-sighted. This was why he had to feel for his way.   Father assisted him over the creek, and brought him into the shanty.   Then the man said, " My name is Heyland ; I am a Methodist minister ; I am hunting for the scattered sheep in the wilderness." Not understanding what he meant, I went up to mother and whispered to her, "If the wolves that killed our heifer find his sheep, they will not be worth much to him when he finds them." She replied to me that the good man did not mean sheep with wool on, but he spoke of the people who were scattered in the wilderness.   Mr. Heyland had prayer, after which he talked to my parents on religious subjects for a while, and then after laying his hand on the head of each one of us children, and devoutly asking God to bless all of us, he went away to visit other families.   Who can estimate the value of such a visit.   Little did Mr. Heyland or my parents think, that after more than threescore years, the coarse-looking, awkward boy, who then stood listening to their talk, would, with a swelling heart and a tear-dimmed eye, write about the visit of the pioneer preacher to one of the pioneer families.

Who can even form a conjecture of the amount of the influence that the Methodist preachers have exerted on the social and religious life of the people of this country.

They have greatly assisted in laying the foundations of the social structure.   They have heard almost the first echoes of the woodman's axe, and they have gone to encourage him in his toil.   They have impressed their teaching and their influence upon the hearts and minds of thousands of the children of the pioneer families of this Province as no other class of men has done. There can be no doubt on the question. The religious element of Canadian society owes very much to Methodism.

Our First School House.

About four years after the founding of the settlement, the scattered population concluded to put up a log building that would serve the double purpose of school and meeting-house. They met together and laid their plans, and in a few days a very comfortable little house was ready for use on the corner of Nathaniel Rossell's lot, where the little village of Ballinafad now stands. This same man gave a burying ground, and then in after years he gave land for a church and parsonage, and a piece for a temperance hall. One way or another this good man gave to the public, and to the Lord, nearly half of the front of one hundred acres. And yet he would blush if called a Christian. He was one of the modest, unassuming kind of men.

After the house was up, the next thing was to find a teacher. It was not long before an old man came along and took the school for six months. His name was Pitcher. He was to have a certain sum for each scholar, and to board around among the people. He was a widower, and he had a boy with' him named Peter, who was to board along with his father, and the price of his board came out of the amounts of charges for scholars.

Well the school started in due time. I wish I could

give a picture of that first assemblage of students in Professor Pitcher's academy for young backwoods hopefuls. The dominie himself was a big fat man, with a florid face and a bald head. He would sometimes go to sleep in his home made and bark-bottom chair. Then Peter would take the water-beech rod out of his father's hand and keep things going till the old man got through his slumbers. The subjects taught were, the alphabet, spelling, reading, and the first lessons in writing. That was all.

My mother had led me through the mysteries of the A B C's and A B ab's, so that I was among the advanced students from the first.

How shall I describe the scholars. No two of them were dressed alike, and scarcely any two had books alike. One boy would have a hat without a rim, and another boy would have one with only half a crown. One girl wore a frock (so called at that time) made of home made linen, and another girl had one made of home made flannel, while still another would be clad in "linsey-woolsey," which was a combination of the two. But in that same school rosy cheeks were very common, and smutty faces by no means scarce nor unpopular.

If the ghost of that school could be called up in one of our present well equipped high schools, what a wonderful contrast would be seen. What a grand illustration of the theory of evolution would be presented. The difference between the school in which Professor Pitcher wielded the beech rod, and the one presided over by one of our learned and worthy B. A.'s, would be about as great as that between Professor Darwin and the long-tailed, chattering little quadruped that he claims for an ancestor.

The first religious services were held in the school house soon after it was completed. Among the ministers whose names I can still recall were Belton, Shaler, Rose, Williams and Demorest. One man, whose looks I remember but whose name I have forgotten, was among the first after Mr. Heyland.

The meetings were held on a week day, and it was surprising to see the way the people would leave their work to attend Divine service. This was continued for several years.

The first religious awakening was brought about in a rather mysterious manner. A man named John Teetzel, who lived near where Acton now is, was thrown on a sick bed. He thought he was going to die. He had been a wicked man. In seeking some one to pray with him, he learned that in all the families for miles around no one could be found to do it. He then thought that he was lost. But just as he was about sinking into despair, the Lord spoke peace to his soul and gave him the joys of salvation. He then and there pledged himself to God that he would consecrate his life to Him. And he faithfully kept his promise.

As soon as he got well, he sought out the Methodist ministers, and they took him into the Church. He at once commenced to hold meetings on Sabbath days around in private houses. A number of persons were awakened and converted. My parents were among the number. For years Mr. Teetzel was a power for good in that section of the country. He long since died in the full assurance of faith, and is now enjoying the reward of the faithful.

The old home of my mother was now offered to my father if he would move back to the old place and take care of my mother's parents in their old age, and let my mother's brother have our lot in the new country. We went back to where I was born and stayed a little less than two years. During my thirteenth year I went with my father and mother to a camp meeting, of which I shall have more to say in another chapter.

We went back again to our home in the bush, as my father got sick of the bargain about keeping the old people, on account of some meddlesome relatives who were not pleased with the arrangement. On our return we found that two years had made changes in many ways. The roads were better, the clearings larger, old neighbours were better off, and several new families had come into the settlement.

My oldest sister and young brother died within a year after our return. I felt the loss of these very keenly. But the heaviest blow of all fell upon me in the fall of 1835, when I had to look on the cold, pale face of one of the best of mothers as she lay before me in the calm repose of death. She had been ailing for two years. The death of my sister and little brother had weighed heavily upon her in her enfeebled state of health. She was very anxious for a while about the seven children that she was leaving behind her, of whom I was the eldest and about seventeen, and the youngest was four years old. But before she died that uneasiness all passed away. She said that in answer to her prayers the Lord had given her all her children, and some day they would follow her to the home above. Oftentimes, amid life's clouds and storms, the remembrance of this dying declaration of a Christian mother has come to me like a voice from the unseen world which seemed to say, " Be strong and courageous and all will come right at last." I never knew how much I trusted in my mother until I stood looking into her grave, and the officiating minister, a Mr. Adams, spoke to me and said, " Young man, you must pray for yourself now, for your mother can pray for you no more." I thought that I had realized my loss before, when I looked at the empty chair in which she used to sit; when I looked at my little brothers and sisters and thought who will take care of them now; when I thought how still the house would be when no mother's footsteps and no mother's voice would be heard any more in it; when I picked up the old Bible that lay on the stand that stood near by her as she lay in her coffin, and remembered that she would never touch that book again, I then thought that I realized my loss. But when I was told that my mother would never pray for me again, it seemed to me that my heart must break. I never till that moment knew just what it was for a young man to face the wickedness and coldness of the world without a mother's prayer. And from that day to the present I never could look into the face of a motherless child, either old or young, and not feel pity for it. Perhaps it is a weakness, but I cannot help it.

In December, 1837, I came very near being caught in a trap.

The air was full of rumours of war. The political atmosphere seemed to be surcharged with slumbering forces that only awaited the touch of an electric spark to cause an explosion that would blow into a thousand fragments the selfish combination that then misruled the country. The family compact had been growing more oppressive and tyrannical from year to year, until the country was becoming exasperated and men were growing desperate.

Myself and two cousins had taken a chopping contract from a Mr. Brown, near Acton. One day a man came to us and showed us a proclamation of W. L. Mackenzie and held out such strong inducement that we concluded to join the patriot forces that were gathering for a march to Toronto. We were fully persuaded that the rising was not to be against the crown and government of Britain. But it was to be against the wicked misgovernment of the family compact. We left our work, and went home to get ready to start for the scene of action. It is said that we want "Old men for counsel and young men for war." In this case, the counsellors proved to be the stronger force. Our fathers soon settled the question for us by telling us the nature of the enterprise we proposed to engage in. They said that instead of gaining the honours of war and the freedom of the country, we would likely get a few feet of rope and a rebel's dishonoured grave. We went back to work feeling we had come near making fools of ourselves. The next week we were called out to join the militia to go to the front, and we readily obeyed the call, being willing to do anything to show our loyalty to the British crown and government.

Some time after the death of my mother, my father married again. My mother's name was Mary Johnston. His second wife was Anna Thompson. She was on the whole a very good woman; but I could not believe that any good could be in a stepmother, so I soon got up a quarrel with her and left home; I never lived at my father's any more. Young people often make serious mistakes that they see the folly of in after life. It was so with me in this.

And now commenced a course of life that I have regretted very much. For a few years I yielded to every bad influence and followed every inclination to run into sinful ways; I was ready for anything that was respectable and not criminal. Anything that I thought was mean I would not do; but that was about the only restraint that I regarded except the criminal law.

During these misspent years I came very near being killed on different occasions through my own recklessness or the carelessness of others; but the Lord's arm was about me though I knew it not, and His eye watched over me though I thought not of Him. He had better things in store for me than to die in sin and be lost forever. I drifted about the country from place to place until I was twenty-two years old. Then I made up my mind to change my habits of life, and seek and serve the Lord. I commenced at once and joined the Church. The people were very kind to me, and although I was among strangers they took an interest in my welfare. Eighteen or twenty young men and women joined the Church at the time that I did. The ministers who held the revival meetings at the time were Revs. E. Bristol and A. Roy. One of them died many years ago, and lies buried in the cemetery of the old M. E. Church, in the village of Brooklin. The other, Mr. Bristol, after an active and very successful career in the Christian ministry, is now a superannuate in the Methodist Church.

Shortly after I joined the Church, an incident occurred which I have looked upon ever since as an interposition of Divine Providence.

I was out of work. On the Grand river good axemen were getting what at that time was looked upon as big pay in the lumber woods. I and my brother concluded to go to the shanties for the winter. We got everything ready and started. When we had gone four or five miles on the way we called at a house for a drink of water. The man had been a lumberman, and more recently a hotel-keeper. He and his wife had been converted lately, and closed up the bar room, and banished the liquor. When I told Mr. Guybeson where we were going, he seemed to be sorry. He asked me if I had ever been in a lumber shanty. I told him that I had been one winter among Frenchmen in the business, but that we had boarded at a farmhouse. He said, "Then you know nothing about shanty life. An older Christian than you are would find it very hard to keep from backsliding in a shanty among the kind of men that you would have for associates there. Take my advice, and don't go. Better work for your board part of the time and go to school the other part, than to run the risk of losing your religion." Before he was done speaking my decision was made to go to school. That was just what I needed. It was strange that I had not thought of it before. We turned about and went back to where we started from. My brother went to work for a farmer, chopping fallow. I soon found a chance to work part of the time, and go to school. The teacher was a young man from the States, as was many of the teachers of that period.

My schooling had been very limited. I could read and write a little, but that was all. I knew nothing of arithmetic, and I had never looked inside of an English grammar. I started to school with a determination to do all in my power to learn as much as possible of everything that was taught there. I went to the school about three months. When spring came I had learned a good deal that I did not know before, and I had formed the acquaintance of the young lady who afterwards became my wife.

The next summer I worked for a man named Grout, at the carpenter trade. In the fall I took the contract for a large shed and stable of a Mr. Wetmore. This was my first job, but I did it well, and my employer was well pleased. Part of the pay I took in board, and went to school again the next winter till the month of March.

A new school was started in the township of Caistor. I was invited to take that school. After consultation with my teacher and others, I engaged for twelve months. When I commenced the school, on the 18th of March, 1843, the snow was very deep on the ground. The Millerites were proclaiming the end of the world. The snow was to turn to pitch, and then catch fire, and this old earth would be turned to ashes. Many people were nearly frightened out of their wits by these alarmists. My school succeeded nicely, and I thought of adopting school teaching permanently. But that was not to be.

On the 22nd of August, 1843, I was married to E. J. Griffin, of the township of Grimsby. She was one of a large connection of Griffins that hails from Smithville, which gets its name from its founder Smith Griffin, who in his day was a very prominent man in that community. I expect it will be conceded without debate that the greatest of the Griffins yet seen is the Rev. W. S. Griffin, D.D., who is now President of the Guelph Conference. But I am of the opinion that the best Griffin is the one that has been looking after me and my affairs for the past forty-three years.

I spoke of the Millerites. Well, I had some experience on that subject. My arrangements with the trustees were that I should "board around." I was staying at the time with the family of Mr. Jacob Kerr. We had been talking about the excitement that the Millerites were causing in many parts of the country. This was on Tuesday night. The next Friday was the day fixed upon for the burning of the world. Mr. Kerr and I came to the conclusion that to a Christian there

was no cause for alarm, inasmuch as being prepared
for death he was ready for the end of the world, or
anything else that could possibly happen.

We had prayer and went to bed. I had not been
long in bed when a man came to me with a roll of
papers in his hand. Whether I was awake or asleep
I cannot tell. The man unrolled one of the papers and
held it up before me and began to explain a number of
dates in it. It was from the prophecy of Daniel, and
it made time run out on the next Friday. Then he
opened the other roll which was from the Book of
Revelation, and by a similar mode of interpretation it
was seen that time would die and all the prophecies
end on the next Friday. He rolled up his papers and
then said, "It will surely come." At once he disappeared.
After the man was gone I considered for a while and
then resolved to go and tell everybody what I saw, that
the world would end on Friday. I got up and dressed
myself, intending to start right out and give the
alarm. I had my hand on the door-latch to go out.
Just then a thought came into my mind that stopped
me. The thought was this: God does not ask unrea-
sonable things. This may be all a mistake. If God
wants me to go and give the alarm, He will give me
other proofs of the fact. I knelt beside the bed and
prayed for further light. Soon the agitation of my
mind passed away. I went to bed again and slept
soundly till morning. I saw no more, and I heard no
more. You ask me what it was? I can't tell. To
me at the time it seemed just as real as anything that
I had ever seen before, or anything that I have seen

since.   Call it hallucination, phantom, illusion, or dream—call it what you like—I know it nearly upset me at the time.   But the world did not burn up and if I am not greatly astray in regard to the unfulfilled prophecies, especially the little two-horned beast and the big ten-horned beast of Revelation, the Irish Home Rule and the Land Questions will have to come to a settlement, and many other abuses that the two beasts have imposed on the world must be removed before that event takes place.   Society will see many mighty changes before the end of the world —changes that it may take centuries to accomplish.

About nine months after I joined the Church, I was appointed leader of the class that I belonged to.

This was a great cross to me.   I was young in years and young in the Church, and it seemed to me that there was not a man in the class but was better fitted for the place than I was.   As an illustration of my weakness as a Christian worker at that time the following fact is given.   While I was working with Mr. J. C. Grout, I boarded with him.   He was a local preacher, and belonged to the same class that I did. One morning, at breakfast time, he gave me the Bible and told me to read and pray.   I had never done it before.   I took the book and began to read.   Before I was done reading an old man in the neighborhood came into the house.   This frightened me.   I finished the reading and we all kneeled in prayer. · Something came over me so that I could not utter a single word. It seemed to me that if the salvation of the world depended on it that morning, I could not pray.   The sweat ran off me like rain, and I trembled in every nerve. We remained on our knees for a while and then got up without a word of vocal prayer being uttered. This incident has often recurred to me when I have had to deal with timid young people. Mr. Grout gave me some wholesome counsel when we were at our work, and I told him I would try again, which I did and succeeded better. Within a month after this, when a vacancy occurred, Mr. Grout nominated me for class-leader and I was put in. I continued to lead that class for thirteen years, and then I left the locality.

Before my time was out in the school that I had taken, my health began to fail, so much so that I was forced to resign the school two weeks before the expiration of the time that I had engaged for.

My wife called in a doctor. He said that I had studied too hard, and he forbade me to look into a book for three months. He told me that I must give up the idea of teaching. He said in my case the mental and physical energies were not sufficiently well balanced to bear the strain of a teacher's life, shut up in a school room. He advised me to adopt a calling that would give me plenty of outdoor exercise. He left me medicine, and I got better after a while. Then I bought some tools and went to work as a carpenter in the summer, and in the winter I worked at cooper work or anything that came in my way that I could do. The result was that I never wanted for a day's work, and my family never wanted for food or clothing.

After ten years of married life I found myself the owner of twenty-five acres of good land, nearly paid for, a good frame cottage and good frame shop, and about four hundred dollars' worth of tools and other things of use about the place. When we started we had not more than one hundred dollars, all told.

But now we met with a drawback. One day when I was from home a young man was working in the shop, and by some means it caught fire and burned up, with all my tools and a lot of work and a large amount of seasoned stuff. On my way home I met a man who told me of my loss. "But," said he, "you will not be left to bear it all alone. The neighbours are going to help you. They are out in two directions already seeking help." When I got home I found the smoking ruins of the results of my toil and my wife's economy and care. When night came the men returned, and it was found they had gotten about one hundred and twenty dollars to help me to buy new tools. But much as I prized the money, I thought more of the spirit that prompted this kind act on the part of my neighbours than I did of it. My two nearest neighbours were the largest givers on the list, namely, Robert Miller and Martin Halstead.

One more incident and I will close this chapter. I was hewing barn timber for Mr. A. P. Buckbee. We had been at it for some days, and we were just finishing up the job. The men had got the scoring all done and were standing around looking at me. I was at the last side of the last stick of timber, and within a few strokes of being done.

I was doing my best so as not to keep the others waiting. All at once Price Buckbee spoke to me sharp and quick, saying, "Hilts, take care." I at once dropped the broadaxe and sprang backwards. That spring saved my life—at least it saved me from a fearful hurt. Before I had time to look up a large limb fell from the top of a tall pine tree, and struck and broke in two on the piece of timber right where I had been hewing. It was about ten feet long and as thick as a large hand pry. If I had tried to straighten up I should have met the falling limb. If I had moved forward I could not have gotten out of the way in time. The only possible way of escape, as we all concluded afterwards, was by the very unusual course of jumping backward. When I looked at the men after the danger was over it seemed to me that their faces were nearly as white as the paper on which I am writing. The first one to speak was Mr. Buckbee. He was not at that time a religious man. But I never have and I never can forget the expression of his face and tones of his voice as he said with solemnity, "Mr. Hilts, you may thank God that you are alive this minute. It must have been He that prompted me to look up just in time. It must have been He that helped me to put the warning in the shortest possible sentence, and it must have been He that prompted you to jump backward as you did and not stop to look up to see where the danger was." I could not understand it then. But now I think I do. God had something else for me to do in the world beside hewing timber and framing barns.

It would give me pleasure to dwell longer on my experiences in the locality where I spent so many days in comparative comfort. But this chapter is long enough, and I must close it. Two years after the shop was burnt we left that place, and in two years more I went into the ministry.

CHAPTER II.

FILLING APPOINTMENTS.

THE phrase "filling an appointment" is very closely associated with our itinerant plan of supplying our people with the means of grace. The Roman Catholic holds high or low mass. The English Church holds Divine service. The Presbyterian holds a diet of worship. The Quaker has a meeting. But the Methodist fills an appointment. These others do work mostly laid out for them by the officials of the Churches to which they belong; but the Methodist preacher has much to do with laying out his own work, and making his own appointments.

It is true that he has a certain field to cultivate, a given territory to work over; but how often he is to preach, and when and where he will do so, are matters that very largely depend on his own decision.

In talking about filling appointments, two things have to be considered. The Indian said that the first thing to be done in cooking a rabbit is to catch it; so the first part of filling an appointment is to get to it. In the past Methodist ministers have done most of their getting around on horseback, or in the cutter and buggy. Perhaps no class of honest men, are more attached to their horses, than are the Methodist preachers, especially those of them who are kept for a long time on country circuits. Often his horse is to him at once a piece of property, a servant, a guide, a conveyance and a friend. It is no wonder that the circuit rider becomes attached to his horse, while so much of his comfort and usefulness depends on that mute assistant.

But I did not start to write an essay on horses. Filling appointments is the theme of this chapter. Well, let me see, my first appointment was a long time ago. It was in this wise: in the class that I first belonged to, there were twenty-five or thirty young people. We arranged for a weekly young people's prayer meeting, to be led by the young men, each in his turn. A list of names was made out, and we took our turn in the order in which our names were on the list. My name was near the bottom, so that I had a chance to see how most of the young men got along before my time came.

Well do I remember when the leader at one meeting stated that my name came next, so that I would be expected to lead the meeting of the following week. That week seemed to pass away with a rapidity that was truly astonishing. The days, it seemed to me, flew by with more than railroad speed. When the eventful day came round, I was, as an Irishman would say, on swither. I was sorely tempted to go away somewhere, so as to be out of the neighbourhood; but then, when I remembered how promptly the other

3

young men had taken their turn, I felt ashamed of myself for having even thought of running away. I resolved to stay and do the best that I could, no matter how hard the task might be. No sooner had I come to this decision, than I felt my heart full of peace and joy. I look back to that event, trivial as it may seem, as one of the turning points in my life. If I had run away from my duty then, there is no telling what my after life would have been. Before my turn came round again, a new class-leader was needed, and I was appointed leader of the class, which position I held until I left the settlement twelve years afterward.

How I Got Embarrassed.

My first appointment as an exhorter was in the house of a farmer named Daniel Burkholder, who lived in the township of Caistor. It was the first time that I went away from my own class to hold meeting; to me it was an event of great importance. I had frequently been solicited by the preachers to try holding forth as an exhorter; but up to that time I declined to do so, fearing that I should only make a failure of it, but I had at last consented, and the appointment had been made for me.

At that time there was an old exhorter by the name of Cable, who lived on Mud Street, near Tapleytown. He was one of the old-fashioned shouting Methodists; a regular little hurricane and thunderstorm twisted together. Well, I got him to go with me to the appointment. It was a beautiful Sabbath morning in the month of June.

When we were going through a piece of bush, Mr. Cable proposed that we should have a prayer-meeting all to ourselves, as a preparation for the work before us. We spent some ten minutes in this way, and then went on to the place. When we got to Mr. Burkholder's house, it was crowded with people and a lot outside that could not get in. By dint of much elbowing we got inside the door. I had once taught school in that section, and nearly all the people were there to hear their old schoolmaster.

I commenced the meeting by giving out the hymn, beginning with "Come, sinners, to the gospel feast." The singing was all that could be desired. Who ever knew singing not to be good when there were half a dozen Burkholders in the audience? But while they were singing a thought came into my mind like this: "If any sinner expects a gospel feast this morning, he will be greatly disappointed." This nearly upset me. Brother Cable engaged in prayer. O, how I wished that I had his talent! But I consoled myself with the thought that human responsibility and human possibility are always equal. We are not expected to do what is beyond our strength and ability. I read a part of a chapter and we sang another hymn. Then came the supreme moment. When the last line was ringing in my ears, like an expiring echo, I found myself standing alone, and all the rest of the people seated. This has always been to me the trying moment.

I commenced to talk to the people. But I got bewildered, so that I could hardly tell what I was saying. This feeling increased till I got into such a state of mental disturbance that I could scarcely distinguish one person from another. Sometimes the faces of the people around me would seem to be as big as barrel heads, and then they. would dwindle down till they looked no larger than the bottoms of tea-cups. In this way I went on for ten or fifteen minutes. Then I called my friend Mr. Cable to take the meeting off my hands. Just then I felt that I would never attempt the like again. But I did try again and again. And I have kept on trying till the present time. But I have never got over those times of nervousness, and I never expect to.

Thrown into a Mud-hole.

The first year I was on the Garafraxa Circuit, there was an appointment on the twelfth line, at the house of John Taylor. One Sunday afternoon I was on my way there I met with a mishap that might have been a serious affair ; but the way it turned out was more amusing than sad. There was a piece of woods to go through, and in the woods was a deep mud-hole. My horse was one that would never go on a walk, either in harness or under the saddle. He had run in a circus ring three or four years, which I suppose was the reason of his objecting to walk.

Well, I was going through this piece of bush. My horse was trotting along, and I was singing,

> " Jesus, my all, to Heaven is gone,
>   The way is so delightful. Hallelujah."

All of a sudden my horse got his feet tangled up in some way, and fell right into the middle of the mud.

When I came to realize the condition of things, I found myself lying just in front of the horse, and on my back, in the mire. My first thought was, that when he got up he would likely jump on me before I could get out of his way. But when he got up he turned on his hind feet and went off on one side, and started into the woods as fast as he could run.

I gathered myself up as quick as I could and ran after the horse, which was soon out of sight. While I was wondering where he would go to, I looked in the direction he went and saw him coming towards me at the top of his speed. When he saw me he ran up and placed his chin on my shoulder—a thing he often did when in the field. He seemed to be pleased to see me all right.

When I took a look at myself, I could not refrain from laughing at the ludicrous figure that I presented. Such a specimen of clerical humanity, clad in a mixture of mud and broadcloth, and booted with a combination of black mud and leather, and hatted with an old-time beaver, in alliance with an aqueous formation of decayed foliage, it would be impossible to find in a part of the country where mud and leaves are only found in limited supply.

I went along till I came to a creek. I tied the horse to a tree, and waded into the water, and washed off all the mud that I could. Then I went on, about a mile further, to the appointment. When I got there I found the house full of people, waiting for me, as I was about half an hour late.

The way that they stared at me when I went into

the house convinced me that there was no use in trying to get them to listen to preaching unless an explanation was first given.   I told the audience what had
occurred and then went on with the service.

Hunting More Work.

Some time after I went to Garafraxa Circuit, Mr.
John Taylor told me that there was a new settlement
in the township of Luther, where there was no preaching of any kind. He offered to conduct me through
about three miles of solid bush, and show me some of
the inhabitants.   After we got through to the first
clearing, Mr. Taylor left me to make my own way.

I went to the shanty that stood near the road, and
made some inquiries. I found four or five women
there, helping a neighbour at some kind of sewing.
Presently I told them who I was and what I wanted,
and asked them if they thought any one in the settlement would open his house for preaching.   The
women said they would be very glad to have some
kind of religious meetings on Sabbath, as the people
were getting wild for want of it; but none of them
had a house at all suitable.   But they all agreed that
the best place to have meeting would be at "Sam
Graham's," as he had the largest house and it would
be most central.

They directed me which way to go, and I started to
hunt up Mr. Graham.   When I had gone about a mile
further I came to his clearing, which was a large one
for a new country.   I found him at work in the fields.
I told him who I was, and what I was after.

He said, " I am glad that you have come. Any one with a Protestant Bible in his hand is welcome to my house for a preaching-place. I am a Presbyterian, but that makes no difference in the case."

I made arrangements to preach in his house once every fortnight on Sabbath. The first time I went there, I found the house full of about as hardy-looking men and women as could be found anywhere. The most of them were in the early prime of life. They were just the sort of population to successfully cope with the hardships of pioneers.

When I looked over the congregation that morning, I saw three persons that I knew. They had been among my young associates in days gone by. Though eighteen years had passed since I last saw them, yet I knew them. Our last time of seeing each other was at a dance. But now, after eighteen eventful years, we meet again, in a back settlement, as Christians, to worship God together. [If Mr. and Mrs. Beals and Mr. Boomer should ever see these lines, they will endorse the statements, and I hope also excuse this personal reference to them.]

What a mercy that God, who forgives penitent, believing sinners, will forgive dancers also—even though one of the light-heeled tribe, by her artful gyrations, did once fascinate a wicked king and kick the head off a holy man.

So far as was known, the sermon that Sabbath morning was the first one ever delivered in the township. Now the centre of Grand Valley Circuit, in the Guelph Conference, is not far from this place.

"A Crabbed Old Man."

Myself and Pascal Knox and William Woodward were once going to a missionary meeting at a place called Mayne, in the township of Wallace. In going from the boundary across to the place, it being dark, we got on the wrong road. We came to a shanty on the roadside. I went in to make enquiries as to our whereabouts, and the proper direction to take.

I found an old couple living there alone. When I asked the way to Mayne, the old man wanted to know what I was going there for—thinking that I was a doctor. On my explaining that I was going there to a missionary meeting, he said in angry tones of voice, "Are you not a Methody preacher?" I said, "Yes, sir: there are three of us, and we have by some means got out of our latitude." "Well, I hope the Lord will head ye's off at every turn. I don't like a thing about these kind o' people," said the old man spitefully.

I said to him, "Mister, I did not come in to hear about the Methodists, for I know a great deal more about them than you do," and I turned to go, telling him that we would try and find our way without his help.

The old lady followed me to the door, saying, "Do not mind him. He is just a crabbed old creature, troubled with rheumatics, and he is so cross that I can hardly live with him."

She gave the desired information, and we went on and found the place, and the house full of people waiting for us.

A Crabbed Old Man.

I commenced my speech that night in this way :—

> Through mud and mire, through rain and snow,
> We never tire, but onward go,
>   And it seems somewhat funny
> That we should come where people walk
> A mile or two to hear us talk,
>   And ask them for their money.

GETTING IN THE FOG.

Whether other men have what may be called pet appointments, I am not able to say, but for myself I can speak without any doubt on that point. On nearly all the circuits that I have travelled, there were one or two places where I could speak with greater freedom and ease than I could at the other appointments. My favourite appointment when I was on the Elma mission was at Trowbridge. I always had a good congregation there, and most of them were religious people. I was preaching there one Sunday afternoon ; the house was crowded. I had my subject well arranged, as I thought, and it was one that I had spoken on before, so that I should have gone through it without difficulty. When I had been talking ten or twelve minutes I seemed to get confused, and to lose the run of my subject. I could not make out what was the matter. The sweat stood in great drops on my face, and I trembled in every joint.

I looked around on the congregation. One good old brother was resting his elbow on his knee, and his chin on his hand. I thought to myself, that man feels so bad at the mess that I am making of my sermon that he is ashamed to look up. On the other side was a young man with a smile on his face. It seemed to me that he was making fun of me. In front of me I saw tears on the face of an old mother in the church. Something said to me, "She feels so badly for you that she is crying." I stopped short. Then I said to the audience, " Friends, I am lost in a fog, and it is no use for me to try to conceal it ; you know it as well as I do. Will you pray for me ?" I finished up I do not know how. Then I left without speaking to a person in the house.

At the evening service I got along some better. But the cloud was not wholly lifted.

Next morning, on my way home, I had to pass through Trowbridge. While doing so I met the school teacher, Mr. B. Rothwell. He said to me, " Mr. Hilts, what was the matter with you yesterday ?" I said " I cannot tell, but I never was in a greater muddle in my life." " Well," said Mr. Rothwell, " I think you were the only one in the house that thought you were muddled. I was paying very particular attention, and I was just thinking how nicely you had your subject arranged, and how well you were getting on with it, when you stopped and said you were in the fog." I have never been able to account for that experience on any rational grounds.

Too Many Fishes.

The late Rev. John Lynch was a North of Ireland man. He was fond of a joke, and sometimes he would indulge this propensity at the risk of a successful retort. At a camp-meeting near the village of Hanover, Brother Lynch was preaching one morning with great earnestness, and with considerable eloquence. He spoke of the mighty forces of nature. Among other illustrations, he referred to the Niagara river, where " it stands on end," and where by the weight of gravitation it has pressed the solid rock, down, down, lower, and lower, until it has become the bottom of an immense basin, into which whole cities might be thrown, and still leave room enough for half a dozen smaller towns. But he condensed all these grand hyperboles into one short sentence. He told his hearers about the " tremendous chasm that the waters had washed out."

In the afternoon it was my lot to preach about the " loaves and fishes." By some slip of the tongue, once in the discourse I got three fishes instead of two. That was too good for Lynch to let pass. He had a chance now at the " presiding elder." I was walking past where he and some others were standing when he called me. He said, " See here, Hilts, where did you catch that third fish that you gave us awhile ago ?" I said, " O, I caught that where Andrew's lad dropped it out of his basket while he was trying to cross that tre-men-ge-ous ka-sum that you dug out this morning."

After a hearty laugh, Brother Lynch said, " Well, that is not so bad for a Dutchman. I guess we are about even now, so we will let the fish go back into the ka-sum."

A Bear in the Way.

When I was on the Teeswater mission I travelled on foot. There were three reasons for this: first, I had no horse; secondly, I could not get to all of the work with a horse; thirdly, it would have been very hard to get feed for a horse. So for a year and a half I went to all my appointments on foot. One Sabbath I was going from Parr's schoolhouse in Culross, to John Crowsten's shanty in Kinloss.

There was a piece of solid bush for two miles of the distance. The road was under-brushed through the bush, but it was not cleared out. When I got part way through I passed a little boy. A little further on a big black bear walked out into the road, and took his stand right in front of me, and only a rod from where I stood. He faced me to all appearance with as little concern as a dog or pig would have done.

The boy came up, and with a scream put his arms around me and cried out, " O, save me from the bear." I had not so much as a pocket knife with me. I saw at once the situation of things. I believed that I could get out of his way, but the boy could not do so. My resolve was taken in less time than it takes me to write it. I had read in books, and I had heard hunters say, that no animal can stand the human eye. I resolved to test this theory. I had no trouble to catch his eye, and I looked sternly into it, with all the determination and will force that I was capable of showing. For a while, perhaps five minutes, it was not possible to say which seemed least concerned, the bear or myself.   But after some time I saw that his eye began to quiver.   I said to myself, " I have got him."   In a few minutes he turned and walked off out of sight.

Twenty years after this I was stopping over night in the neighbourhood.   My host invited me to accompany him to a public meeting, to be held in the interest of the Bible Society.   When we came to the church, which stood at a cross-road where four splendid farms joined corners, I was struck with the familiar aspect of the place.   It seemed to me that I had been there before.   The lay of the land, just at the foot of a little hill, seemed to associate itself with my past life in a way that I could not understand at first;   but when I ascertained what line of road it was on, everything was made clear.   The church stood less than six rods from the spot where I had met the bear in the woods twenty years ago.   I mentioned the circumstance in a few remarks that I was called úpon to make.   After the meeting closed a man came up to me and said, " I have often heard that boy tell about the bear and the man that looked it out of countenance, but we never knew who it was.   That boy is a man now, but he don't live here."

TRYING TO WALK A POLE.

Near the little village of Kady, in the township of Sullivan, there is, or was, a small log church, in which I preached once every two weeks when I was on the Invermay mission.   At that time the road, for a part of the way, was across lots and through the farms of two or three settlers.   In the spring of the year it was

A BEAR IN THE WAY.

hard getting through with a horse; at such times I went on foot. One Sabbath morning I was on my way to that appointment. The snow was just going off, and every low place was filled up with mud and water. I came to where a couple of small poles had been thrown over a deep mud-hole, as a sort of footbridge. In passing over, one of the poles turned, so that I fell my whole length in the mud and water. When I gathered myself up I was in anything but a presentable condition. I went and rolled for a while in the remains of a snow-drift, and in that way I got off the thickest of the mud; then I went on to the church. When I got to the door there were a number of men standing there. One of them said to me, "Look here, mister, if I should come to this crowd looking as you do, every one of them would say, 'Bill Innis had been taking too much tangle-leg.' What shall we say about you?"

"Well," I answered him, "you may say what you like about me, if you will only fix that mud-hole before I have to come again."

LOSING THE DEFINITION.

I cannot say whether other men ever lose or forget any part of what they want to say in preaching, but I have sometimes done so. This has occurred mostly when I was very much absorbed by my theme. At such times the mind is apt to give its attention more to the results than to the details of the subject.

I was once preaching in the village of Mapleton (now Listowel). My theme was the cities of refuge among the Jews. In speaking of them as being typical of Christ, I referred to their significant names as illustrative of His character and offices. I had depended entirely on the memory for the names and definitions. When I came to this part of my discourse I found that I had entirely forgotten one of the definitions. I mentioned the name of the city, and then said to the congregation: " My friends, I confess that the meaning of this name has entirely escaped my memory, and I am sorry to say that I cannot recall it." But help came from an unexpected quarter. Mr. Hacking, who is now an old man, was in the congregation that day. When I mentioned the difficulty I was in, he promptly came to the rescue by calling out the word that was needed to fill up what would otherwise have been a breach in my sermon. I thanked Mr. Hacking, and went on with the discourse. I have no doubt but this little episode caused the people to give more attention to the subject, and to take more interest in it than they otherwise would have done. What made the occurance more noticeable was the fact that my friend was not much of a believer in orthodox teaching ; but as he was a man of some culture, and of a good deal of kindness of heart, he was willing to help even a Methodist preacher when he was in a quandary.

He Did Not Know What to Do.

The first time I went over to Teeswater mission I had some difficulty in finding the way from one appointment to another.

The country was new. There were very few open

roads, and the clearings all being small, there was a great deal of bush to go through, with no better highway than a footpath. One of my rounds was in the following order :—Parr's schoolhouse in the morning ; John Crowsten's shanty at two p.m.; at Mr. Hood's house in the evening. This was our Sabbath's work, Then on Monday, at one o'clock p.m., I preached in Mr. Joseph Hanna's shanty. This was about five miles. from Hood's, and there was only one clearing in the whole distance. There a man by the name of Corigan lived.

The first time that I went from Hood's to Hanna's I was directed as far as Corigan's. There I was to inquire the way to where I wished to go. When I came to his place I met him in front of his house. After learning who he was, I told him that I had been sent to him for direction to the house of Mr. Hanna. He gave me a sort of a comical look, and then said, "I know Mr. Hanna, and I know the way to his place."

"Mr. Hood told me that you could give me full directions," I answered.

"Yes, I could tell you all about it. But, you know, *can* and *will* are not always equal terms," said he, giving me a look that I did not understand.

"Well, sir," I said to him, "I cannot see why there should be any difference between *can* and *will* in this case,"

"I think there is a good deal of difference," said he.

"Well, if you do not tell me, I shall go back to Hood's for further instructions," was my reply.

He gave me another look, and with a smile on his face, he said, "Of course, you are a constable."

"O, no, sir; I am not a constable, nor any other law officer. I am only a preacher, going to Mr. Hanna's to fill an appointment in his house."

"Well, all right. That changes the whole affair. I understand that Mr. Hanna has been having trouble about a yoke of cattle that he got a while ago, and I thought that you were a constable going to annoy him, and if that had been the case, you would have got no directions from me," was his answer.

"I am glad to find that your hesitancy was caused by groundless fears. Now for the directions, if you please," I said, with as much gravity as I could command.

He gave me such clear and definite instructions that I found the place without any difficulty.

Finding a Relative.

The village of Rockwood is on the main line of the Grand Trunk Railway, about five miles east of the city of Guelph. There was an appointment or preaching place there, in connection with the Eramosa Circuit.

To that place I once went with Rev. J. F. Durkee, to preach for him. Most of the audience were entire strangers to me. In looking over the crowd, as I sat in the pulpit, I saw a face that had a strangely familiar look. It was that of a woman, whose hair was turning gray, and who had some of the marks of age upon her face. Departed years had left some of their traces upon her features. But while I felt certain that I had seen that face before, and that at some time I had been acquainted with its owner, I could not make out where or when it was. It was evident to me that the woman had some idea that she knew who I was. I could tell that by the inquiring look that she would every now and then give me.

After a while she turned her head so that I got a side view of her face. As soon as I saw her thus I recollected who she was like. I said to myself, "If Alvira McCombs is in this world, that woman is she." This was a daughter of my mother's sister, whom I had not seen since she was fifteen years old, and that was more than thirty years before.

I stopped in church for class-meeting. When I went out of the door, I found three persons waiting for me to come out. There were Miss McCombs, of former years, now Mrs. Balls, her husband and her daughter. She reached her hand to me, saying, "I came here to listen to a stranger, but when I heard the name of the preacher after I came out of the church, I concluded that we are not only old acquaintances of former years, but we are also relatives. Do you remember your cousin Alvira?"

I said: "Yes, I remember her; and when I looked at you in the church, I concluded that no person could look as much like her as you do and not be either herself or her sister."

"Well," said she, "I am herself, and I am glad to meet you after so many years."

"But can it be," said I, "that the romping, rattle-headed little Alvira has become the motherly-looking woman before me?" But it was so. Thirty-three years make great changes in people, especially when those years span the gap between fifteen and forty-eight. The colour and expression of the eyes, and the outlines of the features, remain the same ; but when one looks for the full, round and ruddy face of fifteen in the wrinkled and careworn features of forty-eight, it is not an easy matter to settle the question of identity.

Meeting an Old Acquaintance.

At one time I had a week-night appointment in the house of William Armstrong, on the boundary line between the townships of Maryborough and Mornington.   The meetings were held on Monday evenings.

One evening after I had closed the service, an elderly man came up to me, and reaching out his hand said, " How are you, old friend ? I am glad to meet you again after all the years that have passed since we last met."

I looked at him for a moment and then said to him, " I have no doubt but you know who you are talking to, but really I do not know who is talking to me."

" You have forgotten me, that is all.   You and I were great friends at one time.   Do you remember Aleck Walker, that once stopped at Thomas Crozier's, near Ballinafad," he said.

" I remember Aleck Walker, but he was smaller than I was," I said to him.

" Yes, that is true, but I have grown since then," was his answer.

" I knew you more from your resemblance of your father than from a remembrance of your own looks. You are as much like what your father was when I saw him last as any two persons can be alike."

I went home with my former friend, and found him to be the possessor of a splendid two hundred acre farm, an excellent wife, and a number of children mostly full grown.

Next morning he invited me out to look around the place. After showing me the barn and out-buildings, he took me through a number of beautiful fields. Presently he said, "All that I have I owe to God and to Methodism. After I knew you, I got to drinking, and went very far down in the path of the drunkard; but I came in contact with Methodism, I got converted, and for many years the Lord has greatly blessed me."

Then, turning to me, he said, "How is it that you are travelling the mission on foot ?"

"Simply because I could not use a horse on my last mission, and I sold it. When I came off the mission, the price of the horse was gone for something to feed and clothe my family, so that at present I have nothing to buy a horse with," I answered. We went into another field where there were a number of horses pasturing. Mr. Walker pointed to a horse and said, "There is an animal that would suit your work; my price for him is eighty dollars. I will give five dollars toward buying him for you ; pay me the other seventy-five dollars when you can."

"Well, my friend," I said, "a horse is what I need very much, but I am afraid that I cannot accept your offer so kindly given." "Why not ?" said he. "You will want an endorser, and I do not like to ask any man to go on paper with me, if I can help it," I replied.

He said, "No, I want no endorser ; if the cloth of a

Methodist minister is not worth as much as a horse, I should be very sorry to be a Methodist." I took the horse home with me, and he was a good one. The Quarterly Board undertook to pay for the horse, and they did so with the exception of about twenty dollars. One man, a Doctor Pattison, gave twenty-five dollars towards the amount; the horse was all paid for within six months after I got him. I might fill many pages in relating incidents in connection with filling appointments; but enough on that subject has been written.

Before closing this chapter I wish to speak of an unfilled appointment, or a disappointed congregation. We will suppose the place of meeting to be a country church; the time, "ten-thirty" on Sabbath morning, in the month of November; the roads about as bad as November roads usually are; the weather as "leaky" as November weather can well be. The congregation is made up of farmers and their families, who have come with teams; besides these, there are a few "city folks," who have came out to spend the Sabbath with some of their country cousins. Now the hands of the church clock point to thirty minutes past ten.

Brother John Smith, not Smithe, goes to the door, and looks in the direction the preacher is to come from, but though he can see a mile up the road, he sees no one coming that looks like a preacher. With a disappointed look, he goes and whispers something to Brother Brown. Then Brother B. announces his intention to help the congregation sing the hymn:

"When I can read my title clear," etc.

When this is done, another interval of a few minutes is followed by Brother Jones leading off with,

" How tedious and tasteless the hours," etc.

By this time the clock strikes eleven.   Another visit of investigation to the door, but without results. Some of the clouds now seem to come inside and fix themselves on the faces of some in the audience. Brother Smith's face, for instance, is growing particularly sombre.   At this point old Brother Simkins sings, with a tone of sadness in his voice :

> " O, land of rest, for thee I sigh,
>   When will the moment come
> When I shall lay my armour by,
>   And dwell in peace at home ? "

Now the clock points to 11.30, good measure.   Just as the old class-leader is about to move the adjournment of the meeting, a young sister over near the front window commences to sing " The Sweet By and Bye." This is taken up by the younger part of the audience. While the echoes of the last verse of this beautiful composition are still rolling along the ceiling, an old lady, of Quaker proclivities, gets up and walks toward the door, muttering to herself, as she supposes, something about young girls being in a great hurry to get into the " Sweet By and Bye."   This is the signal for a general church-emptying.   After which the people go quietly home to dinner.

CHAPTER III.

CHANGING LOCATIONS.

IN these days of conveyances on land and water, run by steam power, the average citizen of Ontario cannot fully appreciate the difference between travelling now and travelling thirty or forty years ago. Then, a move of one or two hundred miles was a matter "of great importance." It involved the employment of time, the outlay of money, the endurance of hardships, the performance of labour, the smashing of furniture, the exercise of patience, and the testing of moral and physical courage, little dreamed of by the railway travellers of the present day. Only those who have tried both the old and new methods of migration can form anything like a correct estimate of the difference there is between them. In the one case a man would be a day or two helping his wife to pack things away in boxes that they had spent two or three days in making. Then the boxes and furniture would be loaded on two or three waggons, and he would lash them on with ropes. Then he would take his wife and as many of the children as possible in the buggy. The rest of the children, if there were any more, would be snugly stowed away in the loaded waggons. When all necessary preparations had been made and the good-byes had all been said, and the final hand-shaking had been done, the front teamster would say, "All ready?" and start. Then two or three days of torture would commence. To watch those waggons as they were drawn over the uneven roads, up and down the hills, over rough corduroys, through bridgeless creeks and sloughs, and quagmires; to have his wife fretting and fidgetting about the things in danger of being broken; to find himself nearly distracted over the question as to which was most likely to occur—the upsetting of the waggon and the smashing of everything, or the going off into hysterics by his poor worried and wearied wife. This was a man's lot under the old-time system of migration.

In the other case, a man puts his goods into a car, pays a little freight, tickets the articles sent, visits among friends for a day or two, takes his family into a palace car, pays the fare, enjoys a few hours' ride, arrives at his destination, hauls his stuff from the station, helps to put things in place, goes to bed at his usual time, feeling more like a man that has been to a picnic than one that had been moving. This is a man's privilege under the new system of migration.

OUR FIRST MOVE.

In the month of June, eighteen hundred and fifty-six, my itinerant life commenced. I was living in the village of Smithville, county of Lincoln, Ont. Here I had been working as a contracting builder, and was doing well. But the Church with which I was connected was greatly in want of men to fill its rapidly increasing work. I felt it to be my duty to preach the Gospel. So I offered myself for the work. Having been in the Church, and having filled the offices of class-leader and exhorter for a number of years, I was known personally by a large number of the preachers. My offer was accepted. I was employed by the Elder, Rev. J. W. Jacobs, and as soon as arrangements could be made, we started for our first field of labour in the ministry. This was Garafraxa, in the county of Wellington. To reach it we had to travel eighty miles. I had never been there.

The road north of Hamilton was all strange to me. We had to go on a waggon. All the help that we could get from railroads was the privilege of crossing under one at Dundas and over one at Guelph.

I hired a heavy team and put a rack on a strong waggon. On this we loaded such a load of furniture as is seldom seen on one conveyance. The balance of our goods we left with a friend, to be taken at some future time. The friend died not long after; the goods we never got.

When we had everything ready to start, a man came to me and said, "I think you are making a great mistake; I do not think you will ever succeed as a preacher. As a man you can succeed almost anywhere, but you will never be a preacher. Now, if you will unload that waggon and go to work in my foundry as a wood worker, I will give you steady work and the highest wages going, as long as you like to stay." I thanked him for his kindness and his liberal offer. But I told him I was unable to take his advice or accept his offer, as I felt that I was under an obligation to obey a call that could not with safety be disregarded, as I felt that the impressions that had been on my mind from my boyhood, and that had grown stronger with increasing years, must have a significance. If I was mistaken, it was a mistake made in all honesty, after much prayerful consideration and many petitions for Divine guidance. But this is a long digression.

I took my wife and children in the buggy, and started on after the team that had gone an hour before. We went to Mr. Martin Halstead's, and stopped for the night in what was known as the Buckbee neighbourhood. The teamster went to his home to stay. He was a son of Mr. Adolphus Lounsbury, who owned the team.

The passing through that place was something of a trial to us. Here it was that my wife was raised. Here we had been married, and we had spent twelve years of our married life here on the farm adjoining the one where we were staying. Here we passed by the place where lay in quiet rest the mouldering remains of one of our babes. Here we passed the house, built by myself, where we had started life together, and where our children had been born. The class that I had led for thirteen years was in this locality. In this settlement were many reminders of my vocation as a mechanic. We had lived here, and we were doing well here.

But we got the "western fever," sold out, went

west, did not like it, came back to Smithville, and lost four or five hundred dollars in the movement, but perhaps it was all for the best.

Next morning we started and went on to Hamilton by noon. We fed the horses and got our dinners, after which we started on and went as far as the village of Freelton. Here we stayed all night. We took an early start and drove on seven miles, and stopped for breakfast. We went on through the town of Guelph to the village of Fergus, and stopped for dinner.

Here we left the gravel road and turned toward the old Garafraxa mission parsonage, which was seven miles away. We got along nicely for about three miles. Then we came to a piece of swampy bush, known as "Black Ash Swamp." The bottom of the roadway seemed to have started on a trip to China, and for half a mile the mud was almost to the hubs of the wheels. The horses were not used to that sort of work, and most decidedly objected to proceed any further in that way.

"STUCK IN THE MUD!"

was the significant cry of the teamster as he called back to me from his perch on top of the load. Here was a difficulty. The horses had drawn the heavy load for eighty miles and were tired. I resolved to seek for help. Going forward through the wood I came to an old farmer, named Cassidy. I told him my trouble, who I was, and where I was going. He very cheerfully sent his son with a large, strong yoke of oxen to our assistance. The cattle were hitched to the load, and in a little while we were through the long mud hole and on the high ground once more. I went in to settle with Mr. Cassidy, but he declined to take anything, saying that he always tried, when it was in his power, to help those who were in trouble.

While I was away seeking help, two of the Felkers from the vicinity of the parsonage came along on their way home from Fergus. On finding out who we were, they took our two boys along with them, and left them at Mr. Lawrence Monkman's, who lived right beside the house we were going to, so that the news of our coming went ahead of us. We went on, and when we came to the place we found Mr. Monkman sitting on the fence waiting for us. We drove the load into the yard, and then we all went home with our new friends to stay all night. After tea we all went to the parsonage and unloaded the stuff, and put it into the house that was to be our home for the next two years. After two years of hard work and a good degree of success on the mission, and after becoming warmly attached to the people, we had to prepare for

Our Second Move.

The Conference was held at Willowdale, on Yonge Street. My appointment was to Elma mission. This was a new field, only one year old. It was about forty miles from where I was living. Its headquarters was a little hamlet on the boundary between the townships of Wallace and Elma, in the county of Perth. It was then called Mapleton. It is now the enterprising town of Listowel. From the preacher that had been there the previous year I got a list of the appointments, and the names and residences of the members. But he could tell me but little about the road that I should go. After gaining all the information that I could, I mapped out the line of travel, and made preparations to move. Two young men, James Robinson and James Loree, volunteered to take their teams and carry our stuff. We gladly accepted their kind offer. We started on a nice bright morning in the month of June. We went through the village of Fergus, where we stopped for dinner. After noon we started again. While we were going through the township of Nichol the clouds poured down rain at a rate that sent every one under shelter who had a place to run to. But for us there was no shelter until we came to the village of Drayton, on the line between Peel and Maryborough. We had a covered buggy, but even that could not keep us dry. And the poor teamsters just had to take it as best they could. The rain came in torrents all the afternoon and all night and the next morning, until ten o'clock. We stayed at the only hotel at Drayton. We were as well used as the condition of things in a new country would admit. Next morning everything looked very gloomy. Water was running in torrents everywhere, filling up the low places and raising the creeks and streams in all directions at an alarmingly rapid rate. At ten the clouds seemed to break and the rain ceased. We started on again, but now travelling was almost out of the question, because of water everywhere, and the mud seemed to be turned into brown putty. Wherever it touched it stuck like paint. We got dinner at a little place called Hollin. We tried the road once more. One of the teams got stuck in the mud, and the other teamster had to hitch on and help it out. Between two and three o'clock the rain commenced again as hard as ever. We went on, as there was no help for it. On the town line between Maryborough and Wallace we found a hotel, where we put up for the night, having gained eight miles and got another soaking. The landlord told us that to take those roads through to Mapleton would be impossible. He said the settlers sometimes went through with oxen and sleds, but he did not think a waggon had ever gone over. I told him that·*we must go through.*

Next morning after breakfast we started. We got along all right for half a mile, then we came to a cedar swamp through which a road had been cut and causewayed. In the middle of the swamp was a large creek. When we came to it we found that about two rods of the causeway had been carried away by the freshet, and a current of clear, beautiful water, about two feet deep and thirty feet wide, was running through the gap. I got a pole and tried the bottom, and found that it was solid. I told the men that we would try it. The forward team was a span of Lower Canadian French horses. They went off the logs into the stream all right, but when the waggon went in they both fell flat in the water, and they could not get up again. The two men and myself had to get into the water to save them from drowning. We got them

on their feet and out of the water.   Then we decided
that the waggons could go no further.

I went back and got a man with a pair of oxen to
hitch to the hind axle and draw the waggon and load
back to the causeway.   I told the men to take the
things back to the hotel and unload them.   Then I
put the saddle on my horse and started for Mapleton
to seek for help, having to make my horse swim three
streams before getting there.

I went to George Maynard, who was the class-leader
at Mapleton.   When I told him who I was and what
I wanted, he said he was glad to see me.   They had,
he said, been in a worry about moving the preacher.
"But," said he, "since you have come so far, we can
surely get your things brought the rest of the way."
We went to see the Steward, Mr. J. Tremain, and they
two agreed to come with their oxen and sleds the next
day to bring a part of our stuff.

I went back to where I left the family, and found
that the teamsters had unloaded and started for home.
The water had spoiled a good deal of our furniture.
My wife and I were in the barn examining our goods
when a man came up to me and looked me in the face
saying, "Are you a Methodist preacher?"   I looked at
him, and I hardly knew at first what to make of him.
He was a fierce-looking man, and his hair stood up on
end as much as hair could do.   I did not know
whether I had found a friend, or unwittingly made
an enemy.   But looking him steadily in the face,
I answered by saying, "I am a substitute for one.
What can I do for you?"   "Come home with me,"

was his ready reply. He said, "My children came home from school and brought the word that a minister and his family were here waiting for teams to come and take them to Mapleton. My wife and I talked it over, and we concluded to invite you to our house. We don't know who you are, nor what branch of Methodism you represent, nor do we care. It is enough for us to know that one of our Master's servants is in need of a friend." I asked him where he lived. He pointed over the field to a house not a quarter of a mile away. I went in and told the landlord that I had found a friend, settled up with him for the trouble we had given him, and went home with Mr. Spaulding, who was a Wesleyan class-leader. We found a genial atmosphere at this Christian home, and had a comfortable night's rest. Both Mr. and Mrs. Spaulding were warm-hearted, intelligent and consecrated Christians. As I lay thinking over the events of the day, the passage, "I was a stranger and ye took me in," seemed to have greater meaning to me than ever it had before.

Next morning, at nine o'clock, George Maynard and John Tremain were on hand with the teams. We loaded on the articles that would be most damaged by remaining wet, for everything was completely saturated; the rest we piled up in the corner of Mr. Smith's barn until the flood subsided. We started; I on horseback and the rest any way that suited them best, as I had to leave the buggy behind. The bush in some places was like a flower-garden, and the children nearly ran wild about the wild-wood flowers. We got over

the creeks and watery places as well as could be expected, and arrived at the house that was called the
Parsonage. The country was new; the first settlers
had gone into these townships in eighteen hundred
and fifty, so that there was not a farm in the two townships over eight years old and not many of them more
than half that age. We found an excellent class of
people on the Elma mission. When we got our things
unpacked we found that much of our clothing was
more or less damaged, while some articles were completely spoiled. This was especially the case with our
hats and bonnets. These had been carefully packed in
the drawers of a bureau. The rain had softened the
glue and the bureau had fallen to pieces, letting the
contents of all the drawers fall together in one mass
of mixed cotton, woollen, fur, felt and feathers. The
ruin was complete. My wife had not a bonnet left
that was fit to wear on the street, and I had not a hat
left that was worth picking up in the road; and there
was no chance to replace them, as there was not a
medium store of goods within twenty miles of us. The
best that I could do was to make a dye of soft maple
bark and green copperas, and color a coarse straw hat,
which made me a Sunday hat, till it was cold enough
to put on a fur cap. My wife got a bonnet "shape"
at D. D. Campbell's little store, and covered it with
silk taken from a dress that she got while I was a
mechanic. That did her while we stayed on the mission. The loss of that move by damage done to furniture was more than fifty dollars.

I had fair success on this charge, and I became

warmly attached to the people, and I did not dislike the place. We stayed there one year, and then came the time to give the itinerant wheel another turn. Then came the marching order for us to pack up and go to the Teeswater mission. When I came from Conference and told my wife where we were to go, I expected to hear some sighs and see some tears, but I was disappointed. She only said, "Well, it is a hard move, so soon after the one we had last year. I think the stationing committee might have done better for us." Then I told her that I had made up my mind to leave the decision of the case with her. If she did not want to face it, I would drop out of the itinerancy, settle down again, and do what I could in a local capacity. Short and emphatic was her answer: "We will go to Teeswater," said she, "if we stick in the mud along the road and half starve after me get there." I said, "Good for you, little woman; that decides the matter; we will go."

Two days after I got home from Conference I started on foot to my new field. I followed the road to examine it. What was called the road for much of the distance was only a temporary sled track, winding here and there through the bush. At other places the road had been opened out, and the worst of the swamps and creeks had been bridged over by the Government. After I had gone over and inspected the whole distance of thirty-two miles, I concluded that it would be possible to go through with a waggon if it was not too heavily loaded. I filled the appointments on the Sabbath. On Monday we made arrangements for teams to be sent the next week to move our things. In taking a survey of the place, and after getting what information I was able, I concluded a horse would be of but little use here. The roads were not in a condition to make riding on horseback either safe or pleasant. On my return to Mapleton I sold my horse. Part of the price went to pay the store bill of the previous year, and the other part was taken in store pay.

I knew that it was going to be a very difficult thing to go through to Teeswater with waggons over the road that I had seen, but to find any better road it would be necessary to go around by Goderich, or else by Walkerton. Either one of these routes would involve over one hundred miles of travel, and a bad road at that. I resolved to try the shorter road at all hazards. When the time came for the teams to arrive only one came. That was sent by a man that was going out to the old settlements on some business of his own. I was expected to drive the team back. We loaded up what we could put on the waggon with safety and started. The road was very rough all the way, but the first six miles were cleared out, and the creeks and swamps covered with corduroy bridges. We got along nicely over this. Then we turned off on a bush road for about six or seven miles. Here everybody had to walk that could do so, and the rest had to be carried.

At length we came to a place where the road went through a quagmire, and the black muck had been turned into a bed of mortar to a greater depth than was consistent with the passage of heavy loads. I got on the load to drive over, and got along all right for part of the way, when both horses fell into the mud and could not get up again. Here was trouble. The waggon sank in mud up to the axles. One of the horses gave right up, and seemed to fancy that his time to escape from whips and bad feed had come. The other horse was a spirited animal, that had no notion of dying in the mud. He made a desperate effort to regain his footing, but in doing this he seemed inclined to make a bridge of his unfortunate companion in distress. This proceeding greatly increased the peril of his mate's situation.

I got down from my elevated position on the load, feeling that for once in my life I had found a "soft place" to light on. I got into the mud and unbuckled and unhitched until the horses were loose from the waggon and free from each other. I sent my boys for help to a place about half a mile distant, where I had seen some men and oxen as I was passing the week before. I got a long pole, and placed one end of it over the one horse and under the other, and then I took the other end on my shoulder. In this way I could keep the ambitious horse from throwing himself on the discouraged one, which was in danger of being buried alive by the struggles of his less submissive mate. While I was standing in the mud and water, an elderly lady came along. On seeing the position of things, she said to me :

" Well, mister, you are in a bad fix. Can I do any-thing for you ? "

I said, " This don't look very much like a woman's work, does it ? "

"No, not much," she said; "but I should very much like to help you, if I could. Do you think you will get those horses out alive?"

I said, "I hope so. It can be done if I can get some help."

"Well," said the old lady, "on my way home I pass the shanties of four or five men. I will send every one of them here in less than an hour."

She did as she promised, and with the help of two other men, who came from another direction, we got the horses out after a hard struggle. But such a queer-looking team I never saw. When they went in one was gray and the other black, but when they came out no one could tell which one was black or gray. With the help of the horses, and some ropes and pries, we got the waggon out. We lost three hours by this mud-hole. We fed the horses and took a lunch in the bush, and then drove on to the home of William Ekins, a local-preacher in the Church that I belonged to. This brother was a whole-souled, warm-hearted Tipperary Irishman, who feared no man but himself, and who dared to do anything that was not sinful or mean. I heard him once say, that the only man in the world that he feared was "Bill" Ekins. If by the help of God, he could keep Ekins out of mischief, he could get along with everybody else.

I never was more sorry for any one than for my wife that night. She was so tired that she could hardly get along at all. She was not much accustomed to travelling on foot. But she had walked fourteen or fifteen miles that day, and had carried a baby in her arms the most of the way. As I looked at her as she sat at the tea-table, I thought that so complete an embodiment of pluck, and perseverance, and energy, and weariness, done up in less than one hundred pounds of feminine humanity, I had never before looked upon. After a good night's rest we started on our way to our new home. Brother Ekins placed my wife on a nice pony of his, and sent a boy along to bring it back. This made it easier for her. We found a better road, too, than we had the day before. But we had a number of corduroy bridges or causeways to go over, which caused us to progress but slowly. We took our lunch that day in the shadow of a pile of saw-logs, on the top of a high hill. The children enjoyed this gipsy mode of doing very much.

After this we got on nicely until within about two miles of Teeswater. Then, in crossing a cedar-swamp where the road was very much tramped over, so that the mud was very deep and sticky, the horses both went down again, and either could not or would not get up. Again I went in and got the horses loose from the waggon and from each other. I sent my wife and part of the children on under the guidance of Ekins' boy. I left my boys to watch the team, and went to look for help. Some distance further on I found a company of men "logging" in a new fallow. They had a good yoke of cattle. After much persuasion, and by promising full pay for the time spent, the owner of the oxen went back with me. When we came to the place, the horses had got up and walked out to hard ground, and were browsing leaves off the bushes. The oxen soon brought the load out of the mud. I paid one dollar and fifty cents to their owner, and in an hour we found ourselves at the little house, only partly finished, that was to be our home for the next Conference year. This mission was in the township of Culross.

The first settlers went into this township in eighteen hundred and fifty-three, so that the oldest farm was only seven years old.

When we tried to start housekeeping with the few articles that we had been able to bring on our load, we found no little difficulty. We had neither bedstead, table nor chair in the house; and a number of other things needed for constant use were conspicuous by their absence. But it is not easy to beat a woman if she has her mind made up to do a thing. My wife soon decided what was to be done. Some benches were made as a substitute for chairs; a large packing-box, covered with table linen, served for a table; the floor was used for bedsteads; and for a cradle, "to rock the baby in," a sap trough was got from Mr. Ira Fulford's sugar bush. As soon as I could get away, I went back to Mapleton for the rest of our stuff. But at that time teams were very scarce; the best that I could do was to gather up a pair of horses, a waggon and harness, the property of four different owners, and a young man to go with me and bring back the team. We started with our load, but one of the animals had done no heavy work since it was brought into the bush two years before. The collar soon began to gall its shoulders, and before we got half the distance this horse refused to draw the load any further. We left the waggon standing in the road, and went two miles further on, and stayed all night. Next morning I borrowed a yoke of oxen from a Mr. Donohoe, with which I hauled the load to his place and put it in his barn, sent the young man back with the empty waggon, and I went home without the stuff. After a while I got a team and a boy from Mr. John Gilroy and a waggon from Mr. Barber. They lived seven miles apart. With this outfit I went and fetched the things. We had been without them about two months. (As this mission is spoken of elsewhere in these pages, I will say no more about it here.) We stayed only one year; then we were sent right back to Mapleton, or more properly, Listowel, as the name had been changed. But the improvement in the road was so great, and our return move was so different from what we found the year before, that we could hardly believe that it was the same road that we had gone over the year before. Rough causeways had been covered with earth, creeks had been bridged, knolls had been levelled down, and low places filled up, so the whole distance was gone over in one day. Teams were sent from Listowel to move the household goods. Mr. P. B. Brown, reeve of Culross, volunteered to go with a double carriage and take the family. We got through in one day, and not ten cents worth of injury was done to anything.

It is surprising what rapid progress is made in a new country, when it is filled up with an enterprising, go-a-head class of settlers. And that was the kind of people that first went into these townships.

During our stay this time at Listowel, there was nothing of an unusual nature that occurred, except the prevalence of typhoid fever, spoken of in another chapter. My success in the work was about an average, nothing special one way or other. We were here but one year, and then we had our appointment for the second time to Garafraxa. This was three moves in as many years. I at first concluded that I was one of the unfortunate men that the people would only tolerate for one year. But then the fact that I was sent to places where I had been before seemed not to harmonize with that idea. I could not understand it, and it was only after I had gained experience, in the stationing of men, that I could account for the strange moves that are sometimes made in the itinerant work.

On my way home from Conference I passed through Garafraxa, and made arrangements for moving. The committee to move the preacher that year was composed in part, of Morris, Cook, and Henry Scarrow, who consented to go with their teams and move us. In this case, too, we found the return journey entirely different from what we had experienced three years before, in going from Garafraxa to Mapleton.

We found improvements in other things as well as roads. When we left there we moved out of an old log-house that had been built in the early days of the mission. On coming back we moved into a nice little stone cottage, that had been built during the pastorate of Rev. J. H. Watts.

On resuming the work on this circuit I was much pleased with the state of the Church. Progress had

been made in other things besides building. Through
the earnest and persevering labours of Brother Watts,
a large number had been added to the Church since I
had left the circuit three years before. Of this man's
work I wish to say, after ample opportunities to observe
its effects, it wears well.

During my former pastorate on this charge, I
received into membership over one hundred new converts. It was very encouraging on my return to find
most of these still on the way, and some of them filling important positions in the Church. Some two or
three had passed away in the full assurance of faith,
and in the joyful hope of a glorious home beyond the
tide. These things gave me great encouragement to
work on for the salvation of men.

We had two very pleasant years, and would have
stayed longer, but at that time the discipline only
allowed two years' pastorate as a rule. The results of
my efforts on this circuit are fully shown in another
chapter. So that I must not particularize here.

Our next move was to Mount Forest. Teams were
sent to move us. We loaded up and started. Before
we had gone one mile, a very painful, if not fatal,
accident was providentially prevented by the activity
of Mr. James Bell, who now lives in Muskoka. He
was walking by the side of one of the loads, on the top
of which a place had been fixed for our two little girls.
They were perched up on the load safely, as we thought.
While we were going through a piece of brush, where
the ground was nearly hidden by beautiful wild-flowers,
the girls became so attracted by what they saw that

they forgot where they were. Just at that moment the front wheels went into a deep rut. One of the girls fell from her seat, and was falling right in front of the wheel. Mr. Bell sprang forward just in time to catch her, and, before he could set her aside, the other girl came right after her sister. But Mr. Bell was so quick in his movements that he saved them both from harm. I was just behind with a horse and buggy, along with my wife and the smaller children, and we saw the whole thing. When I saw them fall I thought they would be instantly killed. I could not see how any earthly hand could save them. But by the mercy of God they were saved. They lived to grow up to womanhood, seek the Lord, witness a good profession, and then go to pluck the flowers of fadeless beauty in the fields of the " sweet by and bye."

Nothing more took place of an unusual character till we got to Mount Forest. We spent rather an uncomfortable year there. A combination of circumstances, which I need not mention here, contributed to make our stay in this place a short one, and an unpleasant one. My manner of doing things was so very different from that of my predecessor, and the style of the people in the town was so diverse from that of those that I had been previously living among, that I was discontented and the people were dissatisfied. I did not want to stay, and the people in the town did not want me to stay, so that our views, after all, were quite harmonious.

When the Conference came on I asked to be moved, and my request was granted. Our next move was to

Invermay.   This was a new mission, only two years old.   It embraced the township of Arran, and extended into the townships of Saugeen, Elderslie and Sullivan.

I liked this place, although it was a hard field to work on account of the distances between appointments.   We found some of the noblest men on the Invermay mission that I have met with in all my ministerial experience.   We remained here one year, and then, by my consent, we went to the town of Meaford, on the shore of the Georgian Bay.   Here I passed some of the pleasantest and some of the saddest days of my life.   But this need not be detailed here, as it is spoken of elsewhere.

We stayed two years, and then we were sent to the village of Thornbury, only eight miles, and also on the shore of the bay.   We were here three years, the discipline having been so changed as to make that the full term.   Then I was placed on the Huron District as Presiding Elder.   We moved back to Meaford, and that was my home during my four years' term on the district.   I was at home on an average two months out of the twelve.   When my district work was done I was again stationed by Bishop Richardson on the Meaford Circuit.   We only stayed one year, and then we went to the fine town of Kincardine, on the shores of Lake Huron.   We sent our goods to Kincardine on a boat, taking good care to have them well insured, as Methodist preachers, as a rule, are not very well prepared to replace articles that may be destroyed by fire or water, and I am no exception to the rule.

We had lived in Meaford and Thornbury for ten

years, and it seemed very much like leaving home when we had to move some eighty miles, and settle again among strangers. This was the case so far as my family were concerned. For myself it was not so. I had frequently been in Kincardine. We stayed in this place nine years. Three years I had charge of the circuit, which was a large one, requiring two men, and six years I was a superannuate, filling one appointment every Sabbath for four years out of the six. As presiding elder, as preacher in charge, or as special supply, I served the M. E. congregation in the town of Kincardine for the term of eleven years.

As we had only moved three times in about nineteen years, we began to fear that we should lose the spirit of the itinerancy, and become stationary in our habits, So we packed up once more, and came to Streetsville, where these pages are written.

In this last move we had an opportunity of testing the advantages of the present system of migration over the old way. We placed our things in a car, took a receipt for them, and then visited among friends for two or three days. Then we stepped into a first-class car, had a few hours' pleasant ride, reached our destination, and found our goods all right and everything safe. I could not help saying to my wife that if this state of things had been in vogue thirty years ago, we would not have had so many articles spoiled and broken as we have lost by moving since we commenced our itinerant life.

CHAPTER IV.

EVERY institution has some set phrases peculiar to itself. Navigation has its wharves, its quays, and its docks; railways, banks, etc., have their presidents, their managers and their agents. The Churches have their synods, their assemblies, and their conferences. Among the Methodists the phrase "Going to Conference" is a very suggestive one. It means a great deal more than the majority of people imagine. There are those who fancy that going to Conference is very much like going to a picnic or a ten days' pleasure party; but to a Methodist minister it is the very opposite to that. To him it means the review of the past, the scrutiny of the present, and the forecast of the future; to him it means a week or ten days of close attention to the details of business, intense thought, earnest discussion, and sometimes harrowing opposition and distasteful decisions; to him it often means the severing of cords that have been strengthening for three years past, and the breaking up of associations that have been widening and deepening month after month during a whole ministerial term according to discipline. It means to him the loss of the sight of well-known faces and of hearing the sound of familiar names.

There was a time when to me the very thought of going to Conference would almost make me shudder. In the M. E. Church, at the time that I joined the ranks of the itinerancy, it was the custom to give every man in the Conference a thorough overhauling in open Conference. The Bishop would ask all the questions that the discipline required, and some that it did not; then he would hand the unfortunate subject of brotherly dissection over to the tender mercies of conferential anatomists to be dealt with according to the whim or caprice of any and every member who might wish to show his ability as an inquisitor, or his ingenuity as a self-constituted detective. No man could, at that time, go to Conference feeling safe, no matter how careful or faithful he had been in his work. He did not know but that the ghost of some duty, overlooked or forgotten, would arise and confront him in the presence of all; he could not tell but that the echo of some unguarded word might come ringing to his ears, and make more noise in Conference than all his prayers and sermons and songs of praise could do. A man was once charged with crime and taken into court; the indictment was read and the crown lawyer made his charge in very strong language, as is usual. The judge asked the prisoner if he was "guilty or not guilty." He said: "When I came into court I really thought that I was innocent of the crime charged against me; but since I have heard the reading of that

6

document, and the speech of that lawyer, I do not know what to think about it."   Just so; a man might go to Conference thinking that his record was not a bad one, and that he might be considered a pretty fair average among reasonably good men; but by the time that Doctor Rake-him-up and some others were done with him, he might doubt if there was a mite of honesty, or a particle of piety in his whole composition. But those days passed away years ago, and the Methodism of this country will never allow them to return.   We now have a better way to reach the same results.   No man should throw out an insinuation that may cast a slur on a brother's good name unless he is prepared to formulate specific charges.

The greatest tongue-lashing that I ever gave a minister was for a matter of this kind.   A young man had been his colleague, and was recommended for admission on trial in the Conference; his superintendent was called upon to give information respecting the young man.   He went on to say that the young man was a fair preacher, and that he stood pretty well among the people, "but," said he, " I have good reason to believe that he is in the habit of receiving letters from a married woman, and I do not know what they are all about."   On enquiry it was found that his statement was entirely correct, but when explanations were given, it came out the letters were from the young man's married sister.   Some of them were on business, and others such as any sister might write to a brother. I concluded that a man like that deserved a talking to, and he got it.

In going to Conference the mode of travel is mostly determined by circumstances. When the Conference is one of very extended boundaries, it becomes a matter of considerable importance to those who live at a distance from the place where its sessions are to be held. The present mode of travel is by railway mostly; but in the past it was not so. I have gone to Conference on the boat, on the cars, on wheels, on horseback, and on foot. The last mentioned is the most independent way of going; then there are no fees to pay, no horse to feed, no wheels to grease, and no one to be thanked; but still I would not advise that way of going, as it is a little wearisome. And I have gone to Conference when it took me three full days' travel to reach it; and I have gone when a few minutes' walk would take me to it.

I have met with interesting episodes before now when on my way to Conference. I propose to relate a few of them. Once I was going from Teeswater to Ingersoll. The country was new and the roads anything but good. I had no horse; I shouldered my carpet-bag and started off on foot. I did not know whether I should have to walk all the way or not. The nearest railroad to me was the Grand Trunk at Guelph or Stratford, and the Grand Trunk did not go to Ingersoll at that time. When I got as far as Listowel I found that the preacher there, Peter Hicks, was going to Conference with a horse and buggy. He kindly offered me a chance to ride with him, which offer I thankfully accepted. We started early in the morning and reached the village of Mitchell by noon.

We fed the horse and got dinner at a hotel. We went on to Stratford and fed the horse. There we inquired the road, and after getting what information we could we started on, intending to go to the home of Mr. T. B. Brown, a local preacher with whom I was acquainted. We got on the wrong road; night came on us and found us in the midst of a settlement of Irish Catholics. At length we came to a little wayside tavern. It hardly could be called a hotel. We drove up to the door and went in. About a dozen men were drinking in the bar-room. We looked around and saw the condition of things, and then went out for a consultation, after inquiring the distance to St. Mary's. We talked the matter over a little, when Hicks said, " I will go in and see if any Orangemen are there." He came out shortly and said, " They are Papists, every one of them, and the landlord is the biggest dogan of the lot." This was not very reassuring intelligence. However, we concluded to stay, as there seemed no help for it. We went in again and asked the landlord if he could accommodate us with supper and bed, and the horse with hay and oats. He said, " You must see the missus about the supper, as it is after hours, but I can promise you the rest." I said to Hicks, " You look after the horse, and I will see about the supper." I hunted up the landlady, whom I found putting away the newly washed dishes. I explained the reason of our coming in so late. I told her that we were very hungry, and asked her to let us have some supper. She very good naturedly set about it, and in a few minutes she had a very respectable meal ready for us. Meanwhile the noise in the bar-room became more boisterous and loud. We ate our supper and then went out to fix up the horse for the night. That being done, we went to our room for the night. We fastened the door and then considered the situation. We could hear from the bar-room every now and then angry words and oaths and imprecations. We could not tell who were the subjects of these anathemas, but we had no doubt they suspected that we were Protestant ministers by the glances that would pass between them as we went out and in through the room.

We did not get into bed until long after midnight, and after the noisy rabble had gone off and the house became quiet. In the morning we did not wait for breakfast, but we went on a few miles and called at a farmhouse and got breakfast. They told us there that we had done well to get away without trouble, as the place was a very rough one. We did not stop there when we came back. The action of the lady on that occasion harmonizes with a statement made by the late Dr. Livingstone in respect to the women in Africa. He says that he never asked a woman a question and did not receive a civil answer, and he never asked a favour that was not courteously granted if in her power to do so.

The first man I met that I knew, as we drove into Ingersoll, was one who was a very popular preacher when I was working as a mechanic. He had been my pastor for two years, and I loved him as my own brother; but he had been expelled for drunkenness some time before. When he saw me, he ran across the street to meet me : with tears in his eyes, and sobbing like a home-sick child, he said, " Oh, Brother Hilts, what would I not give to-day, if I had it, to be as I was when you first met me." My heart ached for that man. He had been one of the most genial and affable men that I had ever known ; but the love of drink was his bane through life. He had inherited alcoholism from his parents, and had not sufficient self-government nor grace to control it. I have been told that he died under the shadow of a tree, on the Pacific coast, as he was trying to make his way to the gold fields of Cariboo.

An Uncircumcised Ishmaelite.

Before the extension of the Northern Railway to Meaford, people had to go to Collingwood before they could take the cars. I was on my way to Conference. which was to meet in Port Perry. While waiting at the Collingwood station an elderly gentleman came up to me and said, " Mister, did you not preach in the M. E. Church in Meaford last night ? " I said, " Yes, sir ; or at least I tried to do so." " Well," said he, " my name is Blank ; I have been from home a while, and I have not been as good as I might have been, so I thought that I would go to church last night. My wife is a member of that church, and she is a good woman, and I think she will be pleased when I tell her that I have gone to church while I have been from home." We went into the car and Mr. B. sat in the seat with me. Presently he said, " Look here, mister, you men like to find a good table to sit down to and a good stable to put your horse in. I have got both of

these at home."   " Well," said I, "the preachers call on
you sometimes, I hope,"   "Yes," he said, "they do
often, and I am glad to have them come.   They call
me the kind-hearted and good-natured "uncircumcised
Ishmaelite."   I told him that I was glad that the
preachers liked him, and that I hoped they would do
him good. "Well," he replied, "I like them well enough,
but either they can't or they won't answer my questions."   I said, "Perhaps your questions are unanswer-
able."   He then said, "Will you tell me how many
folks Abraham and his wife took with them when they
went to Egypt?"   I said, "Sir, I can't tell; I never
studied that question, and I don't think it is found in
any of the arithmetics that I have seen."   He asked
me a number of questions on different subjects, but I
played shy of all of them until he seemed to get a
little nettled.   At last I said to him, "Mr. B., I am too
old to think that I know a great deal, but I can tell
you how to get your questions all answered.."   "How?"
said he.   "The first young man you meet with who
has plenty of conceit, with no beard on his face and
but little brains in his head, ask him and he will tell
you all about it."

By this time we had reached Newmarket.   I stopped
over till the next day.   When I came to the station
in the morning I found Mr. Blank, along with a number of others, waiting for the train.   As soon as I
got on the platform he came to me and said, " Mister,
you dodged all my questions yesterday; now I have
one that I really wish to have answered.   It is this:
"Has a negro a soul?"   I said, "I think he has; he is

a man, and every man has a soul." "Well, how does he come to be black?" I answered that probably climatic influences and habits of life had a good deal to do with making him black. "Hot climates make people dark, and cold climates make them fair," I said. He said, "I don't believe that; for there are darkies in the Southern States whose ancestors came there two hundred years ago, and they are just as black as their forefathers were the day they left Africa." "That may be all true," I answered; "but then the hot climate of the Southern States is not the most favourable surroundings for a negro if you want to bleach him. Have you never seen one in a transition state?" I asked him. "No," said he, "I never have. Have you?" I said, "I think so; at any rate, I have seen men that, for the life of me, I could not tell whether they were faded negroes or tanned white men." Mr. Blank was a very dark-complexioned man. He looked at me for a minute, and then said, "Did you mean that for me?" "By no means sir," I said; "I had nothing personal in my intention. I simply stated a fact in replying to your question, if I had seen a negro in a transition state." The train came up and we parted, and I have never met him since; but after all I could not help liking the man, and I hope he may do well.

A Southern Blasphemer Silenced.

The civil war in America produced a large crop of "bounty-jumpers" and "skedaddlers." The former came from the North as a general thing, and the latter mostly came from the South. Many of these were the sons of Southern gentlemen who thought too much of slavery to let it die an easy death, and too much of themselves to take a soldier's chances in the field of battle to keep it alive.

When the negro was about to be carried to freedom on a wave of blood, these chivalrous defenders of this peculiar institution betook themselves to a land where the bondsman's footprints are never seen, a land where the black man is entitled to "life, liberty and the pursuit of happiness," as well as his white neighbour.

On a sunny day in the spring, one of the Grand Trunk cars going east from Toronto was partly filled with Methodist ministers on their way to Conference. In a seat near the centre of the car there sat a man of striking appearance: he was tall, and straight, and rawboned. His complexion had that peculiar blending of shades of colour that made it hard to tell to what branch of the human race he claimed affinity; his features, too, were a puzzle; his black eye had a look that might indicate cruelty and stoicism; his forehead gave proof of a strong intellect; his mouth and chin were those of a man of an unbending will, while his nose gave the lie to all the rest, and unmistakably proclaimed him a coward.

A number of miles had been passed over without anything to disturb the people or attract attention, when there came a volley of oaths from the man in the centre seat, that made the men look up with astonishment, and the women fairly wilt like a scorched leaf. The terrible words came from the Southerner. Just behind him there sat a minister by

the name of D. Carscaden.   He was a slender man and
not at all strong; but he could not tolerate such out-
rageous blasphemy.   He very gently and kindly informed the swearer that his language was painful to
him and many others in the car.   This only made
matters worse; the man got angry at this.   The string
of terrible oaths that he rolled out beat everything
that I had ever heard, and the look of contempt that
he cast upon poor Carscaden was enough to drive a
stronger man than he was into hysterics.   Just in the
midst of the volcanic eruptions of dreadful words that
one might imagine came right from the brimstone
regions, a hand was laid on the swearer's shoulder;
he looked up to see to whom the hand belonged; he
saw standing in the aisle beside him a man of grand
muscular development and fearless aspect.   He said to
the blasphemer, "Sir, you must stop this at once, or
this train will be slackened up and you will be put
out of the car.   When you are in your own country,
you can do as you please, if people will let you; but
in this country you must behave yourself if you expect to travel in the cars.   Now, not another word of
that sort, or the conductor will be called and you will
go out."

This was another minister, O. G. Collamore; I know
he will excuse my naming him; he is too much of a
man to be ashamed of a manly action.

When Collamore sat down, the Southerner came out
of his seat and walked up and down the aisle for a
few times scanning his new opponent closely, as if to
take the measure of the man.   What his conclusions

were can only be inferred from his action. He went back into his seat. This episode created quite a sensation in the car and everybody felt that the matter was not yet ended.

After a little, the man spoke to the following effect, as nearly as I can recall his words to mind : "Ladies and gentlemen, I owe an apology to you all for the language that I have been using. Whatever you may think of me, don't lay the blame upon my parents ; they taught me better than to speak such words, especially in the presence of ladies. I am sorry for what I did, and I will not do it again."

Every one felt a relief at the turn the affair took, and I think the Southerner had more respect for Canadians than he would if he had been allowed to go on unchecked.

MEETING A MAN OF MARK.

I was not going to Conference at the time that the incident occurred that I am about to relate, but still I was travelling on the cars. The Great Western Railway had but recently been opened for traffic. One morning in the early spring, I was, along with others, sitting in a car at Hamilton station, waiting for the train to start west. An old woman came into the car selling apples. As she passed along the aisle, she came to an elderly gentleman, whose fatherly appearance and kindly look seemed to give the old woman confidence, so that she continued to press him to buy, after he had told her that he did not need any of her fruit. Presently he said to her :

" Madam, have you any children ? "

She answered him, " Indade, sir, I have six of them and so I have, and I their mother, am a poor widdy, and so I am.   And it's to thry and get a crumb for the little dears that I am here selling apples the day, and so it is."

" Well," he said, " how much will you take for all that you have in your basket ? "

She counted them all over and fixed the price. He then gave her the money for them, and said to her :

" Now these apples are mine, to do with them as I please."

" Yes, sir," she said.   " You do what you please wid 'em, only give me back my basket ? "

" Now," said the man, " I am going to trust you to do with those apples as I tell you."

" And what do you want me to do wid them, sir.   I must have me basket anyway."

" I want you to take the apples home and divide them among your children," said he.   " Will you do it ? "

I will not try to give the number, or describe the quality of the blessings that the old woman invoked upon the body and soul of the kind stranger. After she left the train, he said to me :

" Likely she will sell them before she gets home, but if she does, that is her business and not mine.   I gave them to her in good faith for her children, and if she deceives me, and robs them, she alone will be re-sponsible."

The train started, and nothing more was said about

the old woman or her apples. When we got to Paris, the engine ran off the track, and we were detained for about sixteen hours before we could proceed. During the time I got into conversation with the man who bought the apples. Among other things he said to me:

"I try to get into conversation with all classes of people that I meet with. So much can be learned by taking people on their own ground. You are always safe in speaking to people about what they feel a great deal of interest in. You may at any time or in any place speak to a mother about her children. See how quick that woman was drawn out this morning when her children were mentioned. Just so you may speak to a man about his trade or calling. You may speak to an invalid about his sufferings, or to a penitent sinner about salvation, and be sure of a willing listener."

Before parting from this interesting stranger, I said to him:

" Sir, I have been much interested and highly pleased during the time that we have been together. Will you permit me to ask you, where do you live, and what is your name ?"

He answered, with a pleasant smile upon his face: " As to where I live, it is not easy to say. My home is anywhere within the limits of the British Empire, or within the hospitalities of the English-speaking race. But as to my name, it is not so hard to answer Have you ever heard of Alexander Duff?"

I said I had read in the papers about a man of that name, who is a Presbyterian missionary to India."

He said, " I am he."

" Well, sir," I answered, " I am not a Scotchman, nor a Presbyterian, but as a Briton, a Canadian, and a Christian, I must, before leaving you, have a shake of your hand, and bid you God-speed, and I pray that the Lord may guide you on your way and help you in your work."

He thanked me cordially for my good wishes, and we shook hands and parted. I was highly gratified by having seen and conversed with a man who, at that time, was looming up before the Christian world as a star of the first magnitude. I find in his description of his visit to this country a reference to the accident at Paris, but he says nothing about the apple woman and her children.

BAD NEWS AT CONFERENCE.

On my way to Conference I often met with things that interested me. But at the Conference I sometimes heard things that made me sad. It may seem strange that, although I have lost many friends and relatives during the fifty years that have elapsed since the death of my mother, I have only been permitted to attend the funeral of three of them—two children and one grandchild. That is all. The Lord gave us five sons and three daughters. The latter are all dead and are buried in different counties, far apart. One lies beside its maternal grandfather in Lincoln county ; the other two sleep among strangers in the counties of Grey and Bruce.

There are times when itinerants are lost to their

friends. This is caused by removals from place to place, and from neglect in giving information as to present location. There is really no necessity for this in a country with post-offices in every little village. But sometimes people do not communicate with their distant friends, because of the unpleasant truths that they would tell if they sent to inform their friends of the circumstances in which they were placed. Some people will suffer in silence rather than annoy others with a recitation of their troubles. Sickness comes and goes and nothing is said about it. Death takes place in sundered families and no intelligence is given until long afterwards. In my own case the Conference has been a sort of sad medium of communication between the living and the dead. At one Conference I was told of a sister's departure from this life. At another I heard that my brother had died and was buried. At Conference I first heard of the death of my father, my stepmother, my wife's mother and stepfather, besides other relatives.

Ministers are always willing to enlighten each other and to help each other, and to sympathize with and help each other's friends as far as they can. At least, that has been my experience with them. While every person is supposed to have a place in the affectionate regards of the Methodist minister, I think I am not overstating the case when I say that, other things being equal, there is a peculiar drawing on his part to the family and friends of his brother ministers. I am free to confess that it is the case with regard to myself, and I have often heard others say the same.

I have not missed a Conference in thirty years. I have been a member of twenty-eight Annual Conferences, and I have been in my seat at every session from first to last, with the exception of one day. I have been a member of four General Conferences. From one of these I was kept by sickness. I started to go, but I had to return home too sick to go on. But after all, I like very much to go to Conference, and I shall be very sorry if the time ever comes that I am not able to do so, until the time comes for me to answer to my name at the great roll-call of Conference above.

CHAPTER V.

CAMP-MEETINGS.

IF there is any place on earth that is more like heaven than a good live camp-meeting, I should like to hear from it. I would be pleased to know where it is, and on what grounds the claim is made. To commune with nature, is, to a devout mind, a precious privilege. To commune with good people is a blessed means of grace. And to commune with God is a greater blessing than either or both of these. To hold converse with nature, tends to expand the intellect and quicken the sensibilities. To hold friendly intercourse with the good elevates, refines, and stimulates the social and moral elements of our being. And to commune with God purifies and exalts our whole nature, and inspires us to a holier life and loftier aims and a fuller consecration to the service of God.

In the original idea of the camp-meeting we are at the same time, and in the same place, brought in converse with nature, in religious fellowship with the good and in sweet communion with God. I know of no place where the ethical, esthetical, social and spiritual wants of humanity are more fully provided for than at the camp-meeting. There some of the most soul-inspiring scenes that earth can furnish may be witnessed. When a strong religious influence is felt by the assembled worshippers as, with cheerful voices they ring out the melody of their gladdened hearts, where is the soul so dead as not to feel an impulse drawing heavenward? The trees that surround this leafy temple seem to catch the spirit of song, and send back to the ears of the happy worshippers in pleasing echoes the very words they are giving utterance to. The leaves upon the forest trees as they are swept by the ascending currents of air that are heated by the "light-stand" fires, seem to vie with the human singers as they rustle to the praise of Him who gave to them their numbers and their beauty. Even the shadows cast by the trees and limbs that intercept the lights of the camp-fires seem to enter into the spirit of the occasion, and point upward to a realm where darkness is unheard of and shadows are unknown.

My first experience with camp-meetings was many years ago. When thirteen years old, I was permitted to go with my parents to one at a place called Beechwoods, in 1832. At that camp-meeting there were one or two of the Ryersons, James Richardson, one of the Evans, and other preachers both Canadian and American.

There was a camp of Indians on the ground too. They would sometimes sing. That was a source of enjoyment to the younger portion of the audience. The prayer-meetings were in a square enclosure made by placing long poles on the top of posts set at the four angles, so that the poles would be some three feet from the ground. At one corner there was left an opening for entrance and exit.

My parents had a share in a tent, and we remained on the encampment from the beginning to the end of the meetings.

For the first two or three days the novelty of my surroundings tended to banish serious thoughts from my mind. But as the meetings progressed, a number of the young people were converted. My attention was at last arrested by two young girls, I think they were sisters. I saw them go into the place, and kneel, weeping, at the altar for prayer. It was not long till they were both blessed. Then they began to sing "Come, ye sinners, poor and needy." The congregation joined in, and the woods rang with the voices of a hundred or more as they rolled on the old invitation "Come." The singing was after the manner of happy children whose hearts were full of joy and their souls full of melody, rather than like the cold, majestic performances of some of the stately choristers of our times.

I was standing up against the poles and listening to the singing, when my mother came to me, saying, "My son, you are old enough to sin, so you are old enough to be converted; don't you want to come and be saved?" I bent down and crept in under the pole, and went to the penitent form. My mother knelt beside me. And it seemed to me that I had never heard such praying

as she did then and there for me. My father came
and knelt by me, too, and joined his prayers to mother's.
Up till then I had thought that I was not a very bad
boy, but now it seemed to me that every mean and
sinful thing that I had ever said or done was called up
before me just to torture my wounded spirit. 1 tried
to pray for myself, but the words seemed to stop in
my throat and choke me. Despair was fast seizing
upon me, when one of the preachers came and said to
me, " Can't you say, ' Here, Lord, I give myself away,
'tis all that I can do.' " I commenced to say it. Before
the words were spoken, my soul was full of light and
my heart was filled with joy unspeakable. Then I was
converted. And now, after all the intervening years I
look back to that day and that spot with the same
feelings that prompted some one to write,

> "There is a place to me more dear
>   Than native vale or mountain—
> A place for which affection's tear
>   Springs grateful from its fountain;
> 'Tis not where kindred souls abound,
>   Tho' that were almost Heaven,
> But where I first my Saviour found
>   And felt my sins forgiven."

With what thrilling memories I can still declare in
honesty,

> " Hard was my toil to reach the shore,
>   As, tossed upon the ocean,
> Above me was the thunder's roar,
>   Beneath the waves' commotion."

And, as it were, to add to the horrors of the scene,

> "Darkly the pall of night was thrown
>   Around me, faint with terror;
> In that sad hour, how did my groan
>   Ascend for years of error."

And still the night grew darker, and the storm grew fiercer, and the waves rose higher, and the wind grew stronger, and the thunder louder, till,

> "Sinking and gasping as for breath,
>   I knew not help was near me;
> I cried, 'Oh! save me, Lord, from death;
>   Immortal Jesus, save me.'
> Then, quick as thought, I felt Him mine—
>   My Saviour stood before me;
> Around me did His brightness shine;
>   I shouted, 'Glory! glory!'"

The memory of that blessed moment shall not pass away while reason holds her throne, and consciousness performs its wonted task.   And still I say,

> "O! sacred hour; O! hallowed spot,
>   Where love divine first found me;
> Whate'er shall be my distant lot,
>   My heart shall linger round thee.
> And when from earth I rise to soar
>   Up to my home in Heaven,
> Down will I cast my eyes once more,
>   Where I was first forgiven."

I once heard an old man say at a camp-meeting love-feast, that the dearest spot on earth to him was in a ditch under a hedge in Ireland.   There it was where he was converted.

But I fear I have lingered too long on this old camp-ground.   I have been at a good many such places since, but I shall mention only a few of them.

MONO CAMP-MEETING.

During the second year of my itinerant life I attended a camp-meeting in the township of Mono on the Orangeville mission. There were a number of preachers at that meeting. But they are all gone from this country, or from this world, but the Rev. George Hartley, of the Guelph Conference, and myself. I had been extensively engaged in revival work on Garafraxa Circuit, and I enjoyed it very much. I went into the work with all my might at that meeting. I did a good deal at the leading of prayer-meetings.

One night my wife said to me, "Do you know that you are the noisiest man on the ground?" Now, I had always been called one of the still kind of Methodists, and sometimes people had said that my religion was of the Presbyterian type—not much noise about it. But to be told that I was the most noisy one among a noisy lot of men, was something new to me. But when I came calmly to think the matter over I concluded that my wife had told only the truth. But what should I do. I was now fully committed to the work, and it seemed to be doing good. Finally I made up my mind to go through as I had begun.

One afternoon it came on to rain. The outside services were broken up, and the people gathered into a long tent for a prayer-meeting. After a while the Rev. I. B. Richardson, who had charge of the meeting, came to me and said, " We must have preaching now for a change, and you must preach." I said, " All right;

you line a hymn while I hunt a text." I chose the words, "This man receiveth sinners." It was an easy place to preach. The presence of God was among the people. While I was trying to encourage sinners to come to Jesus and be saved, one man was converted as he sat on his seat. He began to praise the Lord at the top of his voice. Others joined in with him, and then some of the preachers started to shout. This was like a signal for a general hallelujah service. In a few minutes my voice was completely lost in the hurricane of sound that came from that tent full of people. There was no more preaching at that time. Mr. Richardson, who had done a good share of the shouting, took charge of the meeting.

The man who was converted was William Bacon, of Melville, in Caledon. He lived a Christian life, and some years ago he died a happy death, and no doubt went up to see the receiver of sinners in His own bright home. At the time that I received the paper that contained the obituary notice of Brother Bacon's death I was in poor health, and I had been harrassed in my mind for some days. I suppose it was a temptation. But it had seemed to me that perhaps after all I had mistaken my calling. I had thought, that if I had kept to a secular pursuit, it might be that now in my old age, with a broken down constitution, I might not be so helpless and so entirely dependent upon others. When I read the article of Rev. G. Clark concerning the conversion, and life, and death of Brother Bacon, I said that will do. If I have been the means of helping one soul into the kingdom, and who has made a safe journey to the home of the blest, my life has not been in vain.

The Melville Camp-Meeting.

Some years after the Mono camp-meeting there was one at Melville on the same circuit. The tent-holders were nearly the same in both cases. Among them were the Hughsons, Johnstons, Wilcoxes, Bacons, and others, whose names I do not now call to mind. The meeting was well attended, and a good work was accomplished. The late Rev. William Woodward was the manager of the meeting; John H. Watts was the stationed minister. I should have said that Rev. Henry Jones was on the circuit at the time of the Mono camp-meeting.

At Melville there were a number of our ministers present. Among them were Revs. W. H. Shaw, A. L. Thurston, J. W. Mackay, E. Will, and some others. Perhaps the most noticeable circumstance there, was the preaching of an Irish local preacher, whose name was Thomas Moore. At the close of the forenoon services one day the Rev. Woodward told the audience that at 2 p.m. the stand would be occupied by Brother Thomas Moore, a preaching farmer from Garafraxa. At this announcement there was no little stir among the leading laymen on the ground. Mr. Moore was by no means prepossessing either in appearance or manner, and he had an awkward and clumsy way of expressing himself in ordinary conversation. Some of the dissatisfied ones came to me, knowing that Moore lived on my circuit. I listened to them until they had said all they felt like saying; then I said to them, " Brethren, I know Mr. Moore ; all that you say about his appearance and manner is true, but I want to say just two things. He is an honest, devoted Christian man, who tries to do his duty everywhere and at all times; and you will be surprised when you hear him." " Well," said they, " what is the sense of putting a farmer up there while there are so many other men here ? " My answer was only one word, " *Wait.*" And they did wait with a good deal of anxiety and some vexation till two o'clock came.

Appearance has much to do with success or failure in the pulpit ; so has a man's manner and his voice. When all these combine to evoke adverse criticism, the chances of success are largely against a speaker. This was to a certain extent the case with Mr. Moore. When the time for the two o'clock service arrived it was raining. The people crowded into a large tent. This was literally packed ; there was hardly room for the preacher to stand inside the tent. People were standing in the doorway, so that the light was very imperfect, making it difficult to read the hymns. The result of this was that Moore made two or three mistakes in reading the first hymn. This only made matters still worse. One minister, who sat beside me, when he heard the way the hymn was being read, got up and went away, saying, " Tut, tut ; that man can't preach."

I became very uneasy, so did other friends of Mr. Moore. He selected as a text the 6th and 7th verses of the 25th chapter of Isaiah. When he read this passage it seemed to me that he must have lost his usual good sense, or he would not have taken such a text in such a place.   I feared an entire failure.

He had only uttered a few sentences when it became evident that he knew what he was doing.   And as he went on, opening up with the subject and explaining the various metaphors found in this highly figurative passage, the audience began to take a deep interest in the discourse.   And as the speaker became more at home in the anomalous position in which he was placed, he seemed to catch an inspiration that carried him away above himself, and beyond anything that his most intimate friends had ever thought him capable of doing.   I had often heard him preach, and preach well ; but in his effort that day I was completely taken by surprise—so was every one else.   Before he got done speaking that was one of the noisiest audiences that I have been in.   Some were shouting, some were weeping, and others praying.   That sermon was talked about more than all the other discourses delivered at that camp-meeting.   One reason of this was found in the contrast between the man's appearance and his work.   Another reason was, the people had expected so little and got so much that they were carried from the lowest degree of appreciation to the highest point of admiration and enthusiasm.   Some time after I asked Mr. Moore where he got that sermon.   I said to him, "I know that you only read the Bible ; but in that sermon are allusions and illustrations not to be found in the Bible."   "Well," said he, "the fact is, when I was a boy, I heard that sermon preached by one of

Ireland's greatest men, and I knew that I could repeat the most of it. So when I was set up to preach before so many preachers and people, I thought I would give them that, as it is so much better than anything of my own." "Well," I answered, "that sermon has given you a reputation. And if you ever go to Orangeville to preach, you will find great difficulty in meeting the expectations of the people."

IN THE THICK PINERY.

When I was on the Garafraxa Circuit the second time, I took my eldest daughter with me, and went to a camp-meeting on the Flamboro' Circuit. The camp-ground was in a thick pinery. As the sun was climbing up the eastern sky, the tall majestic trees would send their shadows clear across the encampment, as if to give us puny mortals the measure of our littleness. And while we were engaged in worship at their base, they lifted their cone-shaped heads half a hundred yards above us, as if to show us how far they had got ahead of us in the upward journey. But like haughty upstarts everywhere, they overlooked the humility of their origin and the smallness of their beginning. They ignored the fact that they once had been so little that a dewdrop falling on them would have bent them, or a fawn stepping on them might have broken them. And another encouraging thought is this. Their present altitude has been gained only after centuries of growth. Give us time to grow, and we, too, shall rise above our present moral and spiritual standard.

Two or three notable incidents occurred at this meeting. One of these was an old woman's conversion. While passing around among the people one day, when the prayer-meeting was going on, I came to an old lady who was weeping bitterly. I asked her what was the matter. Her answer touched my heart.

"O, sir," she said, "I am past seventy years old, and for the first time in my life I realize that I am a sinner. I thought that if I was honest and industrious and truthful, and went to church when I could, I was safe enough. But now I see that I have been labouring under a mistake. What shall I do?"

I told her to go forward to the place where a number of Christians were praying for just such as she felt herself to be.

She said, "I would gladly go, but I am so crippled with rheumatism that I cannot do so without help."

I went and brought two of the working sisters, and they took the old woman to the altar. Before long she was made very happy in the consciousness of pardon. Her shouts of joy and gladness could be heard all over the encampment, she was so very thankful that she had found the light at last after toiling so many long years in darkness.

Another incident that I will mention was connected with the class-meetings on Sunday morning, when a good Presbyterian was made happy. Among the tents on the ground was one that belonged to two families conjointly. One family was Methodist and the other Presbyterian. In that tent I was appointed to lead the class-meeting on Sunday morning. After I had spoken to four or five, I came to the Presbyterian brother, who, with his wife, owned part of the tent. Both of them stayed in for the service. I asked him what good things he had to tell of the Lord's dealings with him. He rose up and said, "I dare not speak as those have spoken; I cannot say that I am a child of God; I do not know my sins forgiven—I wish with all my heart that I could, but in honest truth I cannot. After giving him a few words of counsel, I passed on to others. The presence of the Lord was with us in that consecrated tent on that beautiful Sabbath morning. Souls were blest and hearts were filled with the joy that springs only from an evidence of our acceptance with God.

Before closing we all knelt in prayer. When we arose the Presbyterian said to me, "Sir, will you allow me to speak again?"

"Certainly, sir, if you wish to do so," was my answer.

"Well," said he, "in this tent this morning I have found what I never before thought was for me. Now I know my sins forgiven. My soul is happy, my heart is full. Blessed light shines upon my pathway, and the future is all glorious."

Before the close of the camp-meeting this brother asked me if he ought to leave his church and join the Methodist. I said to him, "By no means. In seeking church relations two questions are to be considered. One is, where can I do most good? The other is, where can I get the most good? Now, if people intend to be more helpless than useful, they should go where they will get the most good; but if they intend to do all they can for God and His cause, they must go where they can do the most good. My opinion is that you can be most useful in your old church, and therefore I advise you to remain there."

She Wanted the Gaelic.

One night I was leading a prayer-meeting in one of the tents. A number of persons came to the penitent form to be prayed for. Among them was a Highland Scotchwoman. She was greatly in earnest about her soul. At length she got into an agony of spirit, and was seemingly on the very border of despair. I was trying to speak to her as best I could. She turned to me and said, "Sir, could you no pray for me in ta Gaelic?" I said, "No, but I will try and find one who can." I called a brother that I knew could speak the Gaelic, and told him what was wanted. He knelt by her side and began to pray in the tongue she had so often heard among her far-off native mountains. The effect was marvellous. In a very short time she looked up toward the stars, threw up her hands and gave one loud shout, saying "Glory," and fell over like one dead.

Some of those in the tent were frightened. But they soon became calm when I told them there was no danger. It turned out that the man that I called in was a near neighbour of the woman's. She lived about half a mile from the ground, and was the mother of a family of grown-up children. The man who I called I think was a Mr. McNevins. He told me next morning that the woman had lain for three hours in the state in which she was when I left them. Then she got up, praising the Lord, and started home. He

and one or two others went with her through the
woods. She went along shouting all the way. When
she got to her home she shouted and praised the Lord
until the family were awakened, and they at first
thought that "mother" was crazy. But she soon told
them what the Lord had done for her, and their fears
were removed.

Effectual Singing.

While the women were clearing off the tea-tables,
one evening, some young girls got together on an
elevated place, and commenced to sing some of the old-
time camp-meeting hymns. At first not much notice
was taken of them ; but one and another joined with
them until there were some twenty-five or thirty
young women and girls in the group. The singing
became louder and more animated as the number
of singers increased. Others, and older ones, now
began to join them, and in a short time the company
had so added to its numbers that it contained not less
than a hundred persons. Men, women and children
were mingling their voices in holy song.

I was standing on the opposite side of the encampment in conversation with another man. We heard a
loud shout, and started to see what it all meant. When
we came to the place, we found the people all in confusion. Some were weeping, some were laughing,
and some were singing ; others were lying on the
ground as if they had been stricken down by an electric shock ; many of them were insensible. Among
the latter was my little girl, who I think was about

fourteen years old at the time. I found her lying with her head on the arm of a stout, elderly woman who was beside her. I took the girl up and carried her into a tent, where she lay for an hour or more before she came to herself. This went on until the time for the evening service; and it was only after two or three fruitless efforts that order could be restored so as to commence the regular service. The Rev. E. Bristol had the control of this camp-meeting.

A MEETING AT ROCKWOOD.

Among the limestone ledges on the south side of Eramosa township is a little village called Rockwood. In a piece of woods near this place at one time there was a very nice place for camp-meetings. One of these I had the pleasure of attending during my second term on the Elma mission. At that time the Church in Loree's neighbourhood was strong and full of life and energy. Many of those who composed the membership at that time have gone away, some are in heaven, some in Manitoba, and some in other places.

The meetings had been going on for two or three days before anything of a specially interesting character took place.

One night after the services had closed, and most of the people had retired, a prayer-meeting was started in one of the tents. In a short time the singing attracted the attention of the people generally, then shouts began to be heard; some parties that had started for home turned back. Many of those in the tents came out to see what was going on. I had gone

into the tent where my wife and I were staying.
With others, I went out to the prayer-meeting. The
tent was a long double one, with a door on both sides
When I came to the place it was nearly full, and a
crowd standing at each door. When I came up to one
of the doors, I was addressed by a fine-looking young
man, who did not like the noise. He said to me,
" Mister, what do you think of all that racket in
there," as he pointed to the end where most of the
noise came from. I looked at him and said, " Were
you ever converted ?" He said, " No, sir, I never was."
" Do you believe in it ?" I asked him. " Yes, sir, I do ;
but I never can be, if I have to do as they are doing."
" Well, my friend," said I, " you need not trouble
yourself on that score; salvation is not noise, but
sometimes a knowledge of salvation makes people
noisy. Get converted first, and then do what you
think is right, He said in great earnestness, " I do
wish that I was a Christian," and turning to me, he
said, " Will you pray for me here ?" " Yes," I said ;
" let us kneel down here." I commenced to pray for
him, and he began to pray for himself. In about two
minutes he was on his feet jumping and shouting and
praising the Lord for what was done for him ; in fact,
he made more noise than any two of the noisy lot
that he was finding fault with a few moments before.
Next morning I met him on the ground, and I asked
him what he thought about the noise after last night.
His answer was, " Well, I never thought that getting
religion was anything like what it is ! Did I make
much noise." " Yes, some," I said ; " but perhaps not
any too much."

8

Just after I parted from the young man, I was standing in the door of the tent, and looking on one of the wildest scenes that is to be witnessed among an intelligent Christian community, when two young women came in weeping as though their hearts were breaking. They knelt down just inside the door. As they came in I saw my wife standing in the crowd and told her to come inside. Now, she never had any faith in people falling down in meeting, and when she saw some who had fallen lying in one end of the tent, she drew back, saying she did not want to go among them. I said, "You can talk to these two girls here; no one is paying any attention to them." "All right," she said, "I will do that." She knelt down by them, and began to talk to them. Soon one of them was set free, and commenced to praise the Lord. My wife gave one loud shout which made me look to where she was. I found her on the floor perfectly motionless. I found no little difficulty in saving her from being trampled on by the men in the tent, who were paying no attention to any one, only each one for himself. Presently, I saw the old brother in whose tent we were staying; I motioned to him and he came to me. We took her up and pressing our way out, we carried her in and laid her on a bed for the night.

Next morning she was all right. I have never since heard any fault-finding from that quarter about falling in meeting or making too much noise. But of late years no one has had much reason to complain on that score. Methodists are getting above that,

A Series of Camp-Meetings.

During the four years that I was on the Huron District as Presiding Elder, we had five camp-meetings. At Hanover there were two, and two on Orangeville Circuit, and one at Teeswater. A number of conversions took place at each one of them.

The ministers on the district were generally good men for such work, and many of the people were in full sympathy with camp-meetings.

One thing that was very remarkable was the good order that prevailed at every one of them. Though hundreds of unconverted people, both old and young, attended these meetings, yet I saw but very little disorder at any of them. It has been sometimes said that people in the back settlements are uncultivated, and lack refinement. Well, however that may be, there is one thing that I am bold to say, and that is, I have seen more lawlessness and rowdyism in one religious meeting held by the Salvation Army in a frontier village than I saw at five camp-meetings in the back counties.

At some of these meetings I have seen English, Irish, Scotch, Germans and Canadians all sitting together on the camp-ground—Methodists, Presbyterians, Baptists, Church of England, and in a few instances Roman Catholics have been heard singing the same songs of praise together.

At a love-feast held at the close of one of the meetings at Hanover, we had an honest Irish Presbyterian, who gave his testimony. He had been in the country only a few days. He said:

"I am a stranger here and in a strange land, but the kindness shown to me since I came makes me feel very much at home among you.   I am a Presbyterian. Since coming here I have learned more about Methodism than I ever knew before.   I have listened to the preaching, I have joined in the singing, I have heard many of the prayers, and I have mingled in Christian conversation, and I find that salvation is the burden of it all.   Before I leave you I want to say that I am with you in the grand old doctrine of justification by faith and in the blessed hope of a glorious home in heaven."

That young man is a brother to the Rev. Robert Carson, of the Guelph Conference.

A Happy Dutchman.

Perhaps no one can make "broken English" sound so much like a foreign tongue as a German.   And yet perhaps no one who breaks the Queen's English can make himself better understood than he can.

At the meeting at Hanover there were some members of the Evangelical Association.   They enjoyed the services very much, and some of them did all they could to help on with the work.   Their strong, manly utterances did good, although their words were broken, and their cheerful, encouraging expressions of faith, and hope, and love, endeared them to our people generally.   But I will endeavour to give one quotation as nearly as I can.

."Mine Gristian frens, ven I leaves old Charmany, I vas vondering if I coot finds zome goot Gristians in dis off avay place. But I am glad to der Master dat I am not in der least disabointed. I hears dis day der same stories of Jesus and His love, as I did in der Faderlandt. O, I am very much happy in mine soul, dis day. Praise der Lord. I am happy."

We all believed him. His face and voice and all about him said that he was happy.

Some Wild Expressions.

At one of our meetings, a lad of some sixteen or seventeen years of age got converted. He had been a pretty wild boy, though brought up by Christian parents. He had a hard struggle to get free. When he got blest he became very noisy and went among the people on the ground, singing and shouting at the top of his voice. I heard him, but I did not pay attention to what he was saying. I had seen so many noisy conversions that I thought but little about his noise. Besides I like strong-lunged children, that let people know when they are in the world.

The next day I met a man on the encampment, who accosted me, saying:

" Mister, did you hear that rhapsody of that young fellow last night ? "

I said: "I heard some one making a big noise, but I was at the time engaged, so that I did not notice what he said."

" Well," said he, " I never heard anything like some of his wild expressions. Among other thing she said, ' I shall dwell with God, and sit upon a throne with Christ.' "

"That," said I, "is a strong expression, but are you sure that it is a wild one?"

"Well, if that is the fruit of camp-meetings, I think but very little of them," said the man.

I replied: "The camp-meeting is not responsible either for the words nor for the sentiment. The words you complain of are the words of a youth. But the sentiment is that of a God."

"How is that?" said he.

"Did you never read the words of Jesus, saying, 'To him that overcometh will I grant to sit with me in my throne, even as I also overcame, and am set down with my Father in his throne.' The only contingency in the case, if a man is converted, is his stability and faithfulness. For to sit on the throne with Christ is a fulfilment of the lad's declaration."

"Well," said he, "I did not know that was in the Bible."

"I suppose not," said I. "But we see how easily men may make mistakes, when they attempt to pick people up before they are down."

The Mark of Cain.

At the Teeswater camp-meeting, which was in Dowse's woods, at Williamson's Corners, in Culross, an interview with a man-slayer gave me some very sad feelings. For a couple of days I had seen a fine looking man on the grounds, who seemed to keep entirely by himself. On making enquiry as to who he was, I was told that he lived in an adjoining neighbourhood, and had the reputation of being a murderer. This gave me to see how it was that he was so much by himself. People were shy of him, and he knew it and felt it. One day he came to me and said, "Sir, I would like to have some conversation with you, if you are willing." We walked out into the bush by ourselves, and sat on a fallen tree. Then he said to me, "Do you recollect hearing of a melancholy affair that took place some few years ago at G.?" "To what do you refer?" said I. He answered with a faltering voice saying, "I mean the killing of poor W. by E." "Yes," I said, "I do remember it. And being well acquainted with some of W.'s friends made me feel a deep interest in the matter. But E. was tried and acquitted on the ground that he only acted in self-defence, if I do not forget the facts." "That is true," he said, "I am E., and at the time I thought, and I still think, that I could only save my life by taking his. But it is a terrible thing to do. I often wish I had not done it. But do you think that there is mercy for me. Can I be forgiven?" "If you sincerely repent and heartily trust in the Lord Jesus you can be forgiven," was my answer. "Well," said he, "I am trying to do the best I can in a lonely way. My neighbours shun me as they would a poisonous reptile. Even the children will run from me as if I was some ravenous beast. My life is a very unhappy one." Poor man, he did not look like a bad character. But he must carry with him the unhappy reflection that he took a fellow-mortal's life, and sent a soul prematurely to its last reckoning. And even though it was done in defence of his own life the remembrance of it must always be like a deadly shadow resting upon the spirit.

This chapter might be indefinitely lengthened by the relation of camp-meeting incidents. But prudence forbids it. One or two things might be said in regard to the contrast between the old camp-meetings and revivals, and those of the present day. But that subject may possibly be treated of in another chapter specially devoted to change and progress.

CHAPTER VI.

REVIVAL MEETINGS.

IN writing on the subject of revivals I shall give more attention to similarity and contrast than to chronological order. Any one at all conversant with evangelistic work, will bear testimony to the statement that every revival of religion has some peculiarity about it that gives it a sort of individuality of its own. While in all genuine revivals there is a general aspect of unity, still there is a specific diversity in the case of each that makes it differ from all others of its kind. This may arise from a variety of causes. The person who conducts the services may adopt methods that will give a peculiar aspect to the work; or the habits and temperaments of the people may, and no doubt they do, affect the work both as regards its magnitude and character. Again, local circumstances and temporary conditions have a decided influence on this kind of work. And the season of the year, the state of the roads, and the severity or mildness of the weather all have more or less to do with the success or failure of revival efforts. Especially is this the case at the beginning of such meetings. Illustrations will be furnished in this chapter by giving instances that have come under my own observation in connection with services held by myself and others.

I have been acquainted with special services from early life. When but a young man I attended the first protracted meetings that were ever held in the township of Erin. They were held in a private house that belonged to a man named Nathaniel Rossell, whose home was both a dwelling-house and meeting-house for a number of years. The results of these meetings held in that little frame house are felt and seen in that locality till the present day, though almost fifty years have passed away since then. Since that time I have been permitted to attend many of these blessed means of grace in different places. But I shall confine myself to my own experiences since I entered the ministry.

My first effort in revival work was a desperate struggle. It seems to me now as I look back to that effort, that it was the Waterloo of my life and work as a minister. If that first effort had been a failure, as for three long and dreary weeks it threatened to be, what would have been my course I cannot tell; very likely I should have become disheartened and have gone no further. And what then? Between six and seven hundred souls converted since then in meetings that I have conducted, would have been left in their sins, so far as I am concerned, and I should have missed the opportunity of leading them to Jesus, and worse than all, many of them might have died in their sins and been lost for ever.

It was on my first circuit. I had been there from

June till January. The people were kind, but the state of the Church was one of lamentable coldness and indifference. The members were respectable, and, in worldly things, enterprising and prosperous ; but they neither realized their duty nor appreciated their privileges as Christians. When I spoke to some of them about holding some revival services, they talked very discouragingly about it. In fact they said it would be of no use. And besides, it would bring us into disgrace among the Church of England people and the Presbyterians. " However," they said, " if you think it advisable, you can try it for a week or two."

With many misgivings I made an announcement to commence revival meetings in the old log church on the sixth line of Garafraxa. The people turned out extremely well, and all seemed quite willing to let the preacher have his way. But for three weeks not the first indication of revival could be seen in that congregation. Not one hearty amen was heard in all that time. There were three or four old brethren that would offer prayer, but their prayers were so cold that they seemed almost to glisten with frostiness. Who has not fairly shivered under such prayer at some time or other ?

Well, during all this time the meeting dragged itself along despite a frigid membership and a weak, timid preacher. During these weeks I would preach and exhort and sing in the church ; and at home I would lay awake at night, and think and pray and sometimes weep, until I got into an agony of soul for the conversion of the unsaved part of my congregation.

It was on the Friday night of the third week of the meetings. The house was filled with an orderly audience. As I went up the old pulpit stairs I seemed to catch an inspiration. I felt confident of success. Before reading my text that night, I told the people that one of three things would be done. " We must have a revival, or these meetings will be kept going till Conference, or I shall wear myself out and become a useless thing on your hands. So," said I, " you may as well wake up and get to work in right good earnest. I mean just what I say."

I think I preached that night as I had never done before, and there was an influence at work among the people that could hardly be resisted. When I commenced the prayer-meeting and repeated the invitation that had so often been given in vain, there was a general rushing toward the penitent bench, there being no altar in the church. The power of God was wonderfully manifested in the conviction of sinners and in quickening and energizing believers. We continued the meetings for three weeks longer, and between twenty and thirty were converted and united with the Church.

Cotton's Appointment.

On the tenth line of Garafaxa was the scene of my next revival. We had an appointment in a schoolhouse here. The settlers were nearly all of one nationality. They were from the North of Ireland, and adherents of the Anglican Church. They had no religious services, only what were furnished them by the Methodists. They were a wild, thoughtless and daring lot of men. They were called by the inhabitants around them, "tenth line blazers." In fact, their reputation for recklessness spread far beyond the limits of their own settlement. But for all this, a more warm-hearted and generous class of men could not be found so long as they avoided the whiskey and did not get out of temper.

When I told one of our men on the sixth line that I was intending to try the tenth line with revival services, he said that to do anything with them a man would need to have strong faith and a ready tongue. "But," said he, "they will not abuse you whether they agree with your methods or not. If you can get William Cotton you will succeed with the rest, as he is a sort of king among them."

When I told the people at the schoolhouse that I was intending to start meetings there, they were completely taken by surprise. I told them that I wanted them to come every night for two weeks, and then if they wished it I would close up. They readily consented to this, and we concluded to commence the next night. After I came out of the house, two women who had once been Methodists said to me, "We are glad that you are going to try to do something for this place, for it is a fact that we are all going to the *bad* as fast as whiskey and bad surroundings can send us. We will do what we can to help you." I said to them, "You can give yourselves fully to the Lord and do what you can for others." They both promised that they would, and they faithfully kept their promise.

On Monday evening the schoolhouse was full, and

we had the best of order. Tuesday evening was the same, only the interest seemed to be increasing. Wednesday evening the house was crowded. After talking to the people and offering prayer, I made arrangements to invite penitents forward. I think I never had a greater task to perform than I had that night, to place a penitent bench and explain to the people what it was for, and what I wanted them to do. But few of the audience had ever seen anything like this before, and it was a great novelty to them.

As I looked into the faces before me, I could see evidence of wonder and bewilderment, and anxiety and expectancy, but I could see no trace of anger. That night four married women came forward. Two of them were the women that had promised to do what they could ; the other two were Mrs. Cotton and Mrs. Smith. This gave the meeting a good start, and I was much encouraged. The next night a number more came forward, and among them was William Cotton, the man who had been represented to me as " king of the tenth line blazers."

From that night the work went on with increasing power. In three weeks some sixty claimed to be converted, and united with the Church ; and the most of them gave proof of the genuineness of their profession by a consistent walk and conversation. The neighbourhood was entirely changed in its habits and pursuits. During the progress of the work I had been somewhat worried about a leader to take charge of these new beginners. None of them had ever had any experience in Church work. But before the meeting closed the Lord provided a very efficient leader in the person of John Cowan, a man who just then came to live in that locality. He was connected with some of these people and acquainted with all of them. He had been a Methodist from his boyhood and a class-leader for some length of time. We got him to take charge of the newly formed class. He was an excellent leader, and he proved to be a great blessing to that locality for years after.

JOHN CONN'S HOUSE.

During my second year on the Garafraxa Circuit a man named John Conn attended a camp-meeting at Orangeville and got converted. He lived on the eighth line. As soon as he got done praising the Lord for his salvation, he came to me on the camp-ground and said, "Now, mister, I am going to serve the Lord, and I want you to come and hold a revival meeting in my new house before the partitions are put up." I told him I would gladly do so. We arranged to commence as soon as the hurry of harvest would be over.

The people in this neighbourhood were mostly of the same race and religion as those on the tenth line. Not more than two or three of them professed to be converted or made any attempt to live right. The services were commenced at the time appointed. The tenth line people came in large numbers to assist in the work. The Lord was with us, so that in three weeks nearly every grown-up person in the settlement claimed to be converted. We formed a class here and appointed John Conn as a provisional leader, with the understanding that John Cowan, who was brother to Conn's wife, should take oversight for a while until there should be a leader developed from among themselves. Some of the best men that I have known among our worthy laymen grew out of the little class that used to meet in that little private house.

ESSON'S SCHOOLHOUSE.

At Esson's schoolhouse we had an appointment, but we had no society. The congregation was a mixture both nationally and religiously. Scotch, Irish, English and Canadians were all represented here ; and the Anglican, Presbyterian and Methodist Churches each had adherents in the audience that met on Sabbath for religious worship in the somewhat commodious school-room. After much consideration and some misgivings, I resolved to try this place with a series of meetings. The trustees readily consented. The teacher at that time was a fine-spirited Englishman, and at once consented to assist in the singing and in looking after the fire and light. The people generally seemed to fall in with the idea of having a revival meeting. They were acquainted with many of the converts both at Cotton's and Conn's.

We commenced the services in the winter, when there was good sleighing, so that people could come from all parts of the circuit. The house would be crowded every night, and the best of order prevailed throughout the entire series. We kept at work for six weeks—every evening but Saturday nights—without one conversion of either old or young. Everybody was disappointed, and I was nearly heartbroken. Such a complete failure I had never seen. What was the cause of such a signal defeat? These questions frequently forced themselves upon my attention, but no answer could be given that seemed to be a satisfactory one. But I found out, on examining myself closely, that I needed just such a lesson. There are people to whom success is more dangerous than opposition, and I expect I am one of them. My former success had nearly spoiled me, for I had got to thinking that I was specially designed for evangelistic work. But this led me to see what a poor, useless thing I was. And another thing that I learned was this, that it is possible to become so fully absorbed for the salvation of others that you lose your own enjoyment. I think that I never came nearer backsliding in heart than at this time. And still another thing I learned, viz., that it is possible to be actuated by motives that we think are entirely pure, when in fact our motives are mixed. My ruling motive was to do the Lord's work in the way that would most bring glory to Him ; but subordinate to this, and almost hidden behind it, I found also a desire to do it in such a way as to bring praise to myself.

I stayed at home and rested one week, and then I resolved to try again, and at once started again in the old log church, where I had the hard fight the year before. The work here commenced to move on from the first night, and this meeting furnished a complete contrast to the one at Esson's schoolhouse. On the third night of these services I passed through an experience that was new to me, and it seemed to shed some light on the subject of my failure in my last efforts. While the prayer-meeting was going on, an impression was made on my mind just as distinctly as if an audible voice had addressed me. I was startled by its suddenness and vividness. The impression put into words was simply this, " Would you be willing to labour here for six weeks without results, as you did at the last place you tried, if God should will it to be so?" After a few moments of deep and prayerful thought, I said, " Yes, Lord, if it be Thy will that I must work on all my life from this night until I die and never see another soul converted, I am ready to do so. Anything that will honour and glorify Thee shall satisfy me." Here I discovered that I had been too anxious about results. The question of success or failure had been more to me than an entire consecration to God as an essential qualification for eminent usefulness. As soon as this decision was made, a flood of glory swept over my soul, and I was unutterably happy.

From that night a mighty impulse was given to the work. The whole community seemed to be moved. The people came in from all directions. Some of them came ten or a dozen miles. The moon was in its grandeur, and the sleighing all that could be desired. Night after night the old church was packed with earnest listeners and happy worshippers. People were asking each other where this thing was going to end. Numbers had been brought into the new life, and many more were earnestly seeking for it. But how often men make mistakes in drawing their conclusions from appearances! While the people and their preacher were rejoicing together over the prospects of a sweeping revival such as our fathers had told of in their day, there came a change as sudden as it was unexpected. A strong south wind and rain set in, and in two days the snow was all gone and the roads became impassable or nearly so, and our meeting had to be closed, or rather it closed itself, before it was two weeks old.

Before dismissing this subject, I will note just two instances in connection with this meeting that I can never forget. One night during the prayer-meeting, I was standing on one of the seats trying to exhort sinners to repent. Presently, I saw a man rise up in the audience, and then another and another, until nine strong men all at once were crowding their way to the altar and weeping over their sins. Some of these men are still working in the Church. Others of them have gone to mingle in the joys of the Church triumphant.

An Old Sinner Saved.

The other instance that I wish to mention, is the case of an old man by the name of Trouten. He had been a Christian in his youth in Ireland ; but he had been a backslider for half a century, and he had gone very far in the ways of sin. His daughter, a very fine young lady, had been converted at the meetings in Cotton's schoolhouse while she was visiting friends in that neighbourhood the year before. Through her the old man was influenced to come to the meetings. He was one of the nine men spoken of above. On the second night after he came forward in the prayer-meeting, we stood up to sing, and while we were singing the verse of one of our good old hymns, that begins with:

> " But drops of grief can ne'er repay,
>   The debt of love we owe,"

the old gray-headed wanderer regained his long-lost faith, and hope, and joy, and love. He made the old house echo, while with his clear, ringing, manly voice he praised the Lord for the mercies that had followed him in all his sinful ways, and that now restored him to the blessed hope of the gospel. This old man lived a useful, happy life for a number of years after this.

A Whole Family Converted.

Time and distance are not essential qualities in the narration of isolated facts, and therefore I shall pass them by in this instance.

I was holding a series of meetings in the village of Trowbridge, in the township of Elma. The audience room was a little schoolhouse. The place was crowded every night. There was a very strong society of Wesleyan Methodists, and a small society of Episcopal Methodists. The former had a snug little frame church, and the latter worshipped in the schoolhouse. The two societies were on good terms, and ready to help each other in their work.

Our meetings had been going on about a week, and there had been some good done; but there seemed to be a little dulness and things were going rather slowly.

Perhaps the overcrowded state of the audience had a good deal to do with this. But one night a woman came forward to seek the Lord. She was very much in earnest, and was a woman of any amount of energy, and of more than average intelligence; she soon found peace, and was made very happy. After giving vent to her gladness of heart in words of praise to the sinner's Friend, the feelings of her rejoicing soul ran out after others. She arose to her feet, and looking around over the audience, she said, as if speaking to herself, yet loud enough to be heard all through the room, "Where is Archy?" Now, Archy was her husband, who sat away in a corner of the house, and was wondering what had come over his wife. Presently, the object of her search was seen by the newly converted woman. She made her way to him, it seemed to me with the agility of a squirrel, and taking him by the hand, said, "Come, Archy, let us start together to serve the Lord." With the docility of a child, he rose and followed her; and in less than ten minutes he too was praising the Lord for his salvation.

Again, the intrepid little woman stood on her feet, and this time the question was, "Where is Ben?" He was her brother who was boarding with her, and teaching the village school. In a few moments she had "Ben" kneeling at the penitent bench, and Archy and others praying for him, and in a little while he too was made happy.

Her next utterance was, "Now, I must have William." This was another one of her brothers, who was also boarding at her house, and attending his brother's school. William was hunted up, and he too was led forward by this energetic sister, and like the rest was soon rejoicing in a sense of pardon. The whole household went home in a happier frame of mind than they had ever enjoyed before.

A Bigoted Young Preacher.

At a place that shall be nameless at present, there was an occurrence that has caused many feelings of sadness to arise in my mind, as memory has carried my thoughts back to the time and place.

In one of the backwoods villages I had an appointment and a small society. We held our meetings in the schoolhouse. The country was new, the people were mostly in sympathy with Methodism in some one of its old-time divisions. The Wesleyans had a good church and a large society in the village. The congregations were made up of the villagers and their neighbours from the surrounding settlement.

The superintendent of the circuit at the time was a true Christian gentleman; but of the junior preacher I can only say that his Christianity seemed to be largely composed of self-importance . and sectarian bigotry.

Revival meetings had been going on in the church for three or four weeks with fair success. They had been closed or adjourned on the Friday night before my appointment in tne schoolhouse. When I came to the place I found the house already full, and the people still coming. I commenced the services. When I was about to announce the second hymn one

of the Wesleyan leaders came up to me and said, " There
are more people outside than there are inside and
they want to come in, but there is no room for
them. We had intended to hold a prayer-meeting in
the church, and it is lighted up. You had better go
into the church and hold your meeting." As we
were going into the door, the class-leader said to me,
" I want you to conduct a prayer-meeting after preaching." My text was, " The simple pass on and are
punished." I tried to illustrate the subject by showing how sinners pass on from one period of life to
another, from one degree of sin to another, from
one means of grace to another, and from one interposition of Divine Providence to another. I spoke of
the calls of mercy when God speaks to men with a
voice more soft and tender than a mother's lullaby.
But men pass on. Then again, He speaks to them in
tones more terrible than the crashing thunder. But
still men pass on, until mercy no longer pleads, and
forbearance no longer stays the lifted hand of Justice.
Then the blow descends and the long delayed punishment comes as in a whirlwind of destruction.

At the close of the address an invitation was given to
all who did not wish to pass on in sin any longer, to come
to the altar. In a short time the altar was crowded
from end to end with weeping, praying penitents.
The power of the Highest seemed to rest on the entire
assembly and the glory of the Shechina seemed to fill
the house. Between thirty and forty came forward
that night to seek the Lord.

Before the close of the meeting the leading officials

said to me, " Our ministers are away from home. One is at the District Meeting, and the other is visiting at the farthest point of the circuit. Can you come and help us till they come home ? " I told them I would do as they wished, and announced for meeting on the next night. On Monday night the house was full again, and there were a number of conversions. During the evening the junior preacher came home, and in passing the church he heard the noise and looked in at the door. But instead of coming in he went off to his boarding place in a pet. After he found out how it came about that I was working in connection with his people, he wrote a very tart and stinging letter to the old class-leader who was the chief offender.

Next night when I came I found the house full and a stranger in the pulpit. A young man who was canvassing in the neighbourhood, and who was a local preacher, had been invited, and had consented to preach. The old leader was not there, and the other officials seemed to be confused and afraid to act. Everybody felt that something was wrong. Only a few knew what it was. The young man in the pulpit did the best he could, but a bishop could not have preached successfully to that congregation. People were asking one another, " How is it that the man who was invited to lead the meetings is pushed aside, and an entire stranger put in the place ? " The tide of bad feeling rose higher and higher as the discourse went on. One after another left the house. By the time the sermon was through, nearly half of the congregation were outside; some were angry and others grieved at what had taken place. It came out afterwards that the junior preacher had that day been around among the officials, and by threats and intimidations had caused them to take the course they did. After some discussion it was decided to go on with the meeting as if nothing had happened. But it was no use. The work was killed as effectually as fire is put out by water. It was chilled to death by the cold wet blanket of bigotry thrown over it by the hand of a young clerical compound of self-importance and sectarian exclusiveness.

The young man in question had a fine personal appearance, a very high order of intellect, a fair education, and he was a fluent and eloquent speaker. But his want of Christian courtesy and brotherly kindness disqualified him to a great extent for the work of a successful minister. He remained in the itinerant ranks for a few years, and then, I think, went to the Pacific coast.

But before he left the country, and two years after the event above described, I met him again, and under entirely different circumstances.

During my second term on the Garafraxa Circuit we had a camp-meeting. The Wesleyan minister on the adjoining circuit, and whose work overlapped mine, was invited to attend the meetings and help us as he could. He was a fine, genial, warm-hearted man, but circumstances forbade his attending in person, so he did the next best thing—he sent his colleague, who was no other than the peppery young gentleman who had shown so much bitterness towards me and my work. When he came on the camp-ground I received him as courteously as I knew how and treated him as kindly as I could. I introduced him to our people and to the ministers present. I also went to the tent-holders and instructed them to give special attention to Mr. McR., and make him feel at home as much as possible while he stayed with us. They did as I told them. He was made welcome to their tents and their tables.

He accepted an invitation to preach. The people were delighted with the sermon. In the pulpit he was clear, logical, and forcible. But he was not of much use to lead a prayer-meeting. But in this he was by no means singular.

Things went on smoothly for a day or two. Then he began to make disparaging remarks to the people about the preachers and their work. This got to the ears of the preachers. There were a couple of high-strung men among them, and the feeling of displeasure began to run high, and there was some danger of an explosion among the clerics. My attention was called to the matter by the late William Woodward, who was the presiding elder at the time. He was a man of gentle spirit and calm deportment. I persuaded Mr. Woodward to take the young critic in hand, and advise him to cease his uncalled-for and ill-timed strictures.

The two went aside, inviting me to go with them.

They talked the matter over in a friendly way, after which the young man thanked Mr. Woodward for his fatherly admonitions ; he also apologized for his unkind and unbrotherly sayings. He soon after bid us good-bye and went away, and I never saw him again.

The unification of our common Methodism has removed the cause of a great deal of the friction that so frequently made things unpleasant in its divided state. This is cause of thankfulness at least.

CHAPTER VII.

REVIVAL MEETINGS.—II.

THORNBURY AS IT USED TO BE.

PLACES, like men, sometimes are reputed to be better than they are, and sometimes worse. That being the case, it is not always safe to estimate a person or place in strict accordance with what Dame Rumour may have to say about them. I found this to be emphatically true of the village of Thornbury, when I went to live there in 1867.

Thornbury was at that time the headquarters of the Collingwood mission of the M. E. Church. When my name was read out by the Stationing Committee, I felt some misgivings about going to it. But I had been long enough in the itinerant work to know that it is not always best for men to choose their own work. So I determined to go and do the best I could for the place. I had been told by a man who was not a Methodist, that it was a very hard place. His words were: "The women of Thornbury are well enough, but the devil and the rumsellers have a mortgage on the most of the men." This, I thought, must be an exaggeration, and I found that, bad as the place was, it was not so far gone as that, for before I was there three months I saw a number of both men and women converted and made happy, though it must be admitted that, for a small village, Thornbury was far from being a model of propriety and order. On the contrary, it could produce as much dissipation to the square rod as any little place that I have seen. But this state of things, I think, arose not so much out of an inordinate love of wickedness on the part of the people, as it did from a lack of special effort on the part of the Churches to help and encourage individuals and families to live right. Everybody seemed to take it for granted that nothing could be done, and so no one tried to do anything for the moral and religious uplifting of that part of the inhabitants of the place who were outside of the Churches.

But God resolved to visit Thornbury in mercy, but in doing so He did not commission some learned divine to teach the people what they ought to do, nor did He send some noted evangelist to arouse the careless, sleeping sinners.

He who takes the weak things to confound the mighty, chose some children in the berry-field to be the instruments in His hands to start a mighty work, in the place. Some little girls, ranging from eight to twelve years of age, went out to pick berries. While thus engaged, one of them spoke of a sermon she had heard on the previous Sabbath, in which something was said about the conversion of children. They talked on for a while, and then they concluded to hold a prayer-meeting, and ask the Lord to convert them. A part of them belonged to a Sabbath-school, taught by a good old Wesleyan, named David Youmans. They gathered into a thicket of shrubbery, and commenced to sing and pray. Before long God heard and answered their simple petitions for conversion, and all of them were blessed and made as happy as they could be.

Some men who were passing by on the road heard the noise and went to see what the children were doing. They found them in a perfect ecstasy of joy and quietly left them without disturbing them. But the story of the children's prayer-meeting soon spread through the village. Some treated the matter with levity. Others were seriously impressed by it.

I had only been there a short time and was a comparative stranger to most of the people. My first Quarterly Meeting came on, and I made arrangements for an all-day meeting, to be held in a nice grove not far from our church. The presiding elder at the time was a live man from Dublin, W. H. Shaw. That day he did grand work. The congregation was large and orderly. One woman was converted, and many of the old professors, both from town and country, were abundantly blessed. We commenced a series of revival meetings in the church at once. The people came out in crowds, and the work of conversion went on from the first. In carrying on the services the band of little workers that had received their commission in the berry-field was a great help to me. Everybody wondered at the clearness of their testimony, and the

A Growing Town (Winter).

fervour and earnestness of their prayers. For a few days these little ones did a good share of praying for penitence at the altar.

During the first week we recorded twelve conversions, and a number more were earnestly seeking the forgiveness of sin. The work went on with increased power from day to day, so that at the end of the fourth week some sixty professed to have been converted, and the religious community was stirred for miles around.

There were two or three things in connection with these meetings that I wish to notice before passing on. One afternoon, at our two o'clock prayer-meeting, there came three squaws from a camp of Indians that were located about a mile from the village. Those women were Methodists from about the Saugeen reservation.

During the meeting the eldest one engaged in prayer in her own language. We could only understand one word, and that was " Jesus." But a more powerful prayer I never heard before or since. It seemed as if the very rain of heaven were falling from a cloud of mercy on every heart in answer to the earnest pleadings of this poor, unlearned daughter of the forest. There were not less than fifty persons present, but at the close of that prayer there was not a dry face in the house.

At the commencement of the third week of our meetings, the altar was somewhat crowded, and we were straitened for room. Some of the leading workers said to me :

" We shall have to put these children in a corner by

themselves, so as to make more room for grown-up people,"

I told them that I was afraid to interfere with the Lord's way of doing His work. But they seemed to insist on it, and I let them have their way. The children were put in a corner by themselves, and the altar left for older people.

For two nights this arrangement was adhered to. The meetings were cold, and dull, and dry, and lifeless. Next night I called the little workers back to the altar and all went well again.

I wish to say here that one of the best helpers in a revival that I have met with among the laymen of Methodism I found in these meetings in Brother Davidson, who came to live in Thornbury about the same time that I went there. He could always be relied on for work either in the pulpit or at the altar. He was a Wesleyan local preacher, and was a good man. In fact, the whole Christian community gave all the help they could in forwarding the work.

One night during the meetings an old woman came to the altar, and I could not help seeing that she made a sensation when she came. The other women drew away from her, as if they were afraid to let their garments touch hers. She was poorly and plainly dressed and was evidently in very humble circumstances. But I felt that this in itself was not any reason why Christians should shun her. She seemed very much in earnest, and she wept as though her heart would break.

After meeting I made inquiry as to who she was. I

10

was told that she belonged to a family in the village and that they had a very bad name, and were looked down upon by every one. I told the people who gave me this information that our duty was to imitate the Master in our treatment of sinners. He never selected special cases, but, on the contrary, He saved any one that came to Him. She might be poor, she might be vile, but she was penitent, and that was a passport to the Lord's sympathy and love, and it ought to be to ours.

Next night she was saved, and she gave a clear and distinct testimony to the fact of salvation from sin. She was very happy. On visiting her and conversing with her, I found that she had been reared in a Christian home, and by Methodist parents, in the eastern part of 'this Province. But like scores of other silly girls she had blighted her life's happiness by an unsuitable marriage. She was married by a Methodist minister to a French-Canadian Catholic. They settled the question of church connection by an agreement to attend no church. They had raised a large family entirely destitute of religious training. When I had learned all this, it was easy to see how it was that parents and children had gone so far astray.

The old woman was very punctual in attending every means of grace after her conversion. For two months we never missed her from any of the services, either by night or by day. At length one Thursday night she was absent from the prayer-meeting. Next Sabbath morning her seat was again vacant. This caused some inquiries, but no one could tell what was the cause of her absence.

On Tuesday I went to her home and found her very sick with inflammation of the lungs and past hope of recovery. I asked her how she felt.

"Oh," said she, "I am hourly sinking, but my soul is unspeakably happy."

Then she reached her hand to me and said, "How can I sufficiently thank the Lord for the protracted meetings. What would I do now if I had not found salvation ? Surely I am a brand plucked from the burning. How wonderful it seems that I am saved after all those dreary years of sin and wickedness."

Next day she died in peace. How often since then have I thought of poor old Mrs. Willot, so nearly lost but saved at last.

In less than a year her husband died with a tumour on his neck. When he found that he must die, he sent for me to come and see him. On going I found him in a very unhappy condition both of body and mind. I asked him what I could do for him.

He said : "I sent for you to teach me how to die, as you taught my wife. She died in peace and I want to die in peace."

I told him that the mercy that had saved his wife would save him, if he would repent and believe as she had done. I found him very ignorant, but ready and willing to be taught. He seemed gradually to grasp the truth, and at length could rejoice in the hope of a future life, based on a sense of pardoned sin. He died soon after calmly trusting in the crucified and risen Saviour. "Almost lost but saved," would be a fitting epitaph for him and for his wife.

McColman's Schoolhouse.

We have lingered about Thornbury longer than was intended. We will now leave it and go to the tenth line of the township of Collingwood, where we had an appointment in McColman's schoolhouse. There was a fair congregation, and a small class of church members.

During my second year on the Collingwood mission I held a series of evangelistic services in that place. I was aware that in the vicinity there were some of the Campbellites or Disciples. But I thought that by judicious management it was possible to avoid coming in collision with them. But in this I was mistaken. Their domain is on the water and along the rivers and streams. And since the earth is about three-fourths covered with water, it becomes very difficult to move in any direction very far without touching their domain somewhere, as I found out in this place, and of which I will speak further on.

In this place, as in Thornbury, the work of revival began at first among the children and youths. Some ten or twelve Sabbath-school scholars, between ten and fifteen years of age, came forward to seek the Lord during the first week, and several of them were happily converted. This gave an impetus to the work and encouragement to the workers. And there were some noble helpers there. One Presbyterian brother— a Mr. Goodfellow—whose two young daughters were among the first converts, did everything in his power to help on the good work.

At the close of the week one brother said to me, " I

am glad to see the children coming to Jesus, but I should like to see the old sinners coming, too."

I said to him: "When you go to clear off a piece of land, you cut the undergrowth first and the large timber afterwards. The Lord is doing so here. He is simply underbrushing now. But He will bring down the tall, strong sinners after a while."

And so it turned out, for in three weeks between forty and fifty professed to be saved from their sins. But this was not accomplished without some opposition from our friends the Disciples. Among them were two who were more than mere laymen, and less than what they call elders. They were in a sense public teachers. After our meeting began to attract the attention of the general public, one or both of these men would be on hand almost every night in a very captious state of mind, if their actions were to be taken as an index to their thoughts and feelings. One night in my discourse I spoke something about the baptism of the Spirit.

After I was done speaking and was about to start the prayer-meeting, one of these men got up and said to me, "You have called up the subject of baptism, and now I want you to clear it up, and let us have no dodging of the matter." I looked at him and said, "Mr. ———, I am no good at dodging, as you call it. But who gave you authority to dictate to me what I shall say or how I shall say it?" At this stage of the proceedings Brother William Houston, a grand sample of a fearless Englishman, started at the top of his voice—which was by no means a weak one—and sung,

"Jesus, my all, to heaven is gone—
The way is so delightful—hallelujah!"

The audience struck right in with him and made the house ring with the voices of men, women and children, while they gave expression to their feelings and sang that grand old hymn, and gave such emphasis to the chorus that nothing but *water-fowls* could resist the influence of the singing. We had a good prayer-meeting after that.

On another occasion, as soon as I was done preaching, the other one of the two men spoken of arose and challenged me to meet him in public debate on the subject of baptism. I told him that I had no time to waste in that way, but if he would wait until these meetings were closed, I would tell him and all concerned what I believed, and why I believed it, on the subject of water baptism. He got on his feet again, and lifting his hand with a Bible in it, and with a look of determination, said to me and the audience, "In the name of this book I demand to be heard." I looked him in the face and said to him, "Sir, you came here without invitation, you have got angry without provocation, and now in the name of the laws of the Province of Ontario, I command you to sit down and be quiet." We went on with our meeting till the close without any more disturbance.

The next day I met this man in the road. He asked me if I intended to take up his challenge. I told him I did not. He said, "It is because you dare not do it; you are a coward." I replied that "Forbearance is not cowardice any more than rashness is courage. The strongest men are the least quarrelsome and the strongest nations are the coolest nations. It is not because I am afraid of you that I decline to accept your challenge, but I am not disposed to spend my time and strength in a useless way. Besides, I am well known in these counties, and if I should engage in a public debate with you it would give a publicity to your views and a notoriety to yourself that you cannot gain if left to make your own way into public notice. I am not going to be an advertising medium for you or any one else if I can help it."

Two weeks after I preached on water baptism, as practised by the Methodists, to the largest crowd that had ever met me in that neighbourhood, and I gave the longest address that I have ever given; but I never heard anything more on the subject while I remained on that charge. Some of the people who were brought in at that series of meetings are among the leading Church workers of that neighbourhood at the present time.

KINLOUGH APPOINTMENT,

on the Kincardine Circuit, was the scene of some four weeks' effort by myself and my colleague, Bro. Thomas Love. The people in this locality were a mixture both nationally and religiously—English, Irish, Scotch, Canadian and Anglican, Presbyterian, Methodist, Baptist and Roman Catholics, all had their representatives and adherents here. A large number of young people attended our services in this place, which made the prospects of success all the brighter.

One peculiarity of this appointment was the lack of denominational attachment on the part of the members of the Church. Another thing that gave a discouraging aspect to the work was the small amount of real and hearty brotherly love and confidence in each other that manifested itself in the community. But still the people were fully up to the average in moral deportment, and some of them were conspicuous in loyalty to Queen and country. Orangeism had a strong hold in the place, and some of the best Orangemen that I have met—and I have seen and known a great many —were found in connection with the lodge at Kinlough.

One of the most prominent men in the place was Mr. Jacob Nichols, deputy reeve of Kinloss township, and Justice of the Peace. He had at one time, I think, been a Methodist, but he was not at this time in connection with the Church. He was a good singer, and was well instructed in vocalization. He took a laudable interest in the young people, and at the time I speak of he had an excellent choir under his tuition.

When we commenced our meetings I asked Mr. Nichols to attend and lead the singing, which he readily consented to do. And during the whole time he and his band of singers did a great deal toward making the effort a successful one. He was one of the best hands at selecting timely and suitable pieces to sing that I have had the pleasure of working with in revival meetings. In this kind of work very much depends on what is sung and how it is sung; but I could rely on Mr. Nichols both as to matter and manner. "A glorious success" was the general verdict respecting our meetings as they were brought to a close at the end of the fourth week. Nearly all the young folks of the Protestant families in the community professed to be benefited, and many of them claimed to be converted. Besides, a number of old sinners were led to turn from the error of their ways.

One young woman who was very active in these meetings, and who was greatly blessed in them, died not long after in the full assurance of faith, and in the hope of the gospel. Miss Mary Rowsam will be remembered when the butterflies of fashion and the votaries of pleasure shall be forgotten and their names have perished. It would hardly be a kind thing for me to close this section without saying something about the homes that I found around Kinlough during the three years of my pastorate on the circuit.

Perhaps, no class of men are so much dependent on homes away from their own residences as the Methodist itinerants. Their appointments are often at a distance from where they reside, so that it becomes a matter of necessity for them to have "homes away from home." This is one of the conditions of itinerant life, and happy is the preacher who can adapt himself to circumstances and make himself agreeable and at home anywhere. These are the men who gain the affections of the people among whom they labour.

Our homes about Kinlough were quite numerous, as they had need to be since one of us had to spend one night every week the year round at some of them, besides all the extras, such as revivals and other week-night meetings. The place was fifteen miles from my home. First and foremost, there is Mr. Nathan Pennel and his wife, called sometimes Aunt Mary. "The meeting-house" stands on a corner of their farm. Their house has been the home of ministers ever since the beginning of the settlement, and they have got rich while feeding the preacher and his horse. By day or by night, their door is ever open to the minister of the gospel.

Aunt Mary, like the Shunammite of old, has a "prophet's room," which she keeps for the preacher, and any one but a preacher who may be allowed to occupy that room must be one of Aunt Mary's special favourites. She told me that she could not read a word before she was converted, which was in middle age ; but she asked the Lord to help her to learn to read His word. She is a passable reader now, and fully up to the average woman of her age in general intelligence, and her knowledge of the Bible is remarkable. She is a great politician—a Conservative—and greatly in favour of Orangeism. May she and Nathan enjoy peace and plenty until their work is done, then in the bright beyond have a home in the Eternal City of God.

Brother James Young, who lives some distance from the church, with his wife was always ready and willing to entertain the preachers and make them comfortable. Mr. Young is one of "Aunt Mary's" particular friends, because he is an Irishman and an Orangeman. He was one of the circuit stewards.

Mr. John Rowsam and his family were always

ready to entertain us, and many a comfortable night I spent with them. Mr. Rowsam has many noble qualities, and I only wish that I could pronounce him faultless, but like the rest of men he gives evidence of human weakness sometimes. His wife and daughter are among the most amiable people to be found.

The Tweedie family were always willing to give the preachers a hearty welcome. They were a family of singers, and made up a part of Mr. Jacob Nichols' choir. The mother and some of the children were Methodists.

One more name I must not forget to mention, John Nichols. He was represented to me as sceptical, but I never found him so, except on the question of Darwinism. He was a little inclined towards that, but he was one of the most intelligent men of that community. I found great enjoyment in talking with him on almost any subject. I think that he must be something more than a "monkey gone to seed."

My Last Revival Meeting.

A combination of circumstances tended to make the closing year of my active work in the ministry an eventful one in more ways than one. Just before the Conference came on, our people in the town of Kincardine had entered into a contract to build an eight thousand dollar church, which to them was a very heavy undertaking. I had been two years on the circuit, and was well acquainted with the wants and wishes of the people.

At Conference it was resolved to cut off two appointments and attach them to another circuit. Against this I protested with all my might; but it was done, and I was left alone on the circuit, with four Sabbath appointments to provide for, and to superintend the building of a new church. This was hard enough, but it was not all. The people at two appointments that had been cut off locked up their churches and positively refused to submit to the new arrangement, so that if these were to be saved to the denomination some compromise must be made. The appointments in question were Kinloss and Kinlough.

The arrangement made was, that I should take charge of both; that I should supply Kinloss with religious services, and Kinlough would be supplied temporarily with preaching from the Teeswater Circuit preachers, and all the financial returns except the salaries should be made in connection with Kincardine. This gave me a large amount of extra work.

Besides all this, there was a great deal of trouble and worry in connection with the building, brought on by the failure of the contractor to fulfil his engagement. To save other parties from heavy losses, we had to assume responsibilities not contemplated when the contract was let. When all these things were put together, I found myself with burdens resting on my shoulders that were more than any man ought to carry; but I resolved to do my best, so that if I failed to succeed it should not be through any lack of effort on my part. The church was completed about Christmas. Dr. Carman and Dr. Stone attended, and took charge of the financial part of the proceedings, as well as the other services. They succeeded in getting over ten thousand dollars promised to wipe out the debt on the church.

According to the contract, no money was due till one month after the building was completed, and then it was all due, and if it was not then paid, of course it would be on interest until paid. Eighty-two hundred dollars would have been amply sufficient to pay off every claim on the day that the church was dedicated; but that amount in hard cash is one thing, and ten thousand five hundred dollars in subscriptions running from one to five years is entirely another thing, as the board of trustees found out to their sorrow. In these wild subscription schemes two important factors are generally lost sight of : one of these is, that interest on unpaid principal continually increases the liabilities, and the other is that shrinkage in the subscription caused by death, bankruptcies and removals from the Province, are all the time causing a decrease in the assets. In the case of which I am now speaking, to make everything safe not less than fifteen thousand dollars in subscriptions would have been needed to provide for debt and contingencies; but I forgot : it is revivals, and not church debts, that I am writing about at present.

About a month after the church was dedicated, there came to me one day a young man about six feet in height, with fine physical proportions, with rather pleasing manners, a fair complexion, dark hair, heavy whiskers, a heavy bass voice, plenty of cheek, and a ready tongue. I am thus particular in describing him because of the important bearing his coming at that

time has had on my own life and on my relation to
the work of the ministry. He claimed to be a travelling evangelist. He showed documents which testified
that he was a local preacher in the great American M.
E. Church.   He also had testimonials from a Methodist minister in Canada, with whom I was acquainted,
and for whom I had great respect as a successful re-
vivalist. I had always kept clear of wandering stars
in the shape of men who were too liberal to belong to
any Church, and yet sought the patronage of the
Churches; but this man was a Church member, which
made his case somewhat different, and in talking with
him I found that he was not willing to work on the
lines of Church work, but he would be a second
Moody.

I told him that I could not think of going into extra
work at that time; that for nine months I had been
under a continuous strain, and was about worn out
and needed all the rest that I could get, and that I
had spent three months in revival work at that appointment since I came to the circuit, as well as many
weeks elsewhere; but it was all to no use. He was not
the kind to be put off without positive rudeness. He
went to some of the officials, and by some means got
them to consent to let him into the Church, with the
understanding that I need not take any part in the
work further than to give directions as to the time and
manner of holding the services. The meetings were
commenced and our evangelist went to work.

During the first week nothing much was done.
During the second week I had to go to Elmwood, on

the Hanover Circuit, to attend a church dedication
and tea-meeting. I was away nearly a week. When
I came home, I found that things were going very
badly, the young man was worse than a failure; the
people were contending, some for him and others
against him. The first man I met after coming home
was an old medical doctor, who often attended our
meetings. He said to me, " If you wish to empty
your new church and scatter the congregation, it can
be effectually done by allowing that brawler to stay
in it for a few weeks, if he conducts himself as he
has done while you were away."

When I heard the statements of a number of members
and others, I resolved to take hold of the affair with a
firm hand. The first thing that I did was to assume
entire control of the services. Then I took the young
man by himself and gave him some fatherly counsel.
I told him that what I was about to say, some honest
man ought to have said to him before he started out
on such a mission. I told him that I did not doubt his
sincerity or piety. But I said, " I think you have
mistaken your calling. Whatever the Lord may
have for you to do, I am satisfied that your work is
not that of an evangelist. You have energy enough,
but it is the kind of energy that breaks what it ought
to soften. You have force, but it is the force that scat-
ters where it should gather. The trouble with you is,
that like a good many others in the Church, you have
got the Moody craze, so that a desire to imitate that
singular man has made you unwilling to do ordinary
Christian work in an ordinary Christian way. Hence

the Church in its local activities and agencies has no field extensive enough for your expanding conceptions of duty. Take my advice and go home, and if you really want to do something for the Lord, He will find you plenty of work that is more in harmony with your capabilities than the holding of revival meetings seems to be." He did not take this very well. But I told him that as I was responsible to the Conference and to the public opinion of the town for what I allowed to be done in the Church, I could not permit him to lead any more meetings there.

Matters had now got into such a state that a powerful revival became an absolute necessity, as it was the only thing that would save the society from serious embarrassments and keep the congregation together. It was resolved to rally our shattered forces at once, and make an advance movement against the combined ranks of our spiritual opposers. We went to work with a determination, God helping us to conquer at any cost.

All personal considerations on the part of both preacher and people were thrown aside, and every one of us felt that the future of our cause as a denomination in the town would be affected by the success or failure of the present effort.

We worked on for three weeks before we regained what had been lost by the operations of the young man who came to us uninvited and went from us unregretted. But at length the goodness of our God was manifested in an outpouring of the Holy Spirit and in the commencement of a mighty work that seemed to shake the town as it had not been shaken for many years before. So people told me. We kept the meetings going for six weeks longer, making nine weeks in all since I took the matter into my own hands. Between sixty and seventy professed to be converted. The membership of the Church was very much strengthened and encouraged, and the congregation was largely increased.

But the effort was too much for me. More than once while the meetings were going on, I found myself unable to walk from the church to the parsonage without help, though the distance was not more than six rods. There was a reason for this. When I came to the circuit three years before I was only partially recovered from a very severe affliction which had nearly cost my life. I ought to have had a year's rest then, but financial considerations forbade me to take it. Then, too, the circuit was a large one, involving a good deal of travel and exposure to bad roads and rough weather. Besides this I had spent about five months in special meetings during the first two years on the circuit, and the third year I had to do more than any man ought to do. And now, as I look back to that year's work, I am not surprised to find myself a broken-down man. When I think of the difficulty I had in filling the regular work, and of the many sleepless nights I spent in trying to devise ways and means to meet and overcome the obstacles that one after another arose in the way of success to the enterprise in which we were engaged, and then on the back of all these the desperate nine weeks' struggle at the close of the year,

11

I only wonder that God gave me strength to bear up under it as long as I did.   If I had my days to live over again after the experience that I have had, I am sure that no Conference or committee would ever induce me to carry so heavy a burden as I did during the last year of my active work in the itinerancy.   But it will all come right "in the sweet by-and-bye."

Before closing this chapter, I will relate an incident of an unusual nature that occurred during the seventh or eighth week of the meetings.   One night, just as I was reading the text, three men came into the church. Two of them took seats just inside the door, the other one walked up the aisle with a hasty and pompous stride, as though he fancied that the whole church and congregation belonged to him.   He took a seat in the forward pew, and right in front of the pulpit, where he could look me squarely in the face, and see every movement of mouth and chin.   He looked at me, and then he took out his book and pencil and began to write.   He was a stranger in the place; I had never seen him before.   He was a large man, with dark complexion, coarse black hair sprinkled with gray, an eye as black as a crow, and one of those peculiar mouths that could enable its owner to pose either as a cynic or a saint.

At first I was a little thrown off my balance.   I did not know who he was, or what he was after.   He might be a wit, looking for subjects to laugh at, or he might be an infidel seeking what he might devour. Or he might be a religious controversialist hunting for an opponent.   When I saw what he was doing I said to the audience, I see there is a gentleman here wishing to take down my sermon. To give him a fair chance, I will announce and read the text again. He took down every word I said. While this was going on, I called up all the knowledge that I had of physiognomy and phrenology, and mentally took the measure of the man. The conclusion I came to was this: "I am not afraid of you, and I shall proceed just as I would if you were not here, only I will be more careful of what I say and how I say it." The man would look at me for a moment, and then take down what I said with the most rapid motion of the hands that could be imagined. As soon as I closed the book he got up in a hurry, put up his book and left the church in the company of the men he came with. One of the men was a leading hotel-keeper in the town.

The next morning, as I was passing the hotel, the proprietor was standing at the door, and spoke to me, saying, "I was sorry for you last night, and I want to explain to you how we came to be there. That reporter is a man who is entirely deaf. He was staying over night here. It was proposed to test his ability to report an address by watching the speaker's face. I knew that you were holding meetings in the church, and I offered to take him there to report the sermon. I thought to have been there before you started, so as to tell you about it, but I was too late. The man is a Frenchman, but speaks English, and he is certainly a wonderful shorthand reporter."

I asked the man if the Frenchman had got a correct report of the discourse. He said it was perfectly correct so far as he could remember. I told him that there was no harm done, and that it was just as well that I did not know the object of their coming, as it would have been harder for me to speak without the temptation to try and do some fine talking, and thus to spoil the whole. I have never seen nor heard of the deaf reporter since.

CHAPTER VIII.

FLOODS AND BRIDGES.

SOME of the experiences of travel are about as rough as they are romantic. Sometimes, on a journey, we meet with incidents that are ludicrous and yet dangerous; and it is not a rare thing that the novelty of a difficulty goes far to conceal the danger that may attend it. In this article I shall give an account of some of my experiences with floods and bridges while itinerating in the new parts of our own country.

The first incident that I will relate is one over which I have often had a quiet laugh to myself when I have thought of it. If my memory serves me right, the Conference was held that year in the village of Palermo. I had left my horse with a friend in Garafraxa, and had gone from Guelph by train. The Conference had closed its session. I was on my way home, or rather to where my home had been the last year, for I had to move to a new place. At Rockwood I fell in with Rev. John H. Watts, who was also on his way to where his last year's home had been. But he had just been appointed to the Garafraxa Circuit, and he intended to stop over and spend the Sabbath on his new field of labour. This circuit was an old and favourite field of mine, so I decided to stay there over Sabbath too. Bro. Watts and I concluded to foot it from Rockwood to the Garafraxa parsonage, as by so doing we would shorten the distance by a number of miles and save quite an item of expense.

Accordingly we started, following one of the concession lines through the township of Eramosa, until we came to the road that runs from Orangeville, on the south side of the Grand River, to Fergus. Here we were directed to follow a certain line which, we were told, would lead to the road running from Fergus to Douglas. We walked on for two or three miles, when we came to the Grand River. It being in the spring of the year, the river was high, the current strong, and the water cold. Here was a dilemma. There had once been a bridge, but it had been swept away by the spring floods. To go back and around by the bridge at Douglas would give us an extra walk of some six or seven miles. The question for us to decide was, " What shall we do ?"

After due consideration we determined to wade the stream. It did not look to be very deep, but was from eight to twelve rods wide and running with a rapid current. I went in first, but before starting I cut a long, stiff cane, and running my umbrella through the loops of my carpet-bag (this before the day of satchels) I swung it over my shoulder, and taking my cane in hand I started for the other shore. I found the water deeper and the sweep of current stronger than I had expected. Had I not taken the precaution to get the cane, I have no doubt but that I should have been carried down the stream and perhaps drowned. However, after a hard struggle, I reached the other side wet to the arm-pits, and pretty well exhausted. I drew off my boots and drained the water out of them, and adopted measures to wring out my clothes.

When I got over I called to Bro. Watts and asked him what he was going to do. I knew that when he undertook anything he was not the sort of man to back out, but I thought I would try him. His answer was characteristic of the man. He said, in a determined manner, "I can go anywhere that you can." "All right, then," I said; "come along." He benefited by my experience so far that he got his garments well above the high-water mark by placing most of them on his head and shoulders before starting in. He got over with less difficulty than I met with. Two facts contributed to this result. He was a younger and stronger man than I was; and in the water the less incumbrance in the way of clothing one has on, the easier will be his progress and the less his danger.

Where we crossed was in the bush, but the mosquitoes were not yet ready to commence their summer's work; so we lay down and rested awhile. We started on again, and in the course of an hour we arrived at the house of Bro. D. Kyle, on the sixth line of Garafraxa. Here we were made welcome by Mrs. Kyle and family. The relation of our watery experiences furnished a good deal of amusement for the young people. However, I never felt that the getting wet or the being laughed at did us any particular harm; but we came to the conclusion that the shortest way is not always the easiest or safest.

A Series of Spring-tide Difficulties.

The Huron District of the Methodist Episcopal Church was a very large one. It included three whole counties and extended into five others. To go over this territory four times in the year, as the presiding elder was expected to do, involved facing some difficulties arising from bad roads and rough weather. For many years this travel had to be accomplished with a horse or on foot.

When I was appointed to the position there were not ten miles of railway within the boundaries of the district. In the spring of the year it was often very hard to meet the appointments on account of the floods caused by the melting of the large quantities of snow that fall during the winter months. One spring I was on my round of Quarterly Meetings and I found myself in the town of Kincardine. On my way to my home in Meaford I was to stop over Sabbath and hold a Quarterly Meeting at Eugenia Falls. I heard that the country was flooded in all directions, and that travel was almost entirely suspended; but I had a good horse and there was a good gravel road nearly all the distance.

I started on Wednesday morning. I intended to make my way to the home of Brother William Cross, in Culross, that day. All went on very nicely for the first part of my journey. But when I called at the

Black Horse Corners for dinner I went to Mr. Harrison's house ; he was the keeper of the post-office, and he told me that four miles ahead, at Riversdale, the road was flooded so that the mails from Walkerton had been brought over in canoes for the last week. This was rather unpleasant news to hear, especially as there was no other road to take. However, there was no help for it. I had often told young men and boys never to say "I can't," until they had tried. After myself and horse had been cared for, I started for the scene of trial. When I came to the place I found that what I had heard was no exaggeration.

The Teeswater, or Mud River, runs for several miles through a low, level, swampy piece of country. At Riversdale, where the Durham Road crosses the river, the flat is nearly a mile wide. A deep ditch was dug out on each side of the roadway and the earth thrown in the centre ; this raised the road some feet above ordinary high-water mark. At this point the stream runs near the high land on one side, and consequently the flat is all on the other side.

When I came to Riversdale and looked down the road, what I saw was by no means reassuring. I saw before me a sheet of water, fully five-eighths of a mile wide, that entirely covered the road. The flood had brought down a number of old logs and stumps that had been lying about on the flats, and they had caught on the middle of the road and stopped there. The road had more the appearance of a pine-stump fence run through a pond than anything else that I can think of.

When I got into the village I spoke to some men who were standing at the door of the hotel, and they told me that no team had passed over the bridge for more than a week. One of the men said that he had been over in a canoe, and he thought it possible to go over with a single rig, if a man had a steady horse and nerve enough to face it. I told him that with me it was not a question of nerve, but a matter of necessity, as I must go over, if that were possible.

I drove on to the bridge across the main stream and got out to take a survey of things. The water was clear, and I could see the road for some distance ahead, and I concluded that there was room for the buggy to go between the row of stumps and the ditch, which was some ten or twelve feet deep. I took off the check-rein and unbuckled the side-straps, so as to give every advantage possible. I took my trunk from under the seat and placed it on top of it, and took off my coat and put it on the trunk, then I got up on top of all and started. The men were standing on the bridge; they said they would wait there until I either got over or needed help. My horse at first was somewhat frightened, but a few words spoken to him in a firm yet kind voice seemed to give him confidence. Sometimes he was half way up his sides in water, and sometimes not above his knees, but he kept perfectly calm and seemed to take in the situation fully. We got safely over, and when I waved my hat back to the men on the bridge as a token that all was well, cheer after cheer came floating over the five-eighths of a mile of water that ran between us.

Just as the sun was going down I reached the house of Brother Cross, and put up for the night after a rather anxious day. Here I was kindly treated and hospitably entertained, and after a good night's rest I was ready for the road again. This Brother Cross is a whole-souled Englishman who, with his Scotch-Canadian wife, always have a place in their home for the weary itinerant.

A Shaky Bridge.

The morning after my adventure at Riversdale, I started on my journey, intending to go that day as far as the village of Hanover. I got to Walkerton about noon, and stopped for dinner at a hotel. Here I was informed that the bridge over the Saugeen River at Hanover had been impassable for more than a week. The mail stage had to take another road, and it went a number of miles out of its way to get around this obstacle. After dinner I went forward, feeling somewhat doubtful of success. When I got within a couple of miles of the place I met a man with a double rig loaded with furniture. I asked him about the bridge. He said that he had come over it, but that it was in a very dangerous condition. I asked him about the flats. He said, "There is no danger there if you keep in the middle of the road ; the danger is at the bridge over the main stream." I drove on to the theatre of strife between human invention and some of the forces of nature. When I came to the place I found that the flats, which were about one-fourth of a mile wide, were entirely covered except the tops of the many stumps that still disputed the right of soil with the cultivators of the land. The scene presented was somewhat picturesque. The water moving hither and thither, as if trying to dodge the stumps—said stumps all the while standing on the spot where they grew, as unmoved as though they were to stand and last for-ever. Little currents and eddies were making music for themselves in ripples among the brush and other things that came in their way, and seemed to fancy that they were infantile rivers and baby whirlpools. Bright sunbeams lightly touched the smiling face of the water as one would pat the cheek of a lovely child.

I awoke from my reverie and started to cross the flats and try the bridge. . I had no difficulty in keep-ing on the road. The water was up to the horse's knees the greater part of the way. When I came to the bridge I found that it was all afloat, and it was kept from going down the river only by the precaution of some of the inhabitants who, with ropes and chains, had fastened it to trees and stumps, otherwise the municipality would have been out of pocket to the amount of twelve or fifteen hundred dollars by the loss of their bridge, besides the inconvenience to the travelling public.

When I drove on the bridge I found that it trembled and swayed to such an extent that I was fearful that it would break loose and go down stream despite the chains and ropes with which it was fastened. I walked over ahead of my horse, and I think that I stepped as lightly as a man weighing a hundred and eighty can possibly do. We got over in safety, but

when I stopped the horse he was all in a tremble.
That bridge had taxed his nerves to a great extent.
I think if the poor brute could have spoken at that
time, he would have said something like this: " It is
much safer to go through deep water if you have solid
ground below you than it is to go over a shaky bridge
with a deep, swift river raging and foaming under it."

I soon after reached the Hanover parsonage, whose
occupants, Bro. and Sister Lynch, kindly invited me
to stop with them over night. I thankfully accepted
their kindly offer, and put up for the night. When I
related the experiences of the last two days, Brother
Lynch, who could enjoy a good laugh as well as most
men, made himself quite merry over the picture that
I presented. But the hearty welcome, coming from a
warm Irish heart, which he gave me, more than atoned
for any soreness that I might feel under the lashing of
his Hibernian wit. I shall have to refer again to this
brother and his excellent wife in these experiences. I
got a good night's rest, and in the morning started for
Eugenia.

A Big Basin Full of Water.

Starting from Hanover in the morning I went on to
the town of Durham, and put up at Dr. Halstead's. I
found the doctor and young people all well, but Mrs.
Halstead was very sick. I always found a cheerful
welcome at Dr. Halstead's either by night or by day.
Here I fed my horse, got my dinner, had prayer with
the sick woman, and started again for Eugenia.

As I was driving out of town I met the mail stage

coming in from the east.   I asked the driver about the road.   He said that I would find great difficulty in getting through.   He quaintly stated the case by saying, "There is a big basin full of water where the road for thirty rods, is covered all of ten feet deep."   He said that in going around through a farm he made his horses swim for a couple of rods, but he got through all right.   I thanked him for the information and started for another fight with floods, cheering myself by the way with the thought that where another could go with two horses I could surely go with one.

I went on through Priceville and Flesherton.   About a mile further on I came to the "big basin."   Here the water was within three feet of the tops of the telegraph poles.   The stage driver could not have found a more appropriate name.   It was a large, round hollow, almost entirely surrounded by hills.   It had an inlet, but it had no outlet.   I had often passed along the road, but I had not noticed this peculiarity.   The road had been made by cutting down the hills and filling up the hollow until an embankment was formed some eight or ten feet high, but now this was from six to eight feet under water.   I found the place where the stage had come out of the fields and turned in, and in a little time I came to the "inlet" of the basin.   This was a spring current made by the melted snow and rains.   It was about thirty feet wide, running swiftly, and the water was very muddy, so that its depth could not be seen.   The banks were some ten or twelve feet high and very steep.   As at Riversdale, I prepared for the worst and drove in; my horse by this time seemed

A Risky Drive.

reckless as to where he went. He was able to touch bottom all the way, but water ran over his back a part of the time. We got over in safety, and got out on the road again all right.

After another four miles of road pretty badly defaced by mud, just as the sun was leaving the last of his beams lingering in the tops of the trees that crowned the hills around the little village of Eugenia, I drove up to the preacher's home and found Bro. Thomas Reid anxiously waiting for the arrival of the often-talked about and much-scolded presiding elder. The genial and kindly welcome of Brother and Sister Reid would drive gloomy thoughts and feelings from the most melancholy dyspeptic that ever brought a saddened face into a happy home. I felt a relief at the thought that for two days I would be at rest, so far as travel was concerned.

On Saturday I learned that the road to Meaford was impassable for a mile in consequence of an overflow of Beaver River at Kimberley. We also learned that all the bridges between Flesherton and Singhampton, on the Durham road, had been swept off, so that it would be impossible for me to go home by way of Collingwood. I told Bro. Reid, when he informed me, that I would dismiss the subject from my mind, and attend to my duties in connection with his Quarterly Meeting, and see what was best to do when Monday came.

On the Sabbath people came in from all directions, and we had a good meeting in the little church. Old Mrs. Purdy, or Aunt Anna as she was frequently called, lived here with her son and daughter. She was an old

Methodist of over fifty years' standing.　She has since gone to her friends across the tide.　R. McLean Purdy, postmaster at Eugenia, did much for his mother's church.

FLOATING CORDUROY.

On Monday morning I started for home, having been absent for more than three weeks.　When I got to Kimberley, and as I was passing through it, a gentleman called to me and said, "You cannot possibly get through the swamp, as the corduroy bridge is all afloat." I said to him, "Sir, I thank you for your kind intentions; but my way is, when I start to a place, I go as far as I can find a track or make one.　I will go on and have a look at the road.　I do not like to give up now." "Well," said my friend, "you will have to come back, and we will have dinner ready when you come."　I went on to the river.　The main stream at this place is small, as the river spreads over the low, flat, swampy land, necessitating a causeway one mile and a quarter in length.　This had been made of logs put side by side on stringers or flat on the ground.　For about half the distance the causeway has been covered with dirt and gravel.

I found the uncovered part all floating so that a horse could not be got over it at all.　I found that by stepping very quickly I could go over without much danger, and I concluded that I could draw the buggy over by hand, if I could only get the horse over.

While I was thinking what to do, two boys came after me, and one of them said that his father sent them to tell me to come back and he would see the

12

horse was got over. When I went the man proposed to put a boy on the horse, and send him a mile back up the river to where a farmer had made a bridge into his premises. He could cross there and go through ten or twelve farms to the side road on the other side of the swamp. This would involve a good deal of trouble, and require the letting down and shutting up of a number of fences; but I could see no other way to do unless I left the horse behind and went on foot home.

The boy started after dinner, and I went to the swamp to take the buggy over. I could see the boy after he got over in the clearings, as the land on that side was very high, just on the face of the mountain. I could see the little fellow steadily moving across the fields. Sometimes he would be questioned a little, but no one interfered with him. I went over the floating logs stepping from one to another, drawing the buggy after me. By the time the boy got around with the horse, I had got over to the covered part of the causeway. I hitched up and drove on four miles and stopped at Bro. R. Gilray's, at Epping. It had taken me all the day to make less than ten miles. Bro. Gilray and family were always noted for their unostentatious hospitality. They are Lowland Scotch. They have a large number of children. One son is a Presbyterian minister in Toronto, and another is reeve of his native township. They are an energetic, moral and prosperous family.

The next morning I started for home, which is twelve miles distant; I got home at noon. After leaving Kincardine, I was four days and a-half on the road. This time was spent in making a trip that has often been done in one day and a-half. My next Quarterly Meeting was at Meaford, so my horse and myself had a rest of a week or more. That was the most watery journey I ever had.

An Involuntary Dive.

When we were on the Teeswater mission, I used to have some exciting times on the river fishing for speckled trout. These splendid fish were plentiful. Wheat and meat being scarce, people caught the trout not so much for sport, or as a luxury, as they did for family necessity. The most noted places for trout-fishing were at Parr's mill and at Carroll's mill-pond; Parr's was three miles from Teeswater, and Carroll's seven, on the Teeswater River.

One day I started to go to Carroll's, and I took a boy with me. We walked as far as Parr's mill, and there we got a flat-bottom skiff that George Parr had made for himself. We went down the river in this. When we got as far as Mr. John Gilroy's, he invited the boy to stop and pick a basket of green peas to take home with us. I went on alone to the pond and succeeded in catching a good string of very fine fish.

When I came back to Mr. Gilroy's the boy had a basketful, and Mrs. G. had the tea ready. We took tea, and then paddled up the stream until we got to where Parr kept his boat. This was in the mouth of a little creek that ran into another creek of a bigger size, which itself enters into the Teeswater. There

THE OLD SAWMILL.

is an eddy at the place, and the whirling water had scooped out a hole fourteen or fifteen feet deep. In trying to run into the mouth of the creek which was very narrow and deep, I missed it. I rose to my feet and placed the oar against the land to push back into the stream, so that I might try to run into the miniature harbour with better success. I made an effort, and I suppose I put on more force than was needed. The boat shot like an arrow into the middle of the eddy, I lost my balance and found that I must either go overboard or upset the boat and spill its contents into the water. It is wonderful how quickly the mind can take in the whole situation at a critical moment. The water was deep, my boy could not swim, the fish and peas would be scattered in the creek, and carried by the current into the river, and I would get as wet as possible. All this I saw at a glance; I chose to get wet alone, and with a spring I went head first over the side into the water, going down until my head struck the bottom. The boy was sitting with his back to me and did not know that I was out of the boat until he saw me come to the surface some distance off, as the boat had moved on after I left it. The work of getting into the harbour was soon accomplished now, myself acting as a tug.

I seems to me that almost everything has a laughable side to it, if one is disposed to see it. When I took in the aspect of things as I came up, I could not help but laugh. The look of wonderment on the face of the boy; myself spouting and blowing like a miniature whale; the little boat rocking and swaying as if to show how easily it could toss a man into the aqueous fluid. After securing the boat we went to the house of George Parr. Mrs. Parr gave me some of his clothes to put on, but on trying them I found they were too small. So there was nothing for it but' to go on home in my wet clothes. We got home all right, and after the usual wifely remark, "I told you to be careful," from the companion of my joys and sorrows, the events of the day became a matter of family history, and I never realized any harm from my involuntary ducking.

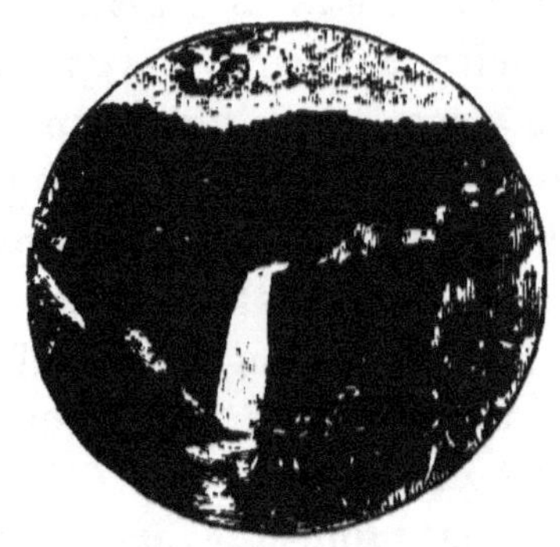

CHAPTER IX.

STORMS AND SNOWDRIFTS.

WELL, what is a snowdrift? The doctor may say it is the grave of a dead snowstorm. The poet will tell you that it is the downy bed in which the storm-king puts to rest his sleeping children. The thin-blooded rheumatic will say it is that which gives him the heaviest chills and the sharpest pains. The wash-woman will declare the snowdrift gives her nice soft water long after the sunny days of spring have melted the snow off the buildings and the fields. If you ask the mischief-loving boy, that stands peering through the fence, and making faces at that other boy that pretends to be hoeing the corn, he will turn and look at you and then give his suspenders a hitch and say, " I like snowdrifts, I do. It is that that gives me the last snowball of the season, and it allows me to take all that remains of itself to wash the faces of Molly and Jennie, as they go tripping to the woods to gather the April flowers. Yes, I like snowdrifts." The snowdrift, like almost everything in this world, has its friends and its foes. The aspect of a snowdrift is affected by the standpoint from which it is viewed. To contemplate it from the inside of a comfortable room, with the thermometer ranging among the sixties, gives rather pleasant ideas of it. But to one wading up to his middle in it, with the thermometer down to ten below zero, there will not be much enjoyment. In the one case there is a feeling of security mingled with a sense of the beautiful. In the other there is a sense of increasing weariness along with the consciousness of possible danger. Few things have a prettier look than a grand drift of pure white snow on a bright sunny day. The glistening brightness that dazzles out in all directions might lead an inexperienced beholder to imagine that it was a thing of more than summer warmth. But to the experienced eye it has a different look. To such the impression made is, that however striking and pretty the thing may be, as an object of sight, it is, after all, like the oration of Bob Ingersoll at his brother's funeral—very brilliant, but very cold.

I know something of snowdrifts, both by theory and by practical experience. Theoretically, it is simply congealed water that has been carried by the wind and left in a convenient place till spring comes. Then it is ready to do its part in getting up a flood to take away somebody's bridge or break up someone's mill dam. Practically, it is like the cold looks and freezing tones of some people in the world—a good thing to keep away from, unless one had a high fever and would be the better of a little cooling.

Some of my experiences with snowdrifts were of a

character calculated to wake up a man's energy if he had any of that quality that is so necessary to winter life in many parts of Canada. Others were sometimes a little risky. But I never was much injured, though I was often incommoded by coming in contact with them. It was during my four years' travel on the district that I found most difficulties with them. I had often to meet appointments twenty or thirty miles distant from each other, and bad roads and stormy weather were not valid excuses for failing to meet them. I never missed an appointment on account of roads or weather. But sometimes I had hard work to get to them.

A Day of Needless Fears.

I found myself one time in the town of Kincardine. On Monday, after the Quarterly Meeting, it began to snow and drift, and for three days and nights the storm raged with relentless fury. My next work was at Invermay. This was forty miles distant from where I was. The snow piled up and filled the road-ways from fence to fence. The Port Elgin stage did not come on Wednesday nor Thursday, so that there was no mail from the north for two days.

On Friday morning I started out from James Ballantine's, telling him that if I could not go through I would come back. It was still blowing a gale, but the snow had ceased to fall. When I got out of the town and reached the Saugeen road that runs north from Kincardine to Port Elgin, I soon found that the storm had overdone its work. The snow being a little damp, it was so packed by the wind that for a good deal of the way a horse could walk on the top of the drift, and not sink deeper than to the fetlocks, and the cutter did not sink the thickness of the runners.

But I also found that when the horse did go down it was no child's play to get him up again. In his efforts to get up he was almost sure to get one of the shafts over his back. Then I must unhitch and draw the cutter away so that he could get up. This I did a number of times that day. But all day present difficulties did not trouble me so much as the dread of one that I imagined was before me. Three miles from Port Elgin the road consists of a deep cut through one of those gravel-hills so common in some parts of the country. If that cut should be filled with show it would present an impassable barrier in the way of further progress. My great anxiety was to reach that place before dark. To do that I drove all day without stopping, except to give my horse a pail of water at noon. About dusk I came to the scene of my expected trouble. To my surprise I saw that all my fears had been utterly groundless. There was not a drift to be seen. The same wind that left such heavy piles of snow in other places, had carried it through the cut. I was reminded of the advice given by some one, which is, " Never cross a river till you come to it." I made up my mind that in future I would not wallow through a snowdrift till I reached it. About seven in the evening I got to Port Elgin and went to old Mr. Bricker's for the night.

Over Covered Fences.

Next morning after my day of groundless anxiety, I started in good time for Invermay. I had to go a long way around, as the shortest road was said to be entirely blocked up. I started out a little behind the stage. I had gone but a short distance when the track went into the fields and continued for nearly two miles over fences, and through door-yards, and barn-yards, until I began to wonder if all the fences had been burned up, as they were nearly all entirely hidden from sight. The road to Invermay was a crooked one. As I went on I found that the track was better broken, until I left the main road. Then there was no track at all since the storm, and I had eight miles yet to go. However, I reached Invermay and drove up to the house of J. W. Dunn just as the members of the Official Board had organized for business under the impression that the presiding elder was somewhere stuck in the snowbanks.

A Four-Mile Drift.

On the tableland between the valleys of the Bighead and Beaver Rivers there is a splendid piece of farming country; but any one who has travelled over this territory, along the fourth line of the township of Euphrasia, in the winter time, will agree with me that it is a wonderful place for snowdrifts.

The distance from "Grier's Rock" to the margin of "Queen's Valley" is about four miles. On both sides of the road there are clearings all the way. I have often seen this roadway full from side to side, so that the fences were covered in and in many places entirely out of sight.   Teams going in opposite directions can pass each other only at the gates of the farmhouses. When two teams are meeting, the one that comes to a gate first must stop and wait for the other to come up. I have had many a tussle with the drifts as I went from Meaford to my work south of there.   On one occasion I was going up the hill at Griersville.   The road is cut down into the rock thirty feet or more, and only wide enough for two teams to pass.   There had been a heavy snowstorm, and the road was filled up on one side ten or twelve feet deep, so the top of the snow looked like one side of a steep roof.

As I was going up my horse got off the beaten track and into the unpacked snow on the lower side.   He rolled over on his back and turned the cutter upside down.   When he stopped rolling he was lying in the acute angle where the inclined plane at the top of the snowdrift met the perpendicular wall of craggy rocks. I only escaped being in the same position with the cutter on top of me by throwing myself out on the upper side as it was going over.   When I got on my feet and saw the condition of things, I concluded the commercial value of my horse at that moment was an unknown quantity.   If he commenced to struggle he would be almost sure to knock his head to pieces against the sharp corners of the rocks.   I saw that the only chance was to keep him still as he was until help should come along from some direction.   I got to his head and by caressing and talking to him I managed to keep him pretty still. It was not long before I saw teams coming. A lot of men and some women were in the sleighs. When they came to the foot of the hill the men left their teams in the care of the women, and came to help me. Shovels were got and the snow dug away, so that in a little while all was right again. After all was over an old farmer by the name of Abercrombie said to me, "Sir, when I came up and saw the fix your horse was in I would not have given fifty cents for his life. He is the coolest horse that I ever saw in trouble, and you are the coolest man that I ever saw have an animal in danger." I said to him, "You must remember that coolness is catching. The man that keeps himself cool can generally control his horse." No harm was done only in the loss of time.

Missing the Way.

I was once going from Singhampton to Horning's Mills in the middle of winter. I had my daughter Anna with me. The roads were badly drifted. We had not gone far from Singhampton when we came to a place where the snow was piled up from six to eight feet on the roadbed. On one side was a piece of bush. The horse soon got down in the snow. I took the girl and carried her off the drift and set her down by the root of a tree, while I got the horse and cutter down from the pathless ridge of snow in which they were partially covered over. I led the horse over old logs and fallen trees for a distance of twenty or thirty rods till we came to a clearing ; then we went across two farms, throwing down the fences in our way. At last we came into a barnyard, where we found a man feeding stock. He told us that we had missed our way and had been on a road that had not been used for some time. He put us on a better road, where a track had been broken through the fields, out to another line where there was more travel.

After we had gone a few miles we came in sight of a man and team with a load of saw-logs. The road was very sidelong where he was. All at once the load capsized, and the one horse fell and the other rolled clear over it, so that the near horse was on the off side and both were lying on their backs with their legs flying in the air like drum-sticks. When we came to the place I let the girl hold my horse and went to help the man. The horses were very restless, and their owner was somewhat frightened. Two men came from the opposite direction, and with their help we soon got the horses on their feet. On a close examination it was found that not a cut or scratch could be seen about them. The man stood and looked at the horses and then at the sleigh for a few moments; then he began to swear like a drunken sailor. After a little I said to him, "My friend, that is a queer way of returning thanks for the safety of your property." He answered, "Well, I know it is not just the thing, but sometimes when a fellow don't know whether to laugh or cry it seems easier to swear than to do either." We soon got to the parsonage at Horning's Mills, and put up for the night with Mr. Will, who was then stationed there.

Bad Harness and Saw-logs.

The next day was very cold and clear. In going through the township of Amaranth we overtook a man with a load of saw-logs. He had a good team and a heavy load, but his harness was old and rotten. The road was drifted full from fence to fence, and the beaten track was a succession of ridges and hollows. In drawing the load out of one of the " pitch-holes " the horses broke their harness. When we came up to the place I saw that there was no chance of getting past until we got to a cross-road fifty or sixty rods ahead.

I never did like to pass anyone on the road, and not try to help him, if he was in trouble. But in this case I could not have done so if I would. Again I gave my daughter the lines and went to help the man. His trouble now became mine as well as his. While he toggled up the harness, I got some rails from the fences and fixed them as pries to help lift the load out of the hollow. After several attempts we succeeded. But we had gone but a few rods when another difficulty met us. The road became so sideling that there was great danger of the load turning upside down, as was done the day before. To prevent this we took a fence rail and made a temporary lever of it by fastening one end of it to the lower side of the sleigh, while the other end reached out some ten feet into the road on the upper side, the rail being placed crosswise of the road. On the end of the lever I perched myself like a squirrel on a limb. The driver stood on the

Bad Harness and Saw-logs.

upper side of the load and managed the team. We found by one riding on a sleigh-rail and the other on a fence-rail, we could keep the load right-side up. We got to the cross-road, and I drove on and left the man with the bad harness to himself.

Soon after we came to Mr. James Johnston's in Garafraxa. When we went into the house, Mrs. Johnston assisted my daughter in taking off her wraps. She found that both of her ears were frozen as hard as a piece of sole-leather. She had neglected to attend to herself while looking after the horse. When I asked her if she did not know that her ears were freezing, she said: "I felt them getting very cold, but I did not say anything, for I thought there was trouble enough just then without me making matters worse by complaining." She was one of the uncomplaining kind. But now she is where frozen ears and chilled bodies are unknown, safe in the home beyond the tide.

Snowdrifts Versus Wedding Bells.

Twelve miles south of the town of Meaford is the home of the Gilray family. One of the daughters of Mr. and Mrs. Gilray was to be married on a certain day to a young man living in Meaford. I was engaged to perform the ceremony, assisted by a brother of the bride, Rev. A. Gilray, who lived in Toronto. Two days before the day of the wedding was one continued snowstorm. The roads were badly drifted before, but the addition of two days' steady snowing and drifting made them almost impassable. Knowing all about the

13

"four-mile drift" on the fourth line of Euphrasia, I did not attempt to go by that road. But, instead, I went by Thornbury, and up the valley of the Beaver River. This was nearly twice as far, but it was not so much drifted. By starting early I reached the place in good time.

When I arrived neither the groom nor the Rev. Mr. Gilray had reached the place. The hour fixed upon for the ceremony came. A number of guests assembled, but nothing was seen or heard of the expected parties.

Meanwhile the would-be son-in-law and a few select friends were floundering in the drifts of the "beautiful" that impeded their movements. They soon became aware of the fact that time was flying, while they were going at a snail's pace. Old Time relentlessly refused to wait, even for a wedding party. And the thought that the swift-winged hours, as they sped on in their unchecked career, seemed to mock the slowness of the anxious plodders through the snow, was almost enough to drive an ardent lover and an expectant bridegroom out of his senses. But Mr. D. Youmans was not the sort of a man to be thrown into despair by a little delay, but no doubt he would have been pleased to send a short message to Agnes, saying, "I am coming," if he could.

At last, after long hours of delay, the party arrived at the old homestead, where a lovely, blushing bride-elect awaited one of them, and the best productions of the farm and the grandest achievements of the culinary art were ready for the whole of them.

But the unpleasant moments of suspense were still to be prolonged. The reverend brother had not yet made his appearance, and every one felt that to proceed without him would be about as unpleasant as it would be for a farmer to bind up a sheaf with a handful of nettles. After waiting another hour a sort of council was held and the conclusion come to was to the effect that either Mr. Gilray had been detained in the city, or else the train in which he travelled was blockaded in the drift somewhere. After due deliberation, it was decided to go on with the ceremony. We did so, and just as we came to the conclusion of it, Mr. Gilray came in, just in time to join in the congratulations. It was an awkward moment. We all regretted the affair. It would have been difficult for any of us to tell, at that moment, whether congratulations for the happy couple, or commiseration for the disappointed brother, were uppermost in our mind. But all concerned accepted the situation with as good a grace as possible. No one was censured, for no one was to blame. Years afterward I met Mr. Gilray in the village of Streetsville, where I went to hear him lecture. We had some talk about old times, and among other things mention was made of his coming too late to the wedding.

A Day to be Remembered.

One morning I started from Mount Forest to Meaford. The mercury was about twenty degrees below zero. I had no idea that it was so cold until I was on the road. When I got to the town of Durham, I turned east towards Priceville and Flesherton. About four miles from Durham, I came up to a lot of children on their way home from school.

Among them were two little midgets that were crying piteously as I came to them. A half-grown girl and a big boy were trying to help them along. I stopped and enquired what ailed the little ones. I was told that they were freezing. I also learned that their homes were one and a-half miles ahead. I said, " It seems to me that their mothers acted very thoughtlessly to send such small children so far on such a day." The answer that I received was, that in the morning they got a ride to the school, and their mothers did not think it was so cold.

I filled my cutter box full of the smallest of the children. The two little girls being my special care, I covered them all up with the robes and drove on. Soon the crying ceased. In a little while everything was changed. Instead of sighs and whimpers there was laughing and singing. Before parting with my little friends, I had the most cheery and jolly load of juvenile humanity that it had ever been my lot to carry.

When we came to the place where I had been directed to let the children off, they scattered in different directions, and scampered to their homes. I went on feeling more pleasure than I should if I had conferred a favor on the greatest man in the country. The day was so intensely cold that when I got to Priceville, I was so nearly frozen that I was forced to stop at the hotel and warm. That was a thing that I had never done before, nor have I done it since. I could stand it as far as a horse ought to go without feed any day in the year, but that day was too much for me.

TEAMSTERS BADLY BEATEN.

From the Black Horse Corners in Kinloss, I once drove to Paisley and Invermay, through one of the worst snowstorms that I have ever seen. The snow was deep before, but it had now been storming furiously for twenty-four hours, with no signs of an abatement. I started about eight in the morning. The storm came from the north-east, so that I had to face it. Nobody was on the road. I only met a man and a dog on the road that day. At that time there was a great deal of teaming of salt and lumber on the old Durham road. In going twelve miles that day, I passed eight loads of salt and nine loads of lumber that had been left sticking in the drift, while the teamsters had found shelter for themselves and their horses in the houses and stables of farmers along the road until the storm should cease.

When I reached the Elora and Saugeen road, I thought it somewhat strange that on such a leading thoroughfare I could see no symptoms of a beaten track; but so it was. However, I turned north and after a hard tussle with the immeasurable heaps of snow that covered the road in some places to the depth of nine or ten feet, I reached the corner at the "Dutch Tavern." Here I had intended to get my dinner and feed my horse; but I went in and looked around a little. I came to the conclusion that if the kitchen and dining-room were any relation to the bar-room I would not be able to eat much. So I got some oats and fed my horse, and went without my dinner. I found here three men and a couple of women and two span of horses blockaded by the storm. They were going to Ainleyville, now called Brussels, and the road that I had just passed over was the way they wanted to go. On my telling which way I came, the landlord told me that the road had been abandoned two weeks before on account of drifts, and the teams, including the stage, had gone another way ; but the blockaded travellers took courage and started on their way. They said if one man and one horse could come through, surely three men and four horses ought to go through. I told them they could do it if they made up their minds to go through.

Before they started, one of them proposed to give three cheers for the old man who had made a track for them. I told him to keep his cheers, for he would need all of them before he reached the next corners, a mile and a-quarter ahead. I do not know how they got along, as I started one way and they the other.

I reached Paisley at seven p.m., and stopped at a hotel, got a good supper, went to bed, and after a comfortable night, got breakfast and then wallowed through the drifts to Invermay, which was eighteen miles distant. I got there in time for the Quarterly Meeting.

THE WILL MAKES A WAY.

From Listowel to Mount Forest there was no great amount of travel at the time that I was presiding elder of the Huron District. In the winter it was often very difficult to go from one place to the other. On one occasion I started from Listowel after a heavy storm of snow and drift. When I got to where Palmerston now is, I turned north towards Harriston in the township of Minto.

The track here was entirely hidden by the recent fall of snow. It looked as if there was no beaten road; but my horse was accustomed to snowdrifts, and by letting him take his own way he would keep on the track pretty well. When I had gone about half a mile from the turn I met two men with a horse and a broken cutter. They were both walking. One was leading the horse and the other going ahead and making a track; but instead of being on the road they were dodging in and out of the fence corners. I at once made up my mind that they were city gents who knew but little about driving horses in deep snow.

When I came up one of them spoke to me and said, "I say, old man, where are you trying to go?"

"Well, sir," I answered, "I am intending to go to Mount Forest by way of Harriston."

He replied, "You may just as well turn back, for you cannot go through."

"What makes you think so?" I asked.

"We have just come from there and know all about it," was his answer.

"Well, sir," I said, "I am an old man, as you can see; I have gone through a great many snowdrifts in my time, and I have never yet turned back on account of supposed difficulties before me."

"There is nothing like a determined will," said the stranger. "Go ahead and perhaps you will get along all right."

"Sir," said I, "somewhere I have read that a good motto is found in this, 'Go as far as you can, either find a track or make one,' and I know of no place where this applies with greater force than in going through snowbanks."

We parted, and I went on my way and they on theirs.

A Message that Never Was Sent.

When I was a boy I got into the habit of saying "I can't" when I was told to do anything, no matter how easy it might be to do it. My mother often tried to break me off the habit, but she failed in doing so.

One day I was going with my father to the barn. Beside the path lay a stick of firewood about a foot thick and thirty feet long. My father had in his hand a switch that he picked up as he was coming along. When we came to the log he told me to take hold of the end of it and lift it. As usual, I said, "I can't," but before the words were fairly spoken he gave me three or four cuts across the shoulders with the whip that made me wince. "Now," said he, "just take hold and try to lift it, or you will get more of this," shaking the switch at me. I took hold of it, and to my utter astonishment lifted the end a foot or more

from the ground.   The secret of this was found in the
fact that a stone was under the log near the middle,
so that the ends nearly balanced.   Whether this was
by design or otherwise I never knew, but it furnished
my father an opportunity to give me a lesson that has
been of use to me in more ways than one.

One winter I found myself at Orangeville Quarterly
Meeting, after an absence from home of over four
weeks.   Saturday and Sunday were very stormy.   On
Monday morning the storm was still raging, with no
appearance of cessation.   I had intended to start for
home that morning.   I was staying at Mr. Abiathar
Wilcox's, about half a mile from the village.   The day
was so rough and the roads so badly blocked up that
I concluded to take the advice of this kind family and
not attempt to go until the storm was over and the
roads opened.

I wrote a copy of a telegram to send home in these
words: "Stormbound at Orangeville; home when
storm ceases; quite well."   With this in my pocket I
started to the telegraph office.   When going through
the gate at the road I recalled the counsel of my father
after I lifted the end of the log, which was, " Never
say you can't until you try."   I turned back and went
to the stable and harnessed my horse, and in less than
ten minutes was on the road.   After a three days'
battle with snowdrifts I got home to Meaford in safety
with the message that never was sent still in my pocket.

A Frost-bitten Official.

From the "Black Horse" Corners in Kinloss to Kincardine on Lake Huron is twelve miles. In the winter time this is frequently "a hard road to travel." With the mercury below zero, and the wind going from forty to fifty miles an hour, persons facing toward the lake need to be well clad or they will suffer from the cold; and even then "Jack Frost" will sometimes steal through unsuspected openings in their habiliments and leave his icy touch on their ears or cheeks or noses.

On one occasion the Rev. J. M. Simpson, who was then presiding elder, and myself, had been holding missionary meetings at Kinlough and Kinloss. We had a stormy night at the latter place, so that very few came out to the meeting. We put up for the night with Mr. and Mrs. John Hodgins. When we got up in the morning we found that the night had left behind it one of the wildest days that we had ever seen. It was Saturday, and our Quarterly Meeting at Kincardine was on the next day. There was no help for it—we must face the storm. As we were about starting Mrs. Hodgins said to me, "You must not freeze Mr. Simpson on that cold road. You have been over it so often that you have got used to it." I replied that he had only one to look after, while I had two—myself and horse.

We started out about 10 a.m., and of all the days that I have ever experienced that was one of the worst. When we got about half way I asked Mr. Simpson if he was cold. He said he was not, and we went on. As we came nearer the lake the storm seemed more severe. We both got cold, and concluded to stop at the house of Henry Daniels and warm, but when we came to his gate it was entirely snowed up. Then we thought to go on and stop at William Purdy's on the next side line, but the snow was so blinding that we passed that without seeing it. We concluded that we were a long while in reaching the side line, but when we found where we were it was inside the corporation of Kincardine and almost home.

Next morning when I met Simpson I could not keep my face straight while I looked at him. His face had the most comical appearance of anything that I had seen of the kind. Wherever the frozen snow had touched, it had left a mark. His face looked as though some one had taken the skin of an Indian and cut it into round pieces ranging from five to fifty cents in size, and stuck them on in grand confusion all over it from top to bottom. When I had laughed at him for a while, he asked me if I had looked into the glass yet since we came home. When I did so I found that I had been making merry at my own likeness, for my face was about as spotted as his. I had been doing what people often do, namely, criticise in others what is most like in themselves. Some of the people said that we were queer looking specimens of clerical dignity and official importance.

CHAPTER X.

WITH THE SICK AND DYING.

THERE is no part of the duties of a Christian minister that is so much calculated to beget in the mind serious thoughts and to stir up tender emotions in the soul as visiting the sick and dying. At least that has been my experience. There are a number of reasons for this. In the first place, there is the voice of nature that speaks in tones of sadness to the heart. What I mean by this is the natural sympathy that almost every creature manifests towards its fellow in the time of suffering. Even the dumb brute is moved by seeing its companion in distress. And mankind is not less feeling than the mute creatures around him. He is a hard man indeed who can look unmoved into the pale face of the sufferer, who lies upon a bed of pain, tossing from side to side in the bitterness of extreme anguish. Another reason for what I speak of is found in our benevolent affections. God has implanted into almost every one a kindly desire to alleviate pain and suffering. Few, indeed, are those callous natures that can contemplate the sickness and pain of any person, and not feel prompted to acts of kindness, pointing to a restoration to health and the removal of pain.

The claims of religion may be named as one more reason why visiting the sick and dying is so serious a matter. Our Christianity enjoins upon us the duty of relieving the distressed and helping the needy as far as we are able to do so. And a conscientious desire to do our whole duty is one of the most efficient prompters to this kind of service. We may do much good in this way, even though our means may be limited and our abilities may be small. There are so many ways of showing kindness to the sick and sorrowing that no one can claim exemption from the obligation to do something.

And then when we think of what lies beyond the sick bed, and the coffin and the grave, it seems that the work of assisting and directing and encouraging those who are about to enter into that unchanging state is the most important employment that a minister or any other Christian can be called to engage in.

The most unpleasant work of any that I have ever found in the line of ministerial duty has been to visit the unsaved sinners in times of sickness or accident. To live without religion is what a great many are willing to do. But to die without it there are but few who dare to. Men and women will live worldly and sinful lives without thought or care. But if death stares them in the face, the hardest hearts begin to feel ; and as they stand upon the last shifting sands of time, the bravest hearts quail and quake in the presence of terrible realities that burst upon their astonished vision.

Then men who have despised the righteous claims of God and pursued the way of the transgressor see their mistake and seek for mercy. Then the man of God is sent for. Then praying people are called in. Then many promises are given and vows made to God, promises that in nine cases out of ten are broken and trampled upon in case the sinner is restored to health.

Sometimes, however, this is not the case, as the following instance will show.

He Would Not be so Mean.

A young married man was lying very low with malarial fever. His medical attendant and his friends got very much alarmed. His young wife was nearly frantic at the prospect of being left a widow, after only a few months of married life. A consultation of doctors was held. One of the two new men called in was an old man of large and long experience in the profession. The conversation was carried on in the sick-room, and the doctors supposed that the man was asleep. But in this they were mistaken. The invalid heard all they said at the conclusion of their deliberations. He was a Universalist and he never had given himself any uneasiness about the future.

The old doctor was the last to give his opinion. He said at length : "I can see no grounds for hope. The young man is going to die, and that before many hours."

The man himself related the case to me years after. I give his own words as nearly as I can :

" When the old man said this, I do not think I could have been more astounded if the earth had opened at my feet. My Universalism was gone in a moment. I felt sure that there was a hell, and I thought that I should be in it in a few short hours. What should I do? Should I now ask the Lord to save me, after I had done all in my power against him? Should I seek for mercy now because I could not do any more harm in the world? Should I desire to go to heaven, when I deserved to be sent to hell? These thoughts ran through my mind in rapid succession. My decision was this: I will not add insult to injury. I will not be so mean as to try and sneak into heaven. I will die and meet the consequences of a misspent life, *but if I get well I will serve the Lord.*" He got well, and a short time afterwards was converted. He has been some years in the Gospel ministry. Hundreds have been saved under his labours. His decision might not have been a wise one, but who will say it was not a manly one? I refer to the first part of that decision.

Almost Fatally Deceived.

In the early part of my ministry there was a man lived near me who was dying with consumption. He lost one wife by that flattering disease, so that he was not ignorant of its deceptive character. He had been respectably brought up under Methodist in-fluences, so that the claims of religion were not unknown to him, but like many others he had lived until middle life without attending to the interests of his soul.

And he was now on the brink of the eternal world—a dying, yet unconverted man. In visiting him I found that he felt safe, although he knew that he was dying. His plea was, "God is too merciful to cast me off." I could not get him to look at any other aspect of the question. Not a word that expressed sorrow for the sins of the past. Not one word about trusting in the Saviour. Nothing about the cleansing blood or the sanctifying Spirit. He was simply relying on the bare mercy of God, without any reference to His other attributes. I was not just satisfied. But as the time passed on he sank lower and lower, yet he kept to that ground of hope; he seemed perfectly willing and ready to die. At last I began to conclude that my doubts were groundless, and what I had looked upon as a thick cloud was only a thin shadow thrown over his real condition, by his mode of expressing himself.

One Sunday night I came home from my evening service. As I was about to retire a message came for me to go and see Mr. M., saying that he was in a fearful state of mind. I went as fast as I could to the place. When I went into the room where he was I found a number of people; they were all weeping, and no wonder. On the bed lay the sufferer, whose bitter cries for mercy might well have moved the hardest heart. As soon as he saw me come into the room he cried out, "O, Mr. Hilts, what shall I do? Here I have been deceiving myself; I thought I was fit to die; that is all a delusion. I am a dying man and yet unsaved, unsaved! What will I do? What will I do?

I sat down by the bedside. He became a little calm. Then I said to him, "John, I am at a loss what to say to you. If you have not been mistaken when you have told me that you were prepared to die, this is a temptation of the enemy. But if you are not prepared to die, this is the work of the Holy Spirit, showing you your danger before it is too late." "O," said he, "this is no temptation; I am not mistaken now. I am dying, and yet in my sins. O, what shall I do?" I talked to him, and read and prayed with him. When we rose up from prayer he said to me, "This can't last long. Don't leave me until I am either dead or saved." I said to him. "I will stay with you as long as you wish. But neither I nor any one else can do much for you now. It is a personal matter between you and your Saviour. Can you not trust him to take away your sins, and fit you for death?" He answered, "I will try."

He lay for a few moments quite calm, and seemed to be in deep thought. Then he commenced, as if he were talking to himself. He said, "I am a sinner; Jesus came to save sinners; I do believe that Jesus will save me; I believe that he will save me now." With what intense eagerness did we catch every word. The dying man went on, "I believe that He is saving me now. O, He has saved me. Glory to His name! I am saved! I am saved!" A happier man I never saw, and a more deeply moved lot of people I never met than those that stood round that bed that night.

One week from that night I was sent for again in the middle of the night. When I went into the room

14

and asked him what I could do for him, he looked up and said, "I do not want anything more here, I am just going. But I sent for you to tell you once more that Jesus saves me, and all is well." He turned over with his face to the wall, and in a few minutes he was gone. John Mockman lives in a brighter world than this.

There was no Getting Away.

I was once sent for to go and see a man that was thought to be near to his end. When I came to the place I found a man well up in years. He was a man of more than ordinary intelligence and culture. He thought he was going to die. When I commenced to talk with him I soon found that he knew more than I did. He had any amount of Scripture at his command. He could state a point and give the proof as readily and clearly as any man that I had ever met with. But for all this I found it impossible to get him to realize his condition as an unconverted man about to appear before his Maker. And yet he knew that he was not prepared to die. He would acknowledge his faults, but did not seem to see anything like transgression of God's laws in them.

He said to me at length: "You see before you a man of a strange experience. God has often laid His hand upon me and brought me very low. But I have always put Him off with promises of doing better; but in every case I have broken my pledges. I am like an unruly boy who has repeatedly offended his father, and has escaped punishment by promises of future obedience. At length the father's patience is exhausted. He takes the lad in hand and there is no more getting away from his strong grasp and heavy hand. The long-delayed punishment comes at last. So it is with me. There is no getting away this time."

He did get off that time. By God's blessing and medical skill the man was once more restored to health and lived some time after this. But he went back into his old ways again. He is dead now; but how he died I am not able to say. How few there are who faithfully fulfil their sick-bed promises.

She did not Die Then.

When people are given up to die by their friends and physicians there is a sort of melancholy pleasure in trying to do all that can be done to make them as comfortable as possible. At such times the kindness of neighbours and friends is manifested in various ways. Everything is done that will relieve the pain of body, or give comfort of mind, so far as it is possible for willing hands and loving hearts to do so.

Prompted by this feeling a man called on me one day to go and administer the sacrament to a woman who was supposed to be in a dying condition. She lived on the far side of the circuit, and was a member of the Church. She was an excellent woman. I was much surprised to learn that she was given up by two doctors. I had not heard of her sickness till then. I lost no time in going to see her.

When I got to the house I found Mrs. C. very sick,

and the family in great distress. The children were greatly alarmed by the prospect of losing one of the best of mothers. Mr. C. was nearly broken-hearted at the thought of losing a true and faithful and loving wife. A number of neighbours were there, and they were lamenting about losing a good neighbour and friend. We proceeded with the administration of the Lord's Supper, the husband and some others taking a part in the solemn rite. During the service the impression was made on my mind that the woman was not going to die at that time; and in praying for her restoration I felt confident that the prayer would be answered.

After the room was vacated by all except Mr. C. and myself, I said to her, " Mrs. C., I feel confident that you are not going to die at this time." Her looks changed in an instant. She said, "Do you think so?" I said, " Yes, I believe that you will be well enough to go to meeting and hear me preach yet before Conference." " Well," she answered, "I am willing to die if the Lord so orders. But if it be His will that I should live a few years more, I would like to do so on account of William and the children." She did get well, and lived some sixteen years after that. She saw her children well provided for, and her husband an honoured and useful man in the Church. Then she peacefully and joyfully went to her rest. And her children called her blessed.

END OF A WILD CAREER.

One day I was splitting some firewood at the door of the parsonage. My attention was directed to a man on horseback who was riding toward me at a rapid rate. When he came up he said to me, "The friend of J. S. wishes you to come and see him. He is dying." Here was a very undesirable call. I knew J. S. to be one of the most wicked young men that I had ever known. His mother had been left a widow in fair circumstances some years before. She had a number of boys of which this J. was the eldest. The mother, like many another good woman, had more heart than head, and more kindness than firmness. She was just the kind of woman to indulge and spoil a lot of boys. The softest mothers sometimes send out the hardest boys. So it was in this case. I had sometimes seen J. walk past the church on Sunday morning. But I never saw him inside a place of worship. I had seen him drunk more than a score of times. I had heard the terrible oaths that came from him. I knew that the doctor had told him some months before that unless he gave up his dissipation he would die before the year was out. Knowing all this, is it to be wondered at that I felt reluctant to go?

I asked the messenger if J. sent for me. He said "No; it was his mother and his brothers." His mother was a member of the Church, and his brothers respectable young men. I could not refuse them.

But what good could I do him? He had lived in sin against God just as long as he could lift a hand or move a foot. He was dying, not by a visitation of God, but as the outcome of his own recklessness. In fact, he was but little less of a suicide than the man who blows his own brains out or cuts his own throat.

I hitched up and went at once. When I got within twenty rods of the house, I heard the moanings of poor J. When I went into the house I found a number of people there. All of them were sad, as well they might be. On a bed in one corner of the room lay a perfect wreck of the once active and strong young man. At each breath came the short ejaculation, " O Lord, O Lord." It was evident that this was not meant for prayer, as his mind was so beclouded that he was quite insensible to everything around him.

We read a chapter and had prayer. Then I tried to get his attention so that I might say something to him about his condition. But he seemed to be entirely oblivious of all surrounding objects. Still his cry at every breath was, " O Lord, O Lord." The way this was said made it sound like the utterances of a soul in anguish, or the bitter outcry of a tortured spirit as it was just about to sink into that night that knows no morning. That plaintive cry seemed like the wailing of despair, and it fell upon the listener's ear like an appealing and warning voice coming up from the regions of the lost.

Before another day had dawned upon our world he died. At the hour of midnight, when the earth was enveloped in its thickest clouds of darkness, the poor abused and suffering body of J. S. sank into the arms of death and his soul entered into the spirit world to meet its God and receive its doom.

Saved at the Eleventh Hour.

On a bright Sabbath morning, in the early summer, I started to my forenoon appointment. When I had gone about a mile I was overtaken by a man who came riding after me on horseback. As he came up he said, "I want you to turn about and come with me."

I asked what was the matter. He said, "Mrs. B. is very low, and the doctor says she cannot live twelve hours. She is unconverted. She is in a pitiable condition, and very much alarmed about her future state. She sent me to ask you to go and see her."

This woman lived some distance in the opposite direction from my work, so that to comply with her request would cause me to disappoint two congregations.

The man who came for me was one of my circuit officials. He said, "I think you had better go. The living can stand to be disappointed better than the dying. And before the day is gone the poor woman may be in eternity."

I turned and went with him. I had sometimes seen this woman and her husband at church. They were respectable people. But they, like thousands in the world, took no interest in a personal salvation. They lived for this world only. When we got to the place we found the house full of people. A number of Christian men and women were trying to help and comfort the penitent sufferer. She was a woman in middle life, with a fair share of intellect, and some amount of culture. She was suffering from some kind of inflammation. She was enduring great pain of body, but her mental distress seemed to be more hard to bear than her physical sufferings. We prayed, and read, and talked with that poor woman till four o'clock in the day. Then she came out of the darkness into light, and out of sadness into joy. Her soul was filled with a heavenly peace of mind and a joy unspeakable sprang up in her heart. O how she talked to her husband, and with what earnestness did she pray for the children she was leaving behind her. Her husband promised her that he would seek and serve the Lord so that he might meet her in that heaven to which she now felt that she was going. Whether he kept that pledge or not I do not know. The woman died that night rejoicing in the hope of a blessed immortality and eternal life. When I next visited the congregations that were disappointed that day I explained to them the reason of my absence. Everybody seemed to be satisfied. Several of the people said to me, "You did right in going to look after the dying first."

A Doctor's Needless Fears.

Sometimes people allow themselves to drift along with the tide of events, and do not know in what direction they are moving, nor how fast they are going. Feeling no uneasiness, they take it for granted they are on the right path. But at length they discover that they have missed the way, and are travelling in the opposite direction from that they intend. Then they become alarmed, and they seek again the path from which they have wandered. They chide themselves for their carelessness, and resolve to do better in the future.

This was the experience of Mrs. F. in her religious life. She had been converted and had joined the Church in early life. She lived a consistent and useful life until she married an unconverted man. They settled in a distant village. She neglected to take her place in the Church, and was so far deprived of Christian counsel and encouragement. For some time things went on smoothly with the young couple. Then a very severe attack of disease brought Mrs. F. face to face with her real state. She saw that she had strayed from the fold and wandered away on the bleak mountains of sin.

In her distress she wanted a minister of her old Church. Being the nearest one to where she lived, I was sent for. The distance was fifteen miles; however, I lost no time in going. I was acquainted with the woman, having been employed to attend her marriage. When I came to her home I found her indeed very low. She was in great pain of body and in great distress of mind. I soon concluded that her case required spiritual remedies more than medical treatment. We had prayer with her, and just then the doctor came. He lived in the same village that I did; we were acquainted. I knew that he took but little interest in religion of any kind, and I had been told that he particularly disliked the Methodist.

After the doctor had attended to his duties and was ready to start away, he called me outside; then he said to me, "I want to caution you before I leave. Be very careful not to excite that woman in any way, as her life depends on her being kept quiet." I said to him, "Doctor, I think I know my business. I was sent for, or I should not be here. The woman is in great distress of mind, and it seems to me that if you can be trusted with my penitent you may trust your patient with me. I shall be prudent but faithful in the discharge of my duty." After the doctor left me Mrs. F. requested that five or six of her Christian neighbours should be invited to come in and hold a prayer-meeting in the evening, as I was to stay all night in the village. They came in as she wished. I cautioned them, and also Mrs. F., against any undue excitement in our devotions; but it was of little use. The well ones did as I told them, but the sick one got into a perfect agony of spirit for a while. We were all uneasy for her safety for a short time. Then everything changed. She found again her lost enjoyment, and with a loud voice she praised the Lord for restoring to her the joys of His salvation. This continued for an hour, and then she went into a peaceful slumber, and rested well all night. Next forenoon the doctor came; when he went into the room he found the sick woman sitting up in bed talking cheerfully with a neighbour. He expressed great surprise at the change for the better. The woman was well in a short time. She insisted upon it that it was the Lord that cured her, not the doctor.

Fear of Death All Gone.

George Maynard was a good man. For thirty years he was a class-leader in the Methodist Church. When an old man, he was thrown on a bed of sickness which proved to be unto death. One day I went to see him, he referred to his feelings on the subject of death. He said, " I know that I was converted when I was a young man. For many years I have had the evidence of my acceptance with God. How is it that I have always had a dread of death ? Can you explain this ? Why should I be afraid of that which I fully believe I am prepared for ?"

" Well," I said, " you know more than I do about many things ; but in this, it seems to me that you are taking too gloomy a view of things. Human nature instinctively shrinks from death ; but by the help of God's grace, even the fear of death may be overcome."

" Do you think," said he, " that I can get dying grace if I ask for it ?"

I said, " Doubtless you will get dying grace when you need it. You know as well as I do, that the help we get to-day will not meet the wants of to-morrow, any more than that the bread we eat to-day will satisfy the hunger of to-morrow. If God gives us grace day by day to live right, we need not trouble ourselves about dying grace until we need it. Then we may rest assured we will get it."

" That is a view of the case that I have not thought of before ; but I see that it is the correct view," was his answer. About a week after this conversation I called again to see him.   When I went into the room I noticed a wonderful change in the expression of his countenance.   His face, it seemed to me, shone with a heavenly light, and an angelic smile rested upon it. As soon as he saw me, he said, "I have been waiting for you to come; I want to tell you that all my fears are gone, and death to me now wears the kindly aspect of a friend, instead of the forbidding look of an enemy.   I want to tell you how it was that I got into this happy frame of mind.

"Two nights ago I lay here alone.   My wife was in the other room attending to her housework.   I was thinking about death.   What a solemn thing it is to die.   How must the spirit feel when it moves out of the tenement it has so long inhabited.   What will be the soul's sensations when it goes out into the untried and unknown state of things and for the first time looks upon its new surroundings and realizes its changed conditions.

"All at once a light darted into my room.   I looked up and seemed to see a shining pathway leading up a gently ascending grade.   With my eyes I followed this shining way until it seemed to be swallowed up by a brightness that is indescribable. Just there I saw one standing whose garments looked like glittering gold bestudded with sparkling diamonds.   In one hand he held a robe that was whiter than snow and a crown that was brighter than the noonday sun.   With the other hand he pointed to these as he looked at me and smiled.   That look and that smile sent a thrill to every fibre of my body and touched every faculty and sensibility of my soul. My shouts of praise brought my wife to enquire what had taken place. The vision vanished, but not the joy. My soul has been in an ecstasy ever since. There is not left a single shadow of the fear of death." He never lost this happy frame of mind until the last. He died within a week after he related this to me. He was a man of sterling character and beloved by all who knew him.

A Mother's Last Conversation.

Among the names whose memory I cannot but cherish is that of Mrs. Ann Gilroy. I first made the acquaintance of her and her family on the Teeswater mission in the year 1858. Some years later she lived in Kincardine when I was stationed there.

We were having a good revival in our church. Mrs. Gilroy and her family all took more or less interest in the meetings. When she could not attend, her son, who lived at home, and three daughters were generally at the services.

One night, on account of not feeling well, she stayed at home. The rest of the family went to meeting. During the evening some one made the statement that "a true Christian is prepared for death at any time. That to such a sudden death simply means sudden glory." Jacob Gilroy noticed this statement. He thought it was an extravagant saying.

When he went home his mother was still sitting by the stove waiting for him and his sisters to come. After the girls retired, mother and son sat up for a while talking about family matters. After they talked some time and were about to retire, the son said, "Mother, are you too tired to tell me one thing that I would like to know before you go to rest?" "What is it?" she said. "Well, it is this: to-night it was said in the meeting that 'true Christians are always ready to die. That to them sudden death is sudden glory.' Now, mother, you have been a Christian ever since I can remember, and I believe that if there are any good people in the world you are one of them. Tell me, now, if you knew that you would die before morning would you not be frightened?" She stood for a short time as if in deep thought, and then said, "I do not think that I would be at all alarmed if I knew that I should die to-night. Why should I be afraid to go to my home in my Father's house? Good night." She never spoke again. In the morning she was found in her bed entirely speechless and motionless, though still alive. Before night she was dead. Some time after this the young man was in the city of Philadelphia. · He had been to a revival meeting and got very happy. He came home to his boarding house, sat on a chair and fell off it, and was dead before his room-mate could get to him. So that both mother and son died unexpectedly. And we hope and believe that both proved by a happy experience that to the Christian "sudden death is sudden glory."

A Night of Sorrow.

One of the most touching events that I have known occurred in one of the new settlements a few years after I entered the ministry.

Typhoid fever was prevailing in the neighbourhood and many were dying of it. There was a family that lived in the bush by themselves. The man took the fever and was lying very low. No one entered the house except the doctor. One night the man died. His wife found herself alone with her dead husband and her two small children, who, all unconscious of trouble, were sleeping in their little cot. The woman's parents lived about three-fourths of a mile off, through a dense piece of woods and over a large stream of water. The stillness of the house and the lonesomeness of the place at length overcame the poor woman's fortitude and courage. She picked up her two children and ran as fast as she could till she came to the creek. In her confused haste she forgot all about the footbridge over it; she waded through it.

She went to her father's door. Through fear of the fever her own parents refused to let her into the house. Then she made her way back to her home as best she could. When she came there she dared not go inside. She sat down on the doorstep with her two little ones in her arms. Next morning when the doctor came he found her still sitting there, soundly sleeping, forgetful of the terrible ordeal through which she had passed. Two men went and carried the dead man out and a few others took and buried him.

A Mistaken Doctor.

I once knew a boy in his teens who was stricken down with typhoid fever. The medical man who attended him was taken down with the same disease just when the boy was at the worst. He sent twenty-two miles for another doctor to come and see himself and his patients.

This strange doctor visited the sick boy, and left orders to give him a certain amount of brandy every hour. The lad kept sinking until he could not be got to swallow the liquor or anything else. I was present when he made his last call (until he called for his pay). He was told that the brandy had not been given, for the simple reason that the patient could not be made to take it. He got angry and scolded the attendants a good deal ; then he went away, saying the boy would not live two hours.

After he was gone, Mr. Hacking, the boy's father, said to me, "I have a great notion to try the water cure, and put William in wet sheets. What would you do if you were in my place ?" I said, "I am not prepared to give any advice in the matter. You heard what the doctor said. From all appearances, I am afraid that his predictions will be verified. So far as the boy is concerned, I do not think that it makes much difference what you do, or what you don't do. I fear he is past being benefited by human help."

The preparations for using the wet sheets commenced at once. I left them, fearing that the boy would die as soon as they undertook to move him. He had been in a stupor for some days, and was seemingly unconscious of everything about him ; but the result of the effort on the part of Mr. H. and family was marvellous. All night they continued their work. Next morning early I went to the house expecting to find the boy dead; but he was still living, and when I looked at him, I could see that he was unmistakably better. That boy got well, and is living yet. The doctor afterwards sued for a very exorbitant fee, and I was called as a witness in the case. The judge allowed him just half the amount asked for, and he paid the cost, the amount having been offered to him, but he refused it.

DEATHS BY ACCIDENT.

When people die, the shock to the surviving friends is not so great as when they are killed by what is called accident. In the one case there is time for the friends to prepare for what they look upon as inevitable. In the other case the suddenness of the unexpected event gives a more crushing aspect to the bereavement.

During my ministry I have been called upon to perform the funeral rites for nine persons who were accidentally killed; six of them were killed by trees and limbs, one at a raising, and two in wells. To particularize all of these would occupy too much space. I will briefly refer to three cases.

DIED IN A WELL.

James Mullen lived in a house built on one of those "gravel hills" so common in some parts of the country. He started to dig a well near the house, and on the side of the hill; he was in the well which had been dug to the depth of eighteen feet, and "curbed" with plank and scantling. His father and his wife

15

were working the windlass one afternoon ; all at once the curbing gave way at the top of the first length of scantling, and the whole thing collapsed. The planks came together a few feet above Mullen's head, thus saving him from being instantly crushed to death by the tons of gravel that burst into the well from all sides. As soon as the first shock was over he called to those above to tell them he was not dead, but said he was badly hurt, and partly covered up with earth. The alarm was given, and men began to come from all directions to assist in trying to get the poor man out. They commenced to dig down to him from the top. Every blow they struck only sent more of the dry gravel sifting down upon the man below. Some fifty men were there ; all night long they toiled, but all in vain to save his life. Once they got so near him he took a cup of water from them between the planks, then a fresh lot of dirt fell in and shut up all the openings. Somewhere about ten o'clock in the morning he called to one of his neighbours and said, "Tell me the honest truth. Is there any chance to get me out alive. The dirt is up to my chin ; I cannot move so much as a finger ; one more shaking down of the gravel will bury me all up. Can you get me out ?"

The friend said to him, "James, you must look to your God for help ; we are doing all in our power, and will do so ; but I greatly fear no human help can reach you in time to save your life."

Shortly after he spoke again, saying, "The dirt is covering me up ;" that was his last word.

When he was at length got out, one of his legs was

broken ; that was all the serious hurt that could be found upon the body. A great concourse of people attended his funeral; I spoke to them out of an upstairs window, that being the most suitable place from which to address the multitude. I saw James Mullen's wife a few years ago ; she was still a widow, though now past middle age.

He Read His Own Funeral Text.

People who have always lived on the front have but little idea what life in the backwoods means. The deprivations of the early settlers are far from being appreciated by those who have never been without schools, and churches, and mills, and stores, and neighbours ; and never is the want of these so severely felt as in the time of trouble and bereavement. A number of years ago a family by the name of Colbeck moved into the north part of the township of Luther. They were Methodists; but now they found themselves away from the means of grace in the public worship of God. They instituted a system of worship of their own. The whole family would take a part in reading at family devotions. One morning the lesson read was the fifteenth chapter of Jeremiah. The youngest son, a young man, read the last verse, which reads as follows: "And I will deliver thee out of the hand of the wicked, and I will redeem thee out of the hand of the terrible." That was the last thing he ever read.

He and his brother went out to the fallow to chop. Before noon a limb fell out of a tree and struck him. He never spoke nor moved.

I being the nearest Methodist minister, was sent for to attend his funeral. At the time I lived on the sixth line of Garafraxa. I had to go about twenty miles to get to the place.

When I came there it was the wish of the mother that the last verse that her boy had ever read should be his funeral text. I could not refuse her, though it allowed me no time for preparation. There were two or three married children settled around the old people. From what I saw of them I took them to be an excellent family. One of the Colbecks is in our ministry, and a member of the Guelph Conference.

Choke-damp Killed Them.

Two dead men in one old well are not often seen·in this country. Such a thing is enough to cause a sensation in any locality. In the vicinity of the Black Horse Corners in Kinloss this scene was witnessed a few years ago.

Two well-diggers undertook to clear out an old well and dig it deeper. They went to the place to commence work. They prepared a windlass. One of them was to go down and do the work in the well, and the other was to work the windlass. When the man in the tub got about half way to the bottom he fell over out of the tub and went to the bottom, where he lay so still his companion thought that he had fainted, or else he was in a fit.

Help was called for. A number of men were on hand in a short time. But the question was, Who would volunteer to go down and bring up the body of the man whom every one now believed to be dead.

At length an old farmer, named Brownscome, who lived on the adjoining lot, offered to go if none of the younger men would do so. He had them to tie a rope tightly around him under his arms. They commenced slowly to let him down. When he reached the point where the other had fallen out of the tub, he seemed to wilt like a scorched leaf, and, slipping out of the rope, he fell to the bottom as lifeless as a lump of lead.

Then it became evident that there was something in the well more than the common air. On applying a test it was ascertained that the well was half full of gas of the most deadly kind. The bodies were taken out by long iron rods with hooks on the ends of them. Mr. Brownscome was an Englishman. He was one of the class-leaders on the Kincardine Circuit. He was an excellent man, but his life was thrown away for want of a little forethought, for if the well had been tested sooner he might have been saved. We buried his remains at Kincardine Cemetery.

How great to him would be the sudden change. One moment surrounded by a group of anxious neighbours; the next moment among the angels and the spirits of just men made perfect. No doubt, to him sudden death was sudden glory.

CHAPTER XI.

TRACES OF THE TRAFFIC.

FEW and far between are the individuals in this country who can claim complete exemption from the effects of the liquor traffic. In no direction can we turn so as not to cross the slimy trail of this monstrosity. It draws itself over the threshold of the peaceful, happy home, and peace and happiness flee from its presence. It drags itself into the workshop, and blows its foul breath into the face of the mechanic, and he exchanges his tools for the drunkard's maddening bowl, and barters his workshop for the drunkard's dishonoured grave.

It goes to the cultivator of the soil and whispers to him of gain and gold, and he turns his acres into sources of supply to the man with the capacious abdomen, the brewer, and the red-faced and blear-eyed distiller.

It sneaks into the grocery store and points its proprietor to the largeness of the profits of the traffic, and he places the whiskey cask in the cellar beside the pork barrel, and the butter firkin, and puts the brandy bottle on the same shelf with mottled soap and friction matches. It gets to the ear of the man who keeps a boarding house and a travellers' home and persuades him that his house and his business will go to ruin unless he connects a bar-room with his dining-hall, and mixes the sale of poison with the sale of food.

It shakes its brawny fist in the face of the politician, and, like Peter in the "judgment hall," he dare not tell nor act the truth. The lawyer is made to believe that his case is made clearer when he wets his brief with whiskey. The doctor is told that his patient has a better chance for life with alcoholic medication than without it. Thus in all directions has it spread its delusions and in every locality has it placed its snares.

This Moloch has set up its shrines upon the hilltops and in the valleys. They are to be found along the country roads and beside the city streets. Everywhere they are to be found. And to these places people go to pay their homage to this deceptive and deceiving demon, and to caress and hug their destroyer.

The mind of a philosoper would fail to grasp, and the imagination of a poet would fail to describe, the dark catalogue of woes that lie concealed in the secret recesses of some of these temples where the rum-god is worshipped.

We will stand awhile and watch the door of one of these inviting places and see who enters. We see that old man of seventy or eighty years, bending upon his staff as he moves along with tottering steps to the bar, were he has often been before. He has become so familiar with the place that he seems like a fixture there more than like a visitor. Poor old man! he will soon go where bar-rooms cease to be a snare. But will the old drunkard be at rest?

Next goes in a man just in his prime. He has a wife and family at home. He loves them. He would shudder at the very thought of harming them. But he has made an entrance in the way that leads to the drunkard's doom. He tarries long and late at night; he then comes out and goes staggering to his home. A dark shadow henceforth hangs over that home for a few years. Then it is broken up. The mother dies with a broken heart. The children are scattered, to find a home among strangers. A few years later the father goes down to the drunkard's and the pauper's grave.

Next there comes strutting up the street a fast youth. He has between his teeth the stump of a cigar at which he is sucking away as if his very life depended on a certain number of draughts per minute.

He swings himself with his cane and cigar into the bar-room. While he dawdles around the tavern he gets the finishing touches to a dissipated character and learns some lesson in vice and uselessness that he did not know before.

He goes from this out into the world to find a thoughtless girl who will be silly enough to link her destiny with his; and when he finds her he will blight her prospects in life, crush all hopefulness out of her heart, drive the roses from her cheeks, turn her cheerfulness to sadness, and send her, as a mere wreck of her former self, to a premature yet welcome grave.

But here comes a woman. See how wistfully she looks into the face of every one she meets. She is seeking some one that she dreads to meet. See how she peers into that bar-room. Some absent one is weighing heavily upon her heart. Who is it? Is it husband, son or brother? We do not know. Or perhaps she is a member of the "Woman's Christian Temperance Union," seeking to save the idol of some other woman's heart.

Look, look! Do you see that little bundle of rags coming up the street? Those rags are intended to cover the person of a little girl, but in this they are only very partially successful. See how she shrinks from those she meets; she pulls up the old rag of a shawl that she wears so as to hide her face from the rude gaze of the men and boys who are idly standing on the sidewalk in front of the bar-room. See again how she tries to conceal that bottle, in which she is forced to carry to her thrice wretched home the devilish stuff that poisoned with its offensive odours the first breath of air that ever entered her lungs, and by its Satanic influence has embittered every moment of her life from then to the present time.

When I think that the poor little creature before us may grow up to be a woman under all the bad influences of a drunkard's unblest home, it makes me sad of heart. But, dear me, where am I getting to? I did not start to write a temperance lecture, but simply to gather up a few pebbles from among the hard rocks that lie along the trail of the rum traffic.

No. 1.—He Wanted a Fiddler.

I was once sitting in a barber shop enjoying a shave when a young man entered. He was very tipsy, as we used to say when I was a boy. I think that the word used now to convey the same idea is "tight." Well, we will say he was "tight." As I said, he came in and began to stagger about the shop, coming once very near where I was sitting. I shoved the barber's hand aside and said to him, "My friend, it makes me nervous to have that sharp razor about my face under existing circumstances." He took the hint, and told the party to sit down and keep quiet. He sat down for a short time; then he began to walk the floor and sing,

> " I will eat when I am hungry,
> I will drink when I am dry,
> And if whiskey does not kill me,
> I will drink it till I die."

Then, turning suddenly to the barber, he called out, " I say, Bob, what will you charge to go to McMurchy's on Wednesday night and fiddle? We are going to have a regular old Virginia breakdown, minus the curly heads and black faces. What will you take and go?"

"Well," said the other, "I will go for six dollars. Is that too much?"

"No; come along."

He started out, but at the door he turned about and said to me, "I say, mister, do I look like a man that has spent one thousand dollars in six months?"

I answered by saying, "When a man drinks whiskey as you seem to do, it is not easy to say how much he will spend."

" Well, six months ago, I had one thousand dollars in cold cash, and to-day I have not *one little dime left.*"

After he went out the barber said, " That fellow has one of the best mothers that the Lord ever gave to a young man, but he is breaking her heart by his dissipation. He has two beautiful sisters who have no superiors in the town, but they are almost distracted about him, their only brother. His father is a good man, too. Six months ago the young scapegrace offered to go to Dakota and take up land, and go to work on it, if he could get the means to do so. His father, taking his words as truth, counted him out the money that he told you of ; but he did not go West, and now his money is gone and he is a nuisance to the place. Before I would do as he has done I would hire some big man to tie a stone to my neck and then put me in a wheelbarrow and trundle it to the end of the wharf and dump me into the lake."

No. 2.—She did not Know what Ailed the Baby.

While passing a house one Sabbath my attention was arrested by hearing my name called with much vehemence. I stopped until a woman came out and said, " O, mister, will yes plase come in and see if you can tell what is the matter wid me darlint of a baby." Now, I knew that this house was one of the lowest kind of groggeries, kept by a man who prided himself on being a Protestant. He could curse the Pope by the hour, and sing about " William of immortal memory," until he was hoarse. He knew as much about the Boyne and William and the Pope as a goose knows about driving a baker's cart, and not much more. I tied my horse to a post and went in to see the "baby." In an old rickety cradle was an infant of a few months old, lying in a stupor. The poor little thing had every appearance of being drunk. In the room were two or three·other children, whose pinched and starved appearance was enough to make one's heart sick to look at them. "What do you think is the matter with the babe ?". I said to the mother. The father was in a corner sleeping off the effects of an all-night carouse with some companions in dissipation.

In answer to my question the woman said, " We do not know what is the matter with the little dear. It will lay sometimes for hours just as you see it now. Thin it will wake up and act as if it was wantin' somethin'. Thin it will pull away at me bosom until I have no more for it. Thin it will turn sick at its stomick and throw up all that it took, and after a little it will cry, and I give it some more of the doctor's stuff, and in a little while it goes into one of the 'spells' again."

I said to her, " Show me some of the doctor's stuff."

She went to a little cupboard and brought a bottle and handed it to me. When I smelt of it, I said " Why, this is only whiskey !"

" Shure, and that is all, sir ! " was her answer.

" And do you give this to your baby every time it cries ? " I asked.

"Yes ; I make it nice and swate for the little darlint."

" Well, my good woman, do you not know that you are killing your baby with this stuff. If you were to strike it on the head with a hammer and knock out its little brains, it would be sure to kill it. But to feed it with this whiskey, as you say you do, will kill it just as surely, though more slowly." The little one died in a few days, and people said, " Poor little thing, it was never strong, and it is well that the Lord has taken it."

No. 3.—A Baby in the Snow.

In a certain locality there lived a farmer who had a drunken wife. Do what he could he could not keep her sober if she could get liquor.

One day they went to town. She had an infant of a few months old in her arms. When they were ready to start home, she had managed to get enough of her favourite to make her tipsy. The man put her and the baby in and wrapped them nicely up in the sleigh robes, and charged his wife to hold on to little Nellie as he had to look after the horses. The snow was deep and the wind was drifting it up in heaps. They had ten or eleven miles to go.

When they got home the man went to help his wife out and found her fast asleep. But worse than that, there was no baby to be found. It had slipped out of its mother's arms and was lost somewhere along the road. The man got one of his neighbours to go with him and they started out to hunt up the lost little one.

After scanning every rod of road for six miles they saw something that looked like the corner of a shawl flopping above the snow. There they found the baby all buried under, but one corner of the wrap that was around it. When he took it up and shook off the snow, the child looked up at him and cooed and laughed as though it was being taken out of its cradle.

No. 4. As good a farm as could be found in the county was the one left to No. 4 by his father. He had learned to drink in early life. Sometimes he would take too much. But not much was said about it. But the habit grew upon him. At fifty-five years of age his farm was gone, his wife was dead, and he was homeless and penniless and almost a vagrant. All through rum !

No. 5 had a good farm given him by his father. He married a good wife. For some years he was a leading man in the Church. Then he lost his wife and took to drink. He married another good wife. He got along for a few years pretty well. But the drinking habit increased. He became reckless about his business; got to horse-racing and other bad ways. He mortgaged his farm for money to spend foolishly. He died while still comparatively young, leaving his wife with his first wife's children and her own to provide for as best she could.

No. 6 kept a hotel on a splendid farm that his father and mother had hewed out of the solid wilderness. He married into a respectable family. He took to drink, and in middle life died a raving maniac, requiring three strong men to hold him in bed while whiskey and *delirium tremens* did their terrible work.

No. 7 was a school teacher without wife or family, He was a man of large intelligence. He was a member of a Church. He gave way to the appetite for drink. He joined the Sons of Temperance to try and get the mastery over this habit. He broke his pledge after having kept it for a year or two. He got on a drunk and never sobered off until deliriums took hold of him. He died, shouting at the top of his voice, " O take away these snakes ! "

No. 8 owned a good two hundred acre farm and kept a store. He was a very clever man. He stood high in the estimation of his neighbours. He was county warden for a number of years. He was a candidate for parliamentary honours, and would have been a very useful man if he had kept sober. He became more and more the slave of drink, and finally died, leaving a large property so involved that his family could not redeem it. His wife in a few years, as I am told, followed him to an untimely grave through strong drink.

No. 9 was a doctor, said to be well read up in medical science. He took to drink. Lost his wife; he married another. She would not allow him about the place when he was drunk. He lost his practice. He became discouraged, and in a fit of despondency he went into a hotel stable, cut his jugular vein, and was found by the hired girl when she went out to milk the cow. He had died alone.

No. 10 was a druggist, and a man of many fine characteristics. He was honest, kind-hearted and truthful ; but drink got the mastery over him, and he died before the frosts of age had begun to bleach his hair, leaving a noble woman to lament his untimely end.

No. 11 was a woman and a wife and a mother. Her husband was a very fine man and an intelligent manufacturer, doing a prosperous business. She took to drink through taking liquor from a doctor as medicine. Everything was done that loving solicitude on the part of husband and friends could prompt or devise to save her. But all to no purpose. Respect for her sex forces me to close the story and draw a veil over the scene.

No. 12 was a man who long took a leading part in everything that was good. But he never could be made to see anything wrong in taking a glass of liquor. As he grew older the love of drink increased so that he was frequently intoxicated. One day while drunk he fell out of his waggon and was killed. The man who, as a class-leader, had formerly often pointed others in the way to heaven, came to his end through drink.

No. 13 was a hotel-keeper. He owned a corner house in a town where I once lived. He took no pains as to what sort of house he kept. He was hardly ever found sober. He became one of his own best customers. One day he became speechless while drunk. He lay in this condition two or three days and then died.

No. 14 was said to be worth twelve or fifteen thousand dollars. When he was getting old he married a widow much younger than himself. He became a hard drinker. He got careless in his business. He would lend his money without security or vouchers. At length he was never sober. He was stricken with paralysis one day and never spoke any more. He died and left his widow to unravel the tangled skein of business as best she could with the help of two or three lawyers. They were quite willing to help her, but somehow it seemed that the most of the ravellings got into the wrong pockets, as usual, and the widow's share was not very much.

No. 15 was a mechanic. He was an honest man generally, but he was given to drink. One night he went home from work and he took with him a jug of whiskey. He asked his wife to drink with him; on her refusing to do so, he produced a bottle of laudanum and commenced to take it. His wife, seeing the word *poison* on the bottle, sprang forward and took it from him. But he took it from her again after a desperate struggle, in which he scratched her hand at a fearful rate to force her to let go the bottle. He swallowed the poison in his drunken madness and died before anything could be done, as no doctor could be got.

No. 16 was a veterinary surgeon. He was a man who would have been a good and useful citizen only for drink. But his appetite controlled his judgment and overruled his conscience. He struggled with his enemy for a while and then fell a victim to this destroyer of thousands. He died, while still a young man, leaving a wife and family to weep over a drunkard's grave.

No. 17 was a medical doctor. He was a man of great skill, and at one time he had a very large and lucrative practice, but he became dissipated in his habits. He lost much of his prestige and patronage. He went on from bad to worse until he died at the age of fifty, leaving a family behind him.

16

No. 18 was the wife of a doctor.   When I commence to write about her it seems to me that I can hear the whispers of a sainted mother and two sisters, and three daughters, now in glory, saying, " Spare our sex. Don't write bitter things about them."   My heart refuses to dictate, and my hand declines to pen the sentences that portray a woman's sins and sad, sad fate through drink.   She died, and that is enough to say.

No. 19 was a capitalist and money-lender.   He was one of the most manly men I ever met, but alcoholism was his weakness and his bane.   And all the influence of a kind wife and lovely children and every consideration that pointed to domestic felicity and financial success failed to check his downward course. His sun of life went down at noon, and the grave received its victim from the hands of the rum-seller ere the hand of age had made a wrinkle upon his brow.

No. 20 was a lawyer who stood well in the profession, with as fine a little woman for a wife as ever presided over a peaceful home.   He was trusted and honoured by his fellow-citizens.   He was successful in his business until the great giant that has conquered so many noble men got him in his grasp.   That grasp was never relinquished until the poor victim died. Then weeping friends and mournful neighbours carried him to the grave.   Everybody knew that the lamp of his life had been blown out by the foul breath of the rum-demon.

No. 21 was a model young man.   He grew up under the careful training of a very strict religious mother. At twenty-one he had never tasted strong drink of any kind. Mothers would point their sons to him as an example of what a young man ought to be. He married a most amiable and excellent wife. The old homestead in which he was born and reared had been put into his hands, along with the care of his aged parents, who were both living. About the age of twenty-five he commenced to drink. At thirty-two he was tippler, a spendthrift, and a rake. At forty his farm was gone, his wife was dead, and the old people had gone in sorrow to their grave. His eldest son died a drunkard before he reached the age of twenty-five. At last accounts the unhappy cause of this wretchedness was still on the road to destruction.

No. 22 was an old man when I first saw him. He had owned a farm, but it had passed out of his hands. He was a very hard drinker. He lived on the outskirts of the town. One terrible night in winter he left the hotel and started to go home; he never got there. The next spring he was found in a gully on the back end of a farm, nearly a mile from his home. He had gone past his own gate, got lost, and wandered off into the fields and died in a drift.

A poor old man one winter night,
Seeking his home with all his might,
While no kind helper was in sight,
  Sank down beneath the snow.
How oft he strove to rise again,
And seek his homeward path in vain ;
How long he lived to suffer pain,
  No one on earth can know.

> 'Tis said that he was fond of drink,
> And sellers did not stop to think
> How soon their customer might sink
>   And die beneath the snow.
> They seem to have but little care,
> If they could but his coppers share,
> Where he might go, how he might fare,
>   *At bedtime he must go.*

No. 23 was a man of strange history. He married quite young, and went at an early day to one of the back townships and secured three hundred acres of bush land of an excellent quality. He faced the difficulties of pioneer life like a hero; he worked like a slave till he got a large clearing and good buildings. In fact, he had one of the best farms in the county of Grey. At last he took to drinking so hard that he made a complete fool of himself. He was a nuisance in the neighbourhood and a terror to his family. His farm passed out of his hands; he and his wife parted; the children were scattered; he sank lower and lower, and the last that I heard of him he was a homeless wanderer, beloved by no one, and remembered only to be despised.

No. 24 was left with a fine property by his father. He was always fond of drink, and took no pains to conceal or control the appetite. He married young. After a few years of fast living and recklessness in spending his money, he found himself a poor man. He went to hotel-keeping for a while, but in a short time he died and left his wife in poverty.

No. 25 was a genius; he had a good farm, and for a

long time got along as well as his neighbours ; but he foolishly sold his farm and bought a hotel in a little village near by. He took to drinking and in a few years died through drink. So far as natural endowments were concerned, this man was capable of becoming anything almost, but the light of intellect and fires of genius were extinguished by the liquid that has darkened so many pages of human history.

No. 26 was an old man when I first met him. He was a general favourite, especially among the children and youths of his acquaintance. He was a slave of the drinking mania. He had neither family nor friends in this country. He was a Frenchman. At length he became a sort of promiscuous helper at two hotels about a mile apart, going from one to the other as necessity or inclination demanded. One stormy night in winter, while in a state of almost helpless intoxication, he started to go from one hotel to the other ; but he never got there. The people where he started from did not know but that he got through in safety, and the people where he was going did not know that he had started, so he was not missed for a week or more. Next spring, when the snow went off, his remains were found in a drift along the fence beside the road. Part of the face had been eaten by the foxes.

No. 27 was an English lady of good social position ; but culture, refinement, social standing, womanly dignity, and religious principle were not a safe environment to save her from the allurements of the liquor traffic. *She died.*

No. 28 was a tailor by trade, and a number one workman. He got entangled in the snares of this deceiver. He lost his wife, then sank lower in his habits. Afterward he married again. In a few months he died calling for drink, and left a wife and family of children to mourn without hope.

No. 29 was a young man, or rather a large boy; but he was fond of drink, and was often intoxicated. In one of his drunken bouts he sat down on the railway track when a train was coming, and he was killed. His career was a short one; but it was long enough to add one more to the hundreds of thousand of the victims of this traffic.

No. 30 was a Canadian woman and the mother of a family. She gave way to drink, and died in a snow-bank.

No. 31 was a man of an influential position in his municipality. He had a good farm. He had a superior wife and a very fine family. He was for years a member of the Church, and an office-bearer in it. He gave way to the appetite for drink and became an inebriate. He sold out his farm, left his family, and went off no one knew where, a wicked and ruined man. Where he is, if alive, or where he died, if dead, are things unknown to his friends.

No. 32 was a doctor well read in medical science. At one time had a large practice. He became a drunkard, and died through drink before he was much past middle age.

No. 33 was a man who had but few equals either as a business man or as a citizen. For a number of years he was at the head of municipal affairs in his township. He owned a very fine property, but drink proved his bane. He died comparatively poor. Through the mercy of God, he was led to seek and obtain forgiveness after he had destroyed his constitution and squandered much of his property. He died lamenting the folly of his life.

No. 34 was the wife of No. 32. She was an exceedingly interesting person; was refined, intelligent and amiable in her manner, and good-looking, if not beautiful in her appearance. She drank, and she died.

No. 35 was a farmer. He was a man of more than average intelligence; he was a hard worker; he cleared up his farm, and raised a large family; but he always loved drink. At last it destroyed him in every way, and he died a poor drunkard.

No. 36 was of the same name as No. 35, though their homes were in different counties, and they were no relation to each other. He was a genial, good-natured man when sober, but when under the influence of liquor he was quarrelsome; but he broke himself down, and died before he was old. He left a wife and family behind him. He was missed by his neighbours when he died.

I shall close this dark catalogue. I might add many more, who have either been entirely destroyed, or greatly injured by the use of legalized poison; but I think that three dozen is enough for one list. I could give the name and location of every person enumerated here, if it were necessary to do so; but it could serve no good purpose to give needless exposure to the sins and follies of the departed. Some in this sad list were relatives of my own, and others were relatives of my friends. I would not like to have their names published to the world.

These unfortunate ones are all relatives of somebody who would not like to have their names made public. For this reason the names are withheld ; but that does in no way affect the truthfulness of the statements made in the above descriptions. The question that meets us right here is, "Who slew all these ?" The only truthful answer that can be given is : these were slain by the legitimate results of a traffic that the Christians of this country have protected by Act of Parliament and licensed for money. The day is coming when the blood of these people must be accounted for. Where, then, will the responsibility rest ? Can all the blame be thrown on the unfortunates themselves, and on their destroyers, the liquor-sellers ? No, not all. The man who upholds the traffic by vote or otherwise will have to bear a share. The woman who favours the traffic by her words or by her actions will have to take a part of this responsibility.

Another question comes up closely related to the former. It is this: "What slew all these ?" These were all slain by a substance that the Rev. Dr. Carry, and others who think with him, claim to be an indispensable ingredient in sacramental wine. The learned Doctor repudiates the use of any unfermented liquid in the administration of the sacrament. In fact, he seems to think it is almost sacrilegious to use the *unfermented* juice of the grape in that solemn rite.

Let us examine the position of those who *assume* so much and *prove* so little on this important and interesting subject. The only new ingredient introduced into grape juice by fermentation is alcohol. So if wine *must be fermented* before it is fit for sacramental purposes, it must be the presence of alcohol that imparts to it that fitness. Now, if it be the presence of alcohol that gives the fitness, then why not use any other liquid in which this qualifying ingredient is found.

For instance, "What is fermented wine?"—It is alcohol and something else—mostly water.

"What is whiskey?"—It is alcohol and something else—mostly water.

Alcohol is the only indispensable ingredient in sacramental wine. Fermented grape juice contains alcohol, and hence it is equal to the demands of sacramental wine. Whiskey contains alcohol, and it is equal to the demands of sacramental wine. Now, since things equal to the same are equal to each other, it follows that whiskey and fermented wine are equal to each other for sacramental purposes.

Doctor Carry and his friends may please themselves in the selection of what they will or will not use in administering the sacrament, but I am happy to be able to say that years ago I gave up the use of alcoholic wine and whiskey for sacramental or any other purposes, only when given as medicine by an honest medical man.

CHAPTER XII.

FIGHTING THE DRAGON.

IN the lonely Isle of Patmos the aged servant of God saw a great wonder, as, by prophetic vision, he scanned the future of the cause of Christ. Looking through the vista of the coming ages he saw a great red dragon work its way into heaven, or into the ecclesiastical organization called the Church.

The dragon was a fabulous monster of antiquity. He was the symbol of heathen superstition and idolatry. He was the embodiment of cunning, craft and cruelty. His existence was fabulous, so was the good that he was supposed to give to his deluded votaries; but the harm that he did was fact. So that in connection with the old-time dragon we have two fables and one fact.

But the old seer looked on down the declivities of time until he saw the dragon cast out of the ecclesiastical world, and thrown among the politicians to be dealt with as his deserts demanded. Before taking his leave, he transferred his power to a seven-headed and ten-horned beast, and left it to work mischief and dis-

aster to the Church, while he transformed himself into
another shape and went into the world to work out
the destruction of millions by a new process.

Of this modern dragon it may be said that his existence is a fact, and the harm that he does is another
fact ; but the good that he promises is only a fable.
So that in his case we find two very ugly facts and one
very delusive fable.

With the old-time dragon we have, at present, nothing more to do ; but of his modern prototype much
more could be said than our space will allow at present.
But though our remarks must be limited, we will say
a few things about it.

No sooner had the dragon found himself floating
down the stream of time than, *like Milton's devil on
the burning sea*, he began to look around for allies and
agencies.   At last he managed to get among the politicians of the time of Queen Elizabeth, and obtained
a monopoly of the liquor traffic, in the shape of a
license granted to the Duke of Essex, giving him the
exclusive right to sell wines to the thirsty thousands
of Old England.   Since then we can trace his slimy
trail through thirty decades of British legislation.

In some respects the liquor traffic and the slave
trade are alike.   They are alike in this—they bring
men into bondage.   The slave of drink is as really a
bondman as any Southern negro ever was.   The difference in this case is, the one is in involuntary servitude,
the other is a consenting party to his own captivity.
The one is enslaved by force, the other is captivated
by fascination.   The one is held by the strong grip of

a lion, the other is charmed by the wily influence of
the serpent. Now, if you break the lion's jaw you
liberate the one, and if you kill the serpent you save
the other.

Slavery and the liquor traffic are alike in that they
subordinate the interest of the many to the gratifica-
tion of the few.

A hundred slaves had to suffer the lash, and toil
and sweat, and live like pigs, and die like dogs, in
order that one man might live in ease and idleness. A
hundred families must suffer want and abuse, and
starvation and disgrace, in order that the liquor-seller
may drive fast horses and sport himself in every way
he likes, and that his wife and children may get themselves into the boots and shoes, and hats and bonnets,
and dresses and shawls that ought to be on the wives
and children of his dupes. The slave trade pressed
most heavily on those who had nothing to do in up-
holding it. The negro and his family were the
sufferers. But they had no share in the profits of the
trade.

The wife and children of the drunkard are the
greatest sufferers from the liquor traffic. But the
makers and sellers of the poisonous compounds get the
money, while these get for their share the rags, the
hunger, the cold, the kicks, the bruises, the disgrace,
and death that are the inevitable outcome of a business that has resting on it the condemnations of
heaven and the maledictions of all right-thinking men
and women, both young and old.

There is nothing in my past life that gives me

greater pleasure than the fact that many years ago, when I was a young man I commenced war with the dragon, and for forty-five years I have been in the conflict, with voice and pen, and by practice and precept have been a total abstainer and Prohibitionist.

When I got married I was president of a temperance organization. I have been associated with every kind of temperance society that has existed in this country. I am among the oldest temperance workers, and in the neighbourhood where I lived at the time I was among the first to take a decided stand on the side of total abstinence.

Jacob Kerr, John Sidy, Robert Miller and myself entered into a compact that we would not tolerate the use of liquor by going to a bee where it was. Soon others joined with us. In about two years from this the use of strong drink at bees was discontinued in that locality.

My work as a temperance speaker has mostly been in the back country. Four out of six counties with which I have been connected with the cause, either in its incipient or advanced stages, have now the Canada Temperance Act in force, viz., Bruce, Huron, Wellington and Dufferin, and I hope that Perth and Grey will soon fall into line. Then all the field of my efforts as a temperance lecturer will be under prohibition. And it must be remembered that it used to cost more in every way to be an advocate of total abstinence and prohibition than it does now. Then the cause was unpopular, and the question new as compared with the present. A man required considerable nerve to stand up in an audience and advocate an unpopular subject, when nine-tenths of his hearers were in sympathy with the opposite side of the question.

I can easily remember when it was very difficult to get a minister of the Gospel to stand on the platform and advocate the claims of temperance. They were either not in favour of the movement, or they were afraid to speak out on the subject. The charge of political interference was a bugbear to many, and the fear of the loss of influence was a terror to others.

There were two classes of men that could and did stand by the cause. These were the obscure men, who had but little reputation to forfeit, and the men of means of their own, who could get along without the people's money if they had to do it. But this latter class was very small.

Of the former class there were more. And they did the best they could, and success has crôwned their efforts. But many of the popular men gave the cause of temperance "a good letting alone" until the cause itself became popular. And another difficulty was that the question was a new one, so that there had not been much light thrown on it by the great luminaries of the world of thought.

To find argument that could stand the adverse criticisms to which every word and sentence of our utterances were subjected was no easy matter. Now, since the greatest minds of the world have fully canvassed the subject in all its aspects and given us their conclusions and the reasons for them, it is an easy matter to find something to say on temperance. Almost anyone can be a lecturer at the present time. But it was not so forty or fifty years ago.

I will now give an account of some of my experiences in fighting the dragon.

FEARFUL SCHOOL TRUSTEES.

In the county of Perth, on the line between Wallace and Elma, and some few miles north of Listowel, is a little village called Molesworth. I am thus particular in pointing out the place because there used to be a very careful and cautious Board of School Trustees living and having authority there.

When I went to Listowel as a missionary, twenty-eight years ago, the country was new, having been very recently settled. But it was not too new to have a good, live lodge of Good Templars in Listowel. I at once joined them and became one of the active workers in the cause.

A young man by the name of Winters, who lived near Molesworth, asked me to go and give a lecture on temperance, in the schoolhouse. To this I consented, and the arrangements were made for a meeting on a certain night.

At the appointed time I and four or five others from Listowel rode out to the place on horseback. When we came to the spot, we found a lot of men sitting on logs around the schoolhouse, which was in the bush. We tied our horses to some saplings, and joined the company, but the door was locked.

On enquiry being made as to why the door had not been opened, it came out that the leading trustee, who held the key, had some very strong objections to allowing a temperance meeting to be held in the school-house. Another trustee was among the men present. He demurred a little at what he called the doggedness of his brother in office.

He asked what kind of a meeting we intended to hold. I explained in a few words what was the routine of a temperance meeting. While we were talking, the man who held the key came up. On being told who I was, he turned to me and said: "Sir, you are a stranger here. We don't know anything about you. You may be a good man or you may not. We can't tell. But before I open the door, I want a guarantee from you that no injury will be done to the house."

I said to him: "Sir, I am a stranger, as you say. I don't know anything about the people around here. They may be all right and they may not. I shall give no guarantee for them. But for myself and those who came with me I will promise that we will not harm the house while we are in it, nor carry anything away from it when we leave it. That is as far as I can go."

By this time between thirty and forty men were there. The door was opened, and we held the first temperance meeting ever held at Molesworth. An effort was soon after made to organize a Good Templars' Lodge. But in canvassing for names the committee met at one house a minister who was visiting among the people. On learning what it was they were trying to do, he advised them to give it up, giving as his reason that the whole thing was only a

"Yankee humbug." One remarkable thing about the meeting at Molesworth was the fact that not a single woman or girl was present. On my mentioning it, the chairman said they did not know that it was a suitable place for women.

An Ex-Reeve in Trouble.

When I went to Meaford the first time, I had only been there a week when I was called on by a Presbyterian elder, who asked me which side I was on in the temperance question.

I told him that I was a practical total abstainer and a thorough Prohibitionist.

"Well," said he, "you are a man after my own heart. I want you to go with me to-morrow to a convention of the temperance men of this township. We are just now on the eve of voting on the Dunkin Bill in St. Vincent, and we shall be pleased to have your help."

We went to the convention, which was held in a grove on the ninth line of St. Vincent. There were four or five ministers there, and a large number of people. The contest was exciting a good deal of attention.

There was a man there who had been the reeve of the township for a number of years, but he had been run out that year. He was at the meeting, and after the ministers had spoken and most of them had left the ground, he came forward to represent the "antis." He was a good speaker and a shrewd, sharp man. He made a very severe attack upon all ministers who took

17

an active part in the contest against the traffic.   He accused them of meddling with politics, and compared them to incendiaries going about with torches in their hands to destroy their neighbours' property, and other things that he said was not at all complimentary to the clergy.

When he got through with his speech he left the stand, picked up his hat and was about to leave the ground.   I called to him and said : "See here, Mr. —, I have something to say about you, and I would be pleased if you would stop and hear it."

" All right," he said.   " Now, I suppose we will have some more torchlight."

" Yes, sir," I answered.   " And sparks, too.   If you don't want the sparks to get into your eyes, you must put your goggles on.   Then everything will look as verdant to you as your arguments do to me."

I took up his statements item by item, as we used to say at Conference.   He stood it for awhile.   Then he and his chums got up and left the ground.   I did not call after them, but I felt like it.   If I had done so I should have said something like this :

> How the sparks fly here and yonder,
>   Lighting where the dust lies thickest,
> Making rummies stop and wonder,
>   Then, try who can "" git " the quickest.

The chairman was a good honest Quaker, Hiram Bond.

A blind girl, Lizzie Stephenson, did good service by singing a number of pieces.   She was the daughter of a hotelkeeper and the sister of another.

As we were going home, William Carnahan, the man that I went with, said: "I am glad that Greer found his match. He is a hard man to cope with, and most people are afraid of him."

"Well," I said, "I am not a very good hand to be afraid of men. But, after all, there is something about that man I like. He is no sneak. I like a man that has the courage of his convictions, whether he agrees with me or not."

The Same Man Again.

Some years after the convention above mentioned, there was one held in the town of Meaford. This time the condition of things was wonderfully changed from what they were at the meeting on the ninth line.

The representative of the "antis" at that gathering was the chairman at this. Now, it would not be fair to Mr. Greer to leave the impression that he had become an advocate of prohibition. This he had not done, and, so far as I know, he has never come to that; but he had become so far reconciled to temperance men and their work that he would consent to preside at one of their meetings—and no better chairman of a public meeting was to be found in that community.

There were people there from all directions and of every class of persons. Hotel men and shopkeepers were there, as well as farmers, merchants, mechanics and professionals. At that meeting I ventured to hint at the plan of compensation, as the safest and surest means of abolishing the traffic. When I spoke of that, one of the hotel men in the crowd called out and said,

"If you temperance men will start on that line, you will at once have three-fourths of hotelkeepers with you, and the other fourth would only be the scum of the trade, and would not be worth any consideration in the matter."

Nothing that I heard since then has changed my mind in regard to 'the inherent justice of compensation, yet what I have seen has convinced me of its impracticability. From the actions of many of the men in the traffic, I have come to the conclusion that if the trade was bought out to-morrow, on a promise not to engage in selling liquor any more, not one in five would keep that promise. I am sorry that the course of action, adopted by the opposers of prohibition, has driven me and others to the decision that nothing but force will successfully cope with this abomination of the nineteenth century, as we have it in this country.

THEY WANTED ONLY LOGIC.

There was a time in this Province, before Confederation, when the municipal council might refuse to license any place to sell liquor of any kind. Then, if people wanted prohibition, they could only get it by electing men to the council board who were in favour of it. The township of Wallace was the scene of a contest of this sort when I was in Listowel. The temperance party resolved to test the matter, and try to elect a majority of good, reliable men who would close up the sale of liquor in the township.

I was invited to lecture on temperance in a schoolhouse, where a large majority of the people were adherents of the Church of England, and nearly all opposed to the temperance movement. When I went to the place I found a house full of very respectable-looking people, who were waiting for me. We opened the meeting in the usual way, and then a chairman was called for. After considerable delay we got one. In a few opening remarks he said: "I don't know much about temperance, but I believe this man is here to tell why we ought to work for old James Bolton and other temperance men." Then he turned to me and said: "Now, mister, we will listen to what you have to say. We want no cant or sentimentalism; we want logic."

On rising up I said: "I am glad, sir, that you want logic. Yourself and your audience look as though you could appreciate sound reasoning, and I hope you and they have sufficient candour to receive an argument even though it does come from a stranger. I shall not appeal to you as Christians, for that might be construed into the cant that you deprecate; neither will I address you in the name of Methodism, for that to many of you would only be another word for fanaticism, but on the broad ground of patriotism I shall base my remarks. Now, I want you to agree or disagree with my first proposition, which is this: 'That which tends to the production of pauperism, crime and misery should be discountenanced by every good citizen.' Will you endorse that?" I said.

After a moment he said: "Yes, that is a true statement of fact, whatever conclusion it may lead to."

" I am glad," said I, " that we have common ground to stand on at the start, for if we agree at first I think we shall not differ at the last. Now my next statement is this : The drinking usages of society tend to the production of pauperism, crime and misery. They tend to pauperism by wasting our resources ; by misdirecting the course of trade ; by enervating labouring men ; by wasting time in tippling and drunkenness ; by using the means of satisfying hunger to make whiskey ; and by needless destruction of property in many ways. They tend to crime by exciting the bad passions, under the influence of which crime is committed ; and by weakening the moral sensibilities by which crime is prevented. Thus they strengthen the downward tendency, and at the same time they break down the barriers of resistance, so that by a double process they send men to the penitentiary, to the gallows and perdition. Will you endorse that statement ? " I asked him.

" Well, I don't see how to do anything else, unless I am to deny or ignore facts, and I am not disposed to do either," was his answer to my question.

" I am very much pleased," said I, " that I have to do with an honest, intelligent chairman, and a logical audience. Now that we are agreed on the two main propositions, the conclusion follows as a matter of course—so that as good citizens we are bound to discountenance the drinking usages of society."

" Well," said the chairman, " I never thought that temperance men had such good ground to stand on in their opposition to the traffic."

"That is because you have never investigated the subject," I said.

"I wish that you would give that address in every school section in the township," said he.

" Well, so far as that is concerned," I said, " you need have no fears. The Rev. Mr. Luke is looking after a part of the township. I am doing what I can. A minister of your own Church will visit some of the sections; and Mr. J. J. Linton, of Stratford, has sent an armful of his papers, called the ' Prohibitionist,' into the township. We intend to prevent the sale of ' dragon juice' in Wallace next year, if it is possible to do so."

I shall close this chapter by giving some extracts from a report of a mass meeting, in the town of Kincardine, the first year of my residence there. It is taken from the *Bruce Reporter*, of Feb. 8th, 1877.

" MASS MEETING !

"Temperance men to the front. Facts and figures in favour of prohibition. The pulpit on the attack.

" A mass meeting of the Congregational Alliance, on Monday evening, was largely attended. The meeting was opened with prayer by the Rev. Mr. Anderson. The chair was occupied by Mr. Ira J. Fisher, who, after stating the object sought by the Congregational Temperance Alliance, called upon the Rev. J. H. Hilts to move the first resolution—which reads as follows :—

" Resolved,—' That the liquor traffic, as hitherto carried on in this and in other countries, has been extensively a source of misery, crime, and every form of degradation, calling aloud for all that can be done by the voice of a strong public opinion, and by wise legislation to regulate and restrain it.'

" Mr. Hilts said that he was coming down from his usual platform to-night. If it had been to prohibit or blot out, instead of regulate and restrain, it would have been better. But as it was, he was proud to defend the temperance cause even on the low level on which it was put.

He was the unrelenting enemy of the liquor traffic —not of the men who deal in it—on account of the number he had seen ruined by it. Sound philosophy would require the abolition of everything that does more harm than good. The best State policy would enjoin the discontinuance of any and every institution that impoverishes and demoralizes the subject. True philanthrophy would lay a firm, though kindly hand, on every class of actions that can result in nothing else than human misery.

" Genuine religion, speaking in the name of God and humanity, would utter its solemn protest against every-thing that tends to nothing better than to make man more wicked.

" We are persuaded that the liquor traffic is the enemy of sound philosophy, of true State policy, of in-dividual happiness and of religion. The whiskey traffic involves a waste of means, and hence it tends to poverty. The amount of grain made use of in 1873 was 1,733,164 bushels. The excise duties and customs in 1873 were $4,762,278. This only indicates the manu-facture and importation, not touching the cost of license ' to sell.' This waste is on the increase, for in 1873, eighteen distilleries made 5,547,062 gallons of spirits. But, in 1875, twelve distilleries made 68,062 gallons more than that amount. Thus, it seems, that while temperance men congratulate the country on the reduction of distilleries, the traffic is really strengthening its position by reducing the number of salient points; while it is throwing all its influence and concentrating all its forces into a few mammoth corporations. Hence, while the necessity for defensive stratagem is made less, the power for agressive warfare is increased. . . . . .

" The amount of spirituous liquors made in 1875, was 5,615,740 gallons, and the malt liquors made in the same year was 11,584,226. Now, if we allow that one quart of this whiskey or one gallon of this beer would keep a man drunk for a day, then the whole amount would keep 120,000 *hors de combat* for a whole twelve months. . . . . These men at $1.00 per day would be worth $36,814,200. . . . .

" In 1874 a committee was appointed by the Senate of the Dominion, to enquire into the propriety of a prohibitory liquor law which was asked for by some 500,-000 of the people of the Dominion. I shall give some extracts from the report of that committee. ' Your committee regard the vast and increasing number of petitions, and the unanimity in the statements and prayer of the several petitions, as indicating the immense and pressing importance of the subject to which they call the attention of the Senate; and the profound and widespread feeling of the need of such

legislation as shall at once check and eventually ex-
tirpate from our land the vice of intemperance which
has so long been and still is a prolific source of crime,
misery, disease and death, and a blight upon the fair
prospects of our young Dominion.'

" The petitioners further state that ' the traffic in
intoxicating liquors is shown by the most careful
inquiries to be the cause of probably not less than
three-fourths of the pauperism, immorality and crime
found in this country.' The evidence gathered by a
committee of the House of Commons last year is
strongly in corroboration of this assertion. It will be
observed here that the committee seems to sanction
the statement of the petitioners.

" Men in official positions agree that intemperance
increases crime. The recorder of Montreal says that,
speaking for himself and associates, ' All are of opinion
with me that, apart from the violations of statutory
law and the by-law of the city, every case tried before
the court, with a very few, if indeed, any exceptions,
arises out of intemperance. The clerk of the court is
of opinion that the proportion of the cases which owe
their origin to intemperance is at least three-fourths.
His first assistant sets the same proportion at seven-
eights, and his second assistant at nine-tenths. My
own opinion corresponds with the latter.'

" He continues : ' The records of criminal courts in all
countries, and the dying declarations of the great
majority of criminals who have suffered the extreme
penalty of the law, all clearly establish the fact that
nearly all the crimes committed, especially those of

greater magnitude, would never have been conceived in the first place, or afterwards have been carried out to perpetration by the offenders but for the baneful effects of intoxicating drinks. Licensing the sale of intoxicating drinks as beverage cannot, therefore, be regarded otherwise than as productive of crime.'

"T. W. Penton, in 1873 the Chief of Police in Montreal, says: 'Mostly all offences are due, either directly or indirectly, to intemperance.'

"Mr. Prince, the Chief of the Toronto Police Force, gives the number of arrests in 1873 for drunkenness and disorderly conduct at 2,952.

"The Chief of Police at Ottawa, Thomas Sangrell, says: 'The number of persons confined in the Police Station in 1871 was 722; of these 591 were intemperate. In 1872 the number was 724; of these 631 were intemperate. In 1873 the number was 936; of these 621 were intemperate.'

"L. A. Voyce, Mayor of Quebec, says 'that in 1871 the number of arrests for drunkenness was 1,217, and in 1872 it was 889, and in 1873 it was 976.'

"James Cahill, the Police Magistrate of Hamilton, says: 'The number of arrests in that city for crimes connected with the liquor traffic in 1871, was 659; in 1872, 868; in 1873, 881.'

"Nor is the bad effects of the use of intoxicating drinks in any way confined, but in all communities it is the same. Lord Hamilton, in the British House of Commons, speaking on the Permissive Liquor Bill, says: 'We have the testimony of the Home Secretary, who acknowledges the evils, and admits that our judges, magistrates, governors of gaols, inspectors of police and every one acquainted with administration of law, concur in the opinion that the greater part of the crime in the land is to be attributed to the curse of intemperance.

"Lord Shaftesbury says: 'Is there any one in the least degree conversant with the state of your alleys, dwellings and various localities, who will deny this great truth which all experience confirms; for if you go into these fearful places, you see there the causes of moral mischief, and I do verily believe that seven-tenths of it are attributable to that which is the greatest curse of the country—habits of drinking and systems of intoxication.'

"The Inspector of Prisons in Belgium says: 'My experience extends over a quarter of a century, and I can emphatically declare that four-fifths of the crime and misery with which in my public and private capacity I have come in contact, has been the result of drink.'

"Mr. Quitelet says: 'Of 1,129 murders in France, during the space of four years, 446 have been in consequence of quarrels and contentions in taverns, which would tend to show the fatal influence of the use of strong drink.'

"Mr. Hill says: 'Every one acquainted with our criminal courts must see the truth of what our judges state day by day and year by year, that by far the greatest number of all offences have their origin in the love of drink.'

"On this head I give the following declarations from

the most intelligent and able judges of the English courts:

"Judge Coleridge: 'There is scarcely a crime that comes before me that is not directly or indirectly caused by strong drink.'

"Judge Gurney says: 'Every crime has its origin more or less in drunkenness.'

"Judge Patterson: 'If it were not for the drinking, the jury and I would have nothing to do.'

"Judge Alderson says: 'Drunkenness is the most fertile source of crime, and if it could be removed the assizes of the country would be rendered mere nullities.'

"Judge Wightman says: 'I find in the calendar that comes before me one unfailing source, directly or indirectly, of the most of the crimes that are committed—intemperance.'

"Mr. Charles Paxton, M.P., a celebrated English brewer, says: 'It would not be too much to say, that if all drinking of fermented liquors could be done away with, crime of every kind would fall to a fourth of its present amount, and the whole tone of moral feeling in the lower orders might be indefinitely raised. Not only does this vice produce all kinds of wanton mischief, but it has a negative effect of great importance. It is the mightiest of all the forces that clog the progress of good. It is in vain that every engine is set to work that philanthropy can devise, when those whom we seek to benefit are habitually tampering with their faculties of reason and will—soaking their brains with beer or influencing them with ardent spirits.'

" This is remarkable language to be used by a manufacturer of the very drink that he complains of. His testimony is all the better from this fact, that he is speaking against his own interest in making those statements.'

" I now have done with these extracts from reports of Parliamentary Committees. But do they not most strongly proclaim the startling truth embodied in the resolution before the meeting ? Can any one be found in the audience, or in the town, who is so blind as not to see the propriety—nay, the positive necessity, of regulating and restraining the traffic in intoxicating drinks.

" What is to become of the noble youth and blooming maidens of our town, if on every corner and in every street they are brought face to face with this deadly foe, whose slimy trail is to be found along the centuries, and whose inky character has blotted the history of our civilization for more than three hundred years. Shall we, my friends, quietly sit down and endorse the doings of this traffic ? Let a person of doubtful reputation come within the circle of your home, and see how soon, and wisely, you would seek to secure your sons and daughters from the danger of being contaminated by contact with such persons.

" But here is a traffic whose reputation is worse than doubtful, whose vile character is well known, and it is asking you to sanction the removal of the very reasonable restrictions which your council in its wisdom imposed upon it last year. Will you consent to this ? Methinks I hear a strong and determined NO from all parts of this hall to-night.

"This traffic comes down to us from ancestral times and it is laden with startling memories, and it unfolds to us many dark and tragic scenes, enacted in princely mansions and lonely dwellings.

"True, it comes to us endorsed by our forefathers, but it is an endorsation obtained by false pretences. It comes to us sparkling with the jewels of wealth, but it glistens with teardrops also. It comes to us sanctioned by the voice of legislation and law-makers, but it is condemned by the cry of countless sufferers. It comes to us singing the songs of gladness, but beneath them are heard the undertones of woe.

"It comes to us in the garb of a friend, but it conceals the pointed dagger of a murderous assassin. It assumes the harmless aspect of the dove, but it glares upon us with the fierce demoniac glitter of the serpent's eye.

"There is not a man or woman here to-night who is not interested in this matter. No one here wishes to feel the crushing and withering influence of the demon traffic.

"There is not a home in Canada but is worthy of a better fate than that of being desecrated by so vile a presence as the evil spirit of the whiskey traffic. Chain up the rum-demon, friends, and support the first resolution."

I may here say that as this was my first appearance on the temperance platform in that town, I made the best preparation that I could. The address was written out at length and given to the meeting in the form of a reading.

After a few words by Mr. Thompson, who seconded the resolution, it was passed almost, if not quite, unanimously.   And it has been so far carried out that at the present time Kincardine and the county of Bruce are under the Scott Act.

In looking back over the past there is nothing that gives me more real pleasure, so far as my own doings are concerned, than the stand that I have taken for forty-five years on the liquor question.   I have done a large amount of talking and writing, walking and singing, and some praying, to help along the good and philanthropic work of saving men from drunkenness. I am glad in my heart that I have done a little toward rolling on the car of temperance, and drying up the foul channels through which this dragon of our times sends out his stinking saliva to besot and poison the slaves of their appetites.

My prayer is, that the time may soon come when from Newfoundland to Vancouver there will not be found one single man-trap in the form of a whiskey den—when the banner of temperance shall float over all the land over which the flag of our Dominion now is waving.   Nay, more, when the banner of temperance, interwoven with the banner of the cross, shall wave in triumph over all the world.

CHAPTER XIII.

AT WEDDINGS.

"DO you intend to say anything about weddings that you have attended?" This question was put to me by a person I was conversing with concerning my "book."

My answer was: "Well, I had not intended to do so, but if I thought I could make it interesting I would write a chapter on weddings."

"No doubt," said my interrogator, "you ministers sometimes meet with amusing incidents on those occasions."

"Yes, that is so," I said. "I have met with some laughable things at weddings. And I have seen other things that were not very amusing."

"If I were you," said my friend, "I think I would have something to say about weddings. It would interest the young people, at all events."

The young people are a very large and important part of the population, and they are worthy of all consideration. I shall therefore try to act on my friend's advice, and say something about those occasions to which the young look forward, if not with fear and trembling, yet with a great deal of anxiety.

My First and Only Wedding.

By this I do not mean the first one where I officiated as minister. But I mean the one where I and another person were "the observed of all observers"—the two most conspicuous persons present on the occasion. I will try to present the scene as it comes back to my memory over the graves of forty-three years. And in doing this I ask the assistance, gentle reader, of your own imagination to give vividness and colour to the picture.

Now, just fancy yourself standing or sitting, whichever you prefer, in the best room of a rural home. There are fifty or sixty present, who are all waiting the entrance of the parties most interested in the day's proceedings.

Presently a door opens and four young people enter and take their positions in the usual way.

Now, take a look at the two who are about to slip their heads into the matrimonial noose. The young man who is anxious to become a son-in-law is about twenty-five years old. He is above medium height. He has dark brown hair, very fine and a little inclined to curl, but not parted in the middle; eyes a dark hazel, and eyebrows heavy, giving a cross look to the features, which are coarse but not repulsive. The nose and mouth indicate a quick temper and an inclination to stubbornness.   A close observer would likely say: "I am not just sure about that little girl being able to manage that fellow. She may possibly lead him, but it is certain she will never drive him."

Now, take a look at the bride. You see she could stand up under the young man's arm. Take a fair look at her; she will bear inspection, she is good-looking. Some say that she is handsome. Do you ask how she was dressed? I cannot tell; I never was good at describing ladies' dresses; besides, on that particular day I had so many other things to think about that I am not able to answer your question; but I presume she was well dressed, since I never heard anything to the contrary. The ceremony was over in a short time; but while the minister was performing it, a sort of petty persecution was going on in the room. An aunt of the bride got a looking-glass and, standing behind the minister, held it up before the parties so that they could see themselves in it; and a cousin of the groom, who got himself where his face could be seen in the mirror, stood and made all sorts of faces at them to make them laugh; but in this he failed—the one was too much vexed to laugh and the other was too much frightened.

Now, I am going to take the risk of being dubbed a poetic failure, or being called a clumsy rider of Pegasus. I give the following as a tribute to the little woman who stood by me on that day :—

MY WIFE'S GREY HAIRS.

How well do I remember now,
  The day that we were wed ;
When auburn locks adorned her brow,
  And beautified her head.
When first I took her to my side,
  And claimed her as my wife,
Her youthful beauty was the pride
  And treasure of my life.

Now, when I see some silver lines
  Run through her golden hair,
It seems to me her goodness shines
  More beautiful and rare
Than when I took her by the hand,
  So many years ago,
And promised by her side to stand
  Through long-life weal or woe.

These whitening tresses on her head
  Speak of the fading past,
And tell of tears of sadness shed,
  Of sorrows that have cast
Their lengthening shadows o'er the way
  That led us on through life,
And tell of many a gloomy day
  Since first I called her wife.

The hardships we together shared,
  The ills that we have met,
Have not her faithfulness impaired,
  Or caused her to forget
Her duty as a good true wife,
  When tossed upon the tide,
Or in the battle's fiercest strife,
  She never left my side.

What though the touch of time may leave
  Some wrinkles on her brow,
What though beneath the weight of years
  Her step becomes more slow ;
Yet still her eye seems just as bright,
  Her voice sounds just as sweet,
While onward to the world of light
  She moves with willing feet.

THREE FRIGHTENED ONES.

The first couple that I married after I was ordained was in Listowel. The groom was a young man somewhere between early manhood and what would be called old bachelorhood. He was a very quiet, sober-minded man, who had a great amount of self-command. The bride was a young lady somewhere in the latter 'teens. She was shy and timid, having been brought up by a very strict and careful mother. She had never been allowed to go into company very much. The appointed day came round ; I went to the house of the parents of the girl. A few of the relatives on both sides were present. When the time came the bride-elect and her mother were in a room by themselves. They were called, but they did not come ; then they were sent for, but do what we would the mother could not be got to come out. I enquired if she was opposed to the marriage, and I was told that she was well pleased about that ; but she would not come out. So we proceeded. I was just about as much frightened myself as any one need to be : I was afraid of making mistakes. When the bride came out and I saw her, I could not see what she had to be ashamed of.

I have not, since then, seen a prettier or neater bride. The mother came out after the ceremony was over and attended the table all right. We have often talked the matter over since then, and we concluded that we all acted more like children than anything else.

In Too Much of a Hurry.

When I lived in Mount Forest I was called to go out into the township of Minto to attend a wedding. The distance was ten miles, the day was all that a cold, blustering winter day could well be. When I got to the place I found the house—which consisted of one large room—full of people. A large cooking-stove stood in the room, and it was literally covered with the preparations for dinner. Such a display of *fowl roasting* I have never seen anywhere since then.

> Turkeys within the stove,
> Turkeys without the stove,
> Turkeys about the stove,
>   Seemed moaning and muttering.
> Turkeys above the stove,
> Turkeys below the stove,
> Turkeys around the stove,
>   Were hissing and sputtering.
>
> Maidens with eyes so bright,
> Old men with failing sight,
> Children with hearts so light,
>   Sat down and pondered.
> Matrons with queenly grace,
> Young men with smiling face,
> All of them in their place,
>   Looked on and wondered.

After everything was ready, the parties took their places and the ceremony was commenced. The whole company seemed to be in a mood for any amount of fun and frolic. I thought there was a little too much levity to harmonize with an occasion of so much importance. I resolved to check it if an opportunity offered. When the bride had responded to the usual questions, the young man darted in front of me, and, putting his arm around her neck, gave her a smack that could be heard all through the house. I placed my hand on his shoulder and pushed him back to his place, saying, " Look here, my friend, this transaction is something more than a farce. You will find it so before you are as old as I am. I will tell you when it is time to do the kissing."

" Well, all right," he said, " but I like to be a little ahead of time."

I answered, " That may be all right, but it don't do to get ahead of time in everything."

When all was over and I was about to leave, I said to the young couple: " Next time you make a ' bee ' to eat roasted turkeys and chickens, try and select a more reasonable day than this, if you have to wait a month to get it."

He Bought Her a Thimble.

When I was living in Thornbury I was called upon, one very cold and stormy night, to marry a couple who came in from the country a distance of eight or ten miles. I offered to go to the hotel where the parties were staying. This the young man objected to, saying that they would drive in with the team, as my house was some distance from the main road. He went away about nine o'clock in the evening, saying that they would be on hand in a few minutes.

We waited till nearly eleven o'clock, and heard nothing of the wedding party. My wife said to me, "I think you are fooled this time. It is likely that young chap just came for a lark." It certainly looked like it. At eleven we retired. We had just got into bed when the parties came and rapped at the door. We got up and let them in, and in a few minutes the twain were made one.

When I asked them what had detained them, they told me that they had been wandering about for an hour or more, having lost the way. They had started to come on foot from the hotel and the track being drifted full they missed it. The girls were nearly tired out. I gave the men a bit of wholesome counsel, and made them promise never to drag their women through the snow like that again. When all was over the young man was going off without offering me any fee. When he had his hand on the door I said to him, "Are you not forgetting something?" He felt for his mitts, looked at his muffler and at his hat and then said, "No, I think not."

"Well," said I, "do you think that it is just the thing to be called out of bed at this time of night for nothing?"

"Well, now, is it not strange that I should have forgotten that?" said he; "how much will it be?"

I told him that two dollars would do.

" Can you change a ten ? " was his next question.

I told him I could not, but I would go with him to the hotel and get the landlord to change it. This was done, and I never saw the parties since ; but I heard from them.

Next morning the bridegroom went into a store and said to the merchant : " I was married last night. You know yesterday was Christmas. Now, I want to buy my wife a Christmas box and a wedding gift all in one."

" Well," said the merchant, " I can supply you with the very thing you want. Only tell me the kind of goods you want."

" Well," said the other, " I am not very particular what it is, only I *must have something nice.*"

Dress goods, shawls, bonnets and various other articles of feminine choice were shown, but none of them would suit. The merchant began to fear that his stock of goods was not up to the requirement of the trade in that locality. While he was revolving in his mind whether he could have a special order filled in time to satisfy his fastidious customer, the young man gave him a sort of knowing wink and asked if he had any thimbles.

" O, yes, how strange that I did not think of that before," said the man behind the counter, as he handed the new benedict a three-cent thimble.

A QUESTION OF FINANCE.

Some time while I had charge of the Kincardine Circuit I went out to marry a couple near Armow. I called at Brother Joseph Shier's on my way. When I was starting Mrs. Shier said to me : "Mr. Hilts, how much will you get to-day for tying the knot ?"

"Well, that depends on two or three things," I said.

She asked me what I meant. I answered by saying, " Some depends on his liberality, some on ability, but more depends on the question of his being a bachelor or widower."

" Why," said my questioner, "what has bachelorhood or widowerhood got to do with it ?"

" I cannot tell you just where the cause is to be sought for, but, as a matter of fact and experience, I have found out that men pay more for the second wife than for the first, and more for the third than either of the other two."

" Well, now, I did not think there was so much non-sense in you as all that," she said.

" My good woman," said I, " it is not nonsense but fact, account for it as we may. Now, if this man is a bachelor and in pretty good circumstances, I will get somewhere from two to five dollars ; but if he is a widower in pretty fair circumstances, I will get some-where from four to ten dollars."

" Well, that beats all. Will you call when you come back and tell me how much you got ?" said she.

I promised to do so, and went on to the place where the wedding was to be. After the ceremony was over, and I began to take the usual statistics for registra-tion, I found that the man had been married before. I felt a little curious to find out whether his contribu-tion on the altar of Hymen would harmonize with what I had been saying to Mrs. Shier. When he handed me the money rolled up in a bit of paper, I put it in my pocket. Shortly after I took my leave I called at Mr. Shier's, When Mrs. Shier asked me about the wedding I told her the man had been a widower. Then she wanted to know how much he gave me. I took out of my pocket the little roll, and when I opened it out it proved to be between four and ten dollars, as I said it would be if the man had been married before.

"Why is it," said the questioner, "that you get a larger fee for second marriages than for first?"

"I think," said I, "that there are sound reasons for it. In the first place, men are older at the second marriage than they were at the first, and therefore they ought to be in better circumstances; and in the second place, we never know how to prize a good thing until we have lost it; and the Bible tells us that 'whoso findeth a wife findeth a good thing.'"

A Tangled Question.

Once I was employed to join together an old couple whose united ages would span about a century and a half. When the old gentleman came to ask me to marry him he seemed to be a little embarrassed. Young men are almost always embarrassed under similar circumstances, but one would hardly expect an old man to be very much disturbed. This old man, however, was somewhat in the condition described by an old Irish friend of mine—"he was all through other." When he told me who was the bride-elect I could hardly believe my ears. I was acquainted with the old lady, and I had so often heard her say that she "wadna hae the bonniest man that ever got himsel' intil a pair o' breeks," I could hardly believe that she would change her mind so much and so soon.

When the day came I went to the house of the widow, and found the old gentleman already there. I said to the old lady, "How is this? You must have changed your mind since you told me that you would not have anybody."

She answered, "Weel, weel; that callant ca'd here twa or three times, and by his cannie moods an' winsome ways he just thro'd me aff' my guard. Then he asked me tae be his ane guidwife, and he gaed and tangled up the question sae that I couldna tell which was yes or which was no. I thocht to say no, but I must have said yes, for he takit me at the word, an' noo I canna gang back on't."

"O, the old fox," said I, "to go and corner up a poor young innocent thing like that, and in the excitement and confusion of one so young and inexperienced to extort a promise to be his, and then hold her to that promise. He ought to be ashamed of himself."

At this mock tirade of mine they both laughed heartily. We soon got through with the ceremony. When I was about to leave I said to them: "Will you two young people take some advice from an elderly man? But no, on second thought, I will keep my advice to myself, for it would be useless to give it, because, no doubt, like other youngsters, you would choose to learn by experience rather than take anybody's advice." At this they had another laugh, and I left them.

A Strange Bridegroom.

I was once called on by a man who lived in the town where I resided. He came to engage me to marry a couple. The young man, he said, worked for him, and the young woman was the daughter of a neighbour. I promised to attend to the matter. Before leaving, the man said to me: "Perhaps the young fellow may not have any funds to pay you, but let that go; I will see that you get your pay." I told him that was all right.

When the time came I went to the house pointed out to me. I found a number of people there, but the bridegroom was not there. I was told that he had been there, but he had gone out somewhere about town to be back in a few minutes. We waited for him till long past the time appointed, but he did not come. Then two men went out to hunt him up. After a while they found him and brought him with them. When I saw the parties standing on the floor together two facts flashed upon my mind. It was evident that they ought to have been married before, and it was equally evident that the girl was throwing herself away. This may seem like a paradox, but most people will understand what I mean.

When I commenced the ceremony the man evidently was ill at ease. I thought once or twice, by his actions, that he would bolt and run; but he stood like one who was just where he did not like to be. The ring was used to please the old people, but when we came to that part where the ring is used, it seemed to me that he cared no more for the hand he was putting the ring on than he would for the hand of an Eskimo.

After the ceremony was over I started to go out. He followed me and said, "I can't pay you to-day, but I will before long." I told him that would be all right. The next week he went off and left his wife. No one knew where he went to. Some time after I met the man who had engaged me to marry them. He said to me: "That young man that you married has gone off and left his wife already, but I kept back enough to pay you when I settled up with him."

I said to him: "Well, sir, I am glad you kept it, but I do not want it. You give it to his wife. She, poor thing, will need it before long; give it to her, for I don't want it."

A Queer Bridegroom.

I was leading a prayer-meeting one evening in the church in Kincardine, when a middle-aged man came up to me, as I was giving out a hymn, and asked me to step to the door for a minute. When we got outside, he said: "I am sorry to interrupt you, but my business is urgent. I want to get married this evening, and, on my inquiring at the hotel for a minister, I was sent to you."

"Very well, sir," I answered, "I can attend to you as soon as this service is over, which will be in half an hour. Where will I find you?"

He said: "We will come to your house if you have no objections. The lady does not like to be married at a hotel."

I showed him my house and told him to come along as soon after nine o'clock as they could.

He went away saying they would be on hand. They were a little late, but they came alone. When I saw the woman I was a little surprised that she should marry the man, but on inquiry it came out that they had been lovers in their young days, but something had come in their way. She had been married to another, and moved west from Ottawa to the new country, and with her husband had settled in the bush. They had succeeded in making a good home. Then her husband had died and left her and her family in comfortable circumstances. The two had lost track of each other for more than twenty years, but that day they had met on an excursion train coming to Kincardine. The man had never married. But he had also come to the new country some years ago. When they met on the train that day, and renewed old acquaintance and talked of the past and found that both were free, the old flame was rekindled. And they resolved to be united before they returned home. But there was something a little strange about the man that I could not fathom. He was either very shallow or very deep, and I could not make out which.

When they stood up and I asked him the usual question, instead of answering he gave me a queer kind of a look that I did not like. It was a sort of a compromise between a grin and a sneer.

I looked him in the eye and said: "Mister, I want a distinct answer to that question."

" Well, what do you want me to say ? " He spoke with some emphasis.

"I want you to say whether you will take this woman to be your wife or not?"

"Why, of course I will. That is just what I am here for.

I said that would do and went on with the service.

They were both past fifty years old. The woman was a fine-looking lady of her age and very respectably dressed. After they were married the man told me that not expecting anything of the kind when he left home, he had not much money with him, but he would pay me a part of the fee, and take my address and send the rest of it.

I told him that would do.   So he took the address, but I fear he lost it, as I never heard from him since.

MANLY HOTEL-KEEPERS.

Some young men have strange notions of true manliness. They will pride themselves on their ability to fool and deceive any over-confiding young woman who is silly enough to trust them. They will boast of their conquests and glory in what is really their shame.

I called them men.   I wish, for the credit of real manhood, to take that back. They are not men. They are simply animals with breeches on. There are no manly feelings in any one who can take pleasure in wronging one who is weaker than himself.

I once knew a case where one of this class was brought to the scratch in a way that he little expected.

He had been keeping company for a long time with

a very clever, industrious young girl, who was entirely respectable. But her people were poor. She was working at a hotel in the village where I lived at the time.

After a while the young deceiver made up his mind to go off and leave the poor girl to bear, as best she could, the result of her over-confidence in him.

The man for whose wife the girl was working was a constable. When he learned from his wife the state of affairs, he started to where the young fellow was. He found him at another hotel and just ready to take the stage for parts unknown.

The constable laid his hand on him and said, " I want you to come with me."

" Where to ? " said the other.

" To my house."

" What for ? "

" To marry Bessie."

" Oh, nonsense ! I won't do that."

" Yes, you will, and that before the sun goes down, and before you get out of my sight."

" I have no money to buy the license or to pay the minister."

The other hotel man now spoke up and said, "I will furnish the money. Come along and get the license. You have got to marry that girl before you are one day older."

And he did, and I was called in to tie the knot. Shortly after they went away to live on some land given to him by his father. She made him a good wife, and he made her a passably good husband. He

19

might have said to her one day when he came in to
dinner :

> Dear Bessie, I am sorry now
>   That I was going away to leave you.
> So to my fate I meekly bow,
>   And hope I nevermore may grieve you.

A Wife for Six Brooms.

About the most unique affair that I ever knew took
place in a village where I once lived. Though I had
no personal connection with the transaction I knew all
the parties. I can vouch for the substantial truthfulness for the statements here presented.

A young couple made up their minds to travel life's
pathway together. They were both very poor, and
neither of them had any wit to spare.

The young man made an apology for a livelihood by
manufacturing splint brooms and axe-handles. He
went to a Wesleyan Methodist minister to engage him
to do the splicing. At that time the *banns* were published instead of getting license in many cases.

After all the arrangements had been made as to time
and place the young man said :

"Mr. Blank, I have no money. Won't you take
your pay in brooms ? "

" O, yes ; anything to accommodate you," said the
minister, who was a lively Irishman and fond of a joke.

" Well," said the other, " how many brooms will I
fetch you ? "

" About a half a dozen."

" Will that be enough ? "

"Yes; you bring along your girl and six good brooms, and I will marry you just as good as I would if you were the richest man in the county."

When the day appointed came, the people along the leading street of the village witnessed a spectacle that elicited not a little merriment.

There was the young prospective benedict with his girl fondly clinging to one of his arms, and on the other shoulder he carried half a dozen new splint brooms of excellent design and finish.

He marched on with as much self-importance as a coloured captain of militia, with as much pride as a six-year-old boy with a new top, and as much solicitude as an old hen with one chicken. The tune that they marched to would suit these words or something like them,

> Clear the track, for we are here,
> Brooms and all, as you may see ;
> We'll be married, never fear,
> For I love her and she loves me.

And they did get married, and the minister got the brooms.

Matrimonial Blunders.

There are a great many foolish marriages in this world. Even sensible people in other things make some strange mistakes in this important matter. If men would exercise as much caution and common sense in selecting a wife as they do in picking out a horse; and if women would be as particular in choosing a husband as in picking out a dress or a bonnet, one half of the bad matches would never have been made.

Some marry without considering the importance of such a step. They think it is a grand thing to have some one they can call their own.

I knew a man once that married a woman the second time that he ever saw her, and within a week of the first time of seeing her. He wanted another and could not get her, and to show her that he could get a wife, he married with less than a week's acquaintance. He lived with his bride just seven days, and then went away, and she never heard from him for three years. He came back to her then, and stayed till he died, which was a number of years after. Some marry for the sake of a housekeeper, and others for the sake of a home. Some marry for money, and others for social position.

But in all these motives for marrying, the question of adaptation is generally overlooked, as when a man wants some one to look after his home, and takes the first eligible woman that comes in his way ; or when a woman wants a home, and accepts the first man that offers her one.

Now, they may or they may not be adapted to each other. There may be incongruities of temperament, differences in religious sentiment, educational biasses of the mind, a want of harmony in tastes and pursuits, and many other peculiarities in one or both that render them unfit companions for each other.

And although two persons may not be adapted to each other, that does not prove that they are not worthy of good companions. It only shows that they have not made the right selection, that is all.

God never intended that men and women should be disposed of like cattle or horses, for the amount of work that they could do, or for the convenience of the buyer or the gain of the seller.

Mutual respect, confidence, esteem and affection should draw people together. While I am no admirer of lovesick lunies, either male or female, I do insist upon it that the affinities that bring people together into this closest of all human ·bonds should be some-thing more refined, pure and exalted, than mere material considerations.

I have known people who, while living with their first spouses, were entirely happy and contented. The man lost his wife and the woman her husband. The two survivors married, and they quarrelled like cats and dogs, making each other perfectly unhappy. They could not agree to live together, and would not consent to live apart.

My advice to all who are thinking of marrying is, Be sure that you are adapted for each other, then go ahead.

CHAPTER XIV.

DOCTORS AND DOCTORING.

SOMETIMES it seems to me that for twelve or fourteen years past I have been, to a great extent, only a fit subject for the doctors to experiment upon. For that length of time I have been suffering more or less from some sort of disabilities. During that time I have been in the hands of a number of medical men in different localities where I have resided.

And here I may say, whatever the doctors that I am acquainted with may think of me, I have learned to esteem them very highly indeed. There was a time when I had but little love for doctors—not much more than I had for lawyers. Then I looked upon both of these professions as merely money - getting institutions.

But an experience, such as but few men have passed through, has given me entirely different views and feelings in regard to the medical profession. My mind is not nor never has been fully settled as to the utility of lawyers in human society. Whether, on the whole, the world would not be better without them is, I think, an open question. But the doctors could not be dispensed with.

I have a very great respect for the medical men that I have become familiar with, not only because of the importance of their work in relieving suffering and saving life; but I respect them on account of the warm sympathies, the sterling principles, and the manly qualities that I have so frequently found in them.

My own personal afflictions, and what the doctors have done for me, will be the subject treated of in this chapter. I know that sickness and pain are gloomy subjects to speak or write about; but my excuse for presenting this part of my experiences is found in their unusual character, and in the uncommon kindness shown to me and mine by medical men, and by the public generally.

I do not write to attract attention to myself, or to elicit sympathy: I have already had my share of both; but a sense of justice to those who have reached out a helping hand in the dark hours of severe trials and afflictions impels me to speak of them, and in doing so I must of necessity speak of myself. With this explanation, I feel confident that the reader will exonerate me from the charge of egotism on the one hand, or childishness on the other.

When my time on the District expired, old Bishop Richardson asked me to take Meaford, which was made vacant by putting its pastor, Rev. R. Sanderson, as my successor in the presiding-eldership. I had already

been there for one term, besides a four years' residence
there while travelling the district.   At the time my
name stood in the list of appointments for Palermo.
My whole ministerial life had been spent in the back
country.   It required no little effort on my part to
sacrifice the chance for a better appointment than I
had ever been favoured with; but the Bishop was
urgent, and I consented.   I thought that I knew the
people of Meaford; but in this I was a little mistaken.
I did not know quite all of them, as I learned with a
sad heart afterwards.   When I came home from Conference, I found opposition that was as unexpected as
it was unmerited.   But I resolved to go on and do my
duty at all hazards, no matter what might come in the
way, the Lord helping me.

My colleague and I laid our plans for a year of hard
work.   We intended to go over the entire circuit with
a series of revival meetings; but those plans were
never put into execution.   I had just gone once over
the round of appointments when I was taken sick
with what seemed like a fever.   After two or three
days, Dr. Maclean was called.   On examination he
prescribed for fever; but for several days there was
no change for the better.   The remedies did not seem
to produce the desired effect.   One day I called the
doctor's attention to a secret trouble that had been
slowly developing for years past, caused by an old
injury which had been received while breaking in an
unruly horse.   As soon as the doctor saw the true
state of the case, he said, "You may rely upon it,
that thing is at the bottom of all your present diffi-

culty.   Why did you not come to me about it sooner?
However, I will do the best I can now to help you;"
and the first thing he did was to perform a bit of
surgery. This gave at the time but a temporary
relief. For five months I was an invalid in the doctor's hand. Some of the time I could fill my work
in part, and at other times I could do nothing. In the
meantime my colleague, Mr. Thomas Love, worked
with all his might to keep up the interest of the work
on the circuit.   He held one series of revival meetings
alone, and there were a number of conversions.

As the summer advanced it became quite evident
that one of two things was inevitable. Either I must
submit to a very critical and tedious operation or give
up all hopes of a recovery. Believing as I do, that
men are in duty bound to live as long as they can in
this world, I concluded to take the chances of a dangerous operation.

Dr. Mackintosh, of Meaford, and Dr. Hunt. of Clarks-
burg, were called to assist Dr. Maclean in the difficult performance. After three hours and a half of
intensely anxious work, their task was completed, and
their patient alive; but my nervous system has never
fully rallied from the effects of that three and a half
hours under the influence of chloroform.

I have never been able to exercise the same amount
of self-control that I could before, and I have not the
same power of endurance; but still I have great
reason to be thankful to God for medical skill and
human kindness. Dr. Maclean could not have been
more kind and attentive if I had been his own brother.

Through all my afflictions, both of myself and family, during our seven years' residence in Meaford, he never accepted a single cent as remuneration for his services. Many an earnest prayer has gone up from my heart for the safety and happiness of the doctor and his family. Neither did the other two doctors exact any pay for the assistance they gave. The people, too, showed the greatest kindness to me and my family in our time of trouble. May the Lord reward them for it, and guide them to the home above where affliction and suffering are things unheard of.

REMOVAL TO KINCARDINE.

At the end of the Conference year I was sent to Kincardine. Three years of hard labour there, with health only partially restored, finished up my work in the active ranks of the itinerancy. My strength gave way so that I was compelled to take a superannuated relation to the Conference.

And yet three different medical men, after they had examined me, each one in his own office, said they could find no symptoms of organic disease or functional derangement. The whole system seemed to be run down. That was all that they could say. Dr. Secord, of Kincardine, said, in his blunt, outspoken manner. "You are like an old ox that is half starved through the winter and then overworked in the spring." I said, "Doctor, you have hit the truth, I think. But the starving is not for lack of food to eat, but it is for want of an appetite to eat it. I can hardly tell any difference in the taste of articles of diet, and I never get hungry. What I eat is forced down, for I know that I must eat or die." The doctor prescribed for me and in a few months I so far recovered as to be able to do some work both by preaching and otherwise.

But other trials and difficulties were in store for us. Our married daughter, Mrs. Prentice, had taken cold while cleaning out a new house that they had built, the plaster of which was only partially dry. The cold culminated in consumption. She lingered along for two years and then died, leaving behind her four children. Her home was at Heathcote. Our other daughter had been with her sister the most of the time of her illness, or about a year and a half. When she came home after the funeral, it was easy to see that the same disease had marked her for another victim. I said to my wife, "That new house is going to cost us both of our daughters." And so it came out at last.

But the summer that our second daughter died I passed through a strange experience. The first intimation that I had that anything was going wrong was a noise in my head that sounded like the dashing of the waves of the lake against the shore, or like men sawing with a cross-cut saw. After a few weeks I found my head getting dizzy. This grew on me very gradually, until I was unable to walk with steadiness. Then, in a few days more, a weakness seemed to seize upon every nerve and muscle of my body, and I was completely helpless. For four weeks I was in this condition. I was perfectly conscious, but I seemed to be living in the region of the purely emotional. I had but little control of my feelings. When any one came to see me it seemed to overcome me so that some-times I would weep like a child and could not tell what it was about. All this time I had not a particle of pain. When any one would ask me how I was, my answer generally was, " All right. A person that has no pain and no condemnation surely should have no complaints." My appetite was good ; food never tasted better than it did at that time, though my wife had to feed me like a child. The doctor told her from the first that my case was hopeless, but in this he was destined to be disappointed. At the end of the fourth week I told the doctor one day that I was getting bet-ter. At first he seemed incredulous, but after trying two or three tests, he said : " You really are getting better. I will come again in a day or two and see how you are, as I do not want you to take one dose of medicine more than is absolutely necessary. When he came to see me again I was out in the garden under the trees. When he came out to me he said ; " This is a most wonderful thing ; you are really going to get well."

I said to him : " Doctor, some of the people say that it is in answer to prayer."

" Well, well," said he, " it is in answer to something, but I think it is to be attributed to a good constitution and a sober life."

But it was after I could get up and stand on my feet that I found just how far down I had been. I was greatly taken by surprise one day when I took up a book to find that I could not read a single line. The letters seemed to run all together. I tried to write on

a piece of paper, but I could not make a single letter.
I would find myself sitting at the table with a knife
and fork and teaspoon in my hand. To decide which
of them I wanted to use would cost me a greater
mental effort than it ever did to frame the outline of a
sermon when I was well.

While my strength returned our sick daughter grew
worse, and on the twenty-fifth of August, 1882, she
went home. The last words she ever spoke on earth
were, " Jesus has come to take me home." While writing
this, I have in my desk the breastplates taken from
two coffins. On the one is carved, "Philura Maud
Prentice, died on the 22nd of November, 1879, aged 30
years and nine months." On the other are the words,
"Eliza Ann Hilts, died August 25th, 1882, aged 30
years." The bodies of these two sisters are sleeping,
one on the banks of the Georgian Bay, and the other
on the shores of Lake Huron, far apart. But their
spirits are among the shining ones along the banks of
the river of life.

Before leaving this part of my narrative I must
pause a little and bestow a just meed of praise on one
who has stood faithfully and courageously by me in
many a sore trial—one who, although she has her
foibles and weaknesses like other mortals, has on many
occasions exhibited the noblest characteristics of the
true wife and mother. During those dreary weeks
while I was lying helpless in one room, and our dying
daughter in another, my wife had the care of both of
us on her hands, and for seven weeks she never got
one night's rest in her bed.

I used to look at her and wonder how she could be so calm and composed under such an unusual strain both of body and mind. To be thus taxed to the utmost limit of human endurance and still remain so completely self-possessed, might be looked for in one whose heart was adamant and whose nerves were steel. But it could hardly be expected from a tender mother and a devoted, sympathising wife. But the Lord gives strength and grace for every emergency to those who trust in Him according to His word. I should have mentioned that for the three years past I had one appointment in the town every Sabbath. While I was laid up this time, Rev. Simon Terwilliger, who then resided in the town, kindly took the work for me until I got able to resume it.

ANOTHER BREAKDOWN.

Under the successful treatment of Dr. Secord I so far recovered that the next spring I undertook to assist Rev. D. L. Scarrow in the work on the circuit. It was arranged that I should take charge of the two eastern appointments, namely, Blackhorse and Kinlough.

I was to go out on the stage on Saturday, preach at both places on Sunday, and go home again on the stage any day that suited me. The proprietors of the stage —Messrs. John Kaake and Thomas Stewart—kindly allowed me to go out and in for single fare. Some one of the congregation would generally take me from one place to the other on the Sabbath. When this was not convenient I walked. I followed this up during the three summer months and I enjoyed it very much.

On the first Sabbath in September I was at my work apparently all right. In the morning I preached and led the class at Kinlough. Then Mr. John Nicols took me to the afternoon appointment where I preached and led the class again. Then I went home with Mr. Anderson, where I stayed all night. On Monday forenoon I went to Mr. Joseph Armstrong's, and I was around with him until the stage from Walkerton came along. Then I started for home. I felt as well as usual until we got within a mile of the little village of Bervie, seven miles from home. All of a sudden a sharp pain took me in the back of the neck just below the base of the brain. At first I thought but little about it, but in a few minutes it seemed to dart up into my head, and the pain became most excruciating. Then I turned sick and began to vomit as though I had had a large emetic.

As we came into the village I told the driver that I could not go home. He said if I would go on he would drive through as fast as the horses could go. I told him it was no use: I could not go on. He then asked me which hotel I wished to go to. I told him not to take me to either of them, saying, "I do not wish to die at a tavern, if I can help it. But take me to Mr. William Temple's; I think they will let me in." They were a young couple that I had married a few years before. When I came to the door, Mrs. Temple met me. I told her that I was too sick to go home, and must find a shelter somewhere. She helped me into the house and said they would do all they could for me.

I asked Mrs. Temple to call William and get him

to go for Dr. Bradley, who lived in Bervie, and then telegraph to her brother, Francis Sellery, to bring out my wife. That was five o'clock on Monday afternoon, and it is the last thing that I remember until Wednesday afternoon. It did seem to me that if all the pains that I had ever suffered were concentrated in one sharp hour it could not equal the intensity of anguish that I was enduring when I went into the house that day.

On Wednesday evening, about seven o'clock, I seemed to wake up out of sleep. It seemed to me that I had only a short nap; but I felt better. The pain in my head was nearly all gone. I thought that perhaps, I could get along without the doctor, as he had not come yet. I had not opened my eyes yet, and, supposing that I was still at Bervie, I was somewhat surprised to hear my wife and another woman of Kincardine talking in the next room. I thought, " How is this that they are here so soon ? " Just then I opened my eyes and, to my great astonishment, found myself in my own bed at home; but when or how I got there I had not the slightest idea. I called my wife, and asked her how long I had been home, and how I came. She said, " You have been here about and hour ; but don't you know how you came home ; don't you remember when we came to the gate and helped you out of the carriage, you said you could walk alone, and you came into the house and lay down on the bed." I had no remembrance of anything of the kind. In fact, those fifty hours seem to have gone and not left the faintest impression upon my memory, as I cannot recall a single thing that occurred during that time; but those around me all this time say that I was able to talk and answer any question just as well as ever. They were all greatly surprised when I told them that I could not remember what occurred.

Some time after I got better, I saw Mr. Temple, and he told me of some things that took place at his house. He said, "My wife sent for me to the shop and requested me to come at once and bring the doctor with me. I found him on the street, and we ran to my house as fast as we could. He looked at you for a minute or two, and then said, "Mr. Hilts, you are a very sick man." Mr. Temple said my reply was, "Doctor, I did not send for you to tell me that, for I knew all that before you came; but can you not give me something to ease this dreadful pain in my head?" The doctor said he could, and started to go out. When he got to the door, I called him back and said, "Doctor, what is the matter with me?" He said, "I cannot tell just yet; but it is a very severe attack of some kind." Then I said, "Well, doctor, the trouble is in the head; I had some kind of brain trouble last year, and Dr. Secord gave bromide of potassium."

Dr. Bradley was at a loss to know what to do. On Tuesday morning he went to see Dr. Secord, and when he told him about the case, he asked what he had given, and what was the effect produced. On being answered, he said to Dr. Bradley, "That old man ought to have died last year, according to all the declarations of medical science. You will see he will come through

this. You will find him better when you go back."
And so it proved to be.

After I got home, Dr. Secord attended me. I recovered very slowly, and had to give up all kinds of work for a while. In the meantime I moved from Kincardine to Streetsville. But one word more about Dr. Secord. He attended me and my family during the nine years of our residence in that town, and when I would ask him about his bill, he would turn off to some other subject; but before I left the place I told him I would like to know how matters stood between us. He said, "You owe me nothing; I am working my way to kingdom come by doctoring old ministers, free of charge." I hope he may succeed in reaching that place; but I also hope that he may not find another "old minister," or young one either, that will draw as largely on his good nature and his science as I have done. Success to him.

MORE SURGERY.

During the summer and fall of 1885, I felt that something was going wrong with me; I grew weak and lost in flesh; my appetite became poor and I seemed to be running down generally.

Then a severe and racking cough set in. My wife became uneasy, and sent for Dr. Ockley, of Streetsville. He came, and brought with him his son, Dr. Ockley, jun., who was home on a visit to his parents at the time. After examination, they said that the trouble was caused by a pleuritic affection of the right lung. In fact, the amount of aqueous fluid in the pleura was so great that it prevented almost entirely the action of the one lung, and pressed the other against the heart so as to dangerously interfere with its functions.

At first, it was decided to adopt the usual mode of treatment by blistering; but after taking into consideration the progress that the disease had already made, and the danger of a fatal termination unless relief was speedily afforded, they proposed a quicker method of treatment. To draw the water off with instruments was a shorter and less painful way of combating the disease than the old tedious and weakening process of a series of blisters. This plan was adopted, and it afforded relief in an hour, by removing from the lung seven imperial pints of water. The cure after this was rapid, and so far as can be ascertained now after ten months, it is permauent.

Dr. Ockley, like the others, would make no charge, only for medicine which was administered.

CRITICAL PERIODS.

People talk sometimes about the critical periods in life. We hear of one crisis here and another there as we are passing from the cradle to the grave. I think that I have gone through no less than four critical periods in the last twelve years. It is about that length of time since the affair in Meaford. And I was told, after that was all over, that three or four times during the operation the two younger doctors stepped back and said: "There is no use in doing any more; the man is dead." But Dr. Maclean thought otherwise, and so it proved. " But," said he, when he told me, " four or five times we had you down to the death line. There is not more than one in a thousand that would have lived through it."

At the time that I lay so long helpless in Kincardine, Dr. Secord told me, after I got better, that he had never known of any one getting well who was in the same condition that I had been in. When Dr. Bradley was called to see me at Bervie, he said to Mrs. Temple : "The old man will die at your house. He is too sick to be moved." And at the time of my last attack the doctors said it was very doubtful if I would have lived a week longer if I had not been relieved.

So, kind reader, you see that when, at the beginning of this chapter, I spoke of being a subject for the doctors to practice on, I was not talking at random. I know what it is to look my wife in the face and realize that she will very likely be a widow within an hour. When the chance of life is only as one in a thousand, it seems to be well-nigh hopeless, but human nature clings to that one chance till the last moment, and faith proclaims that, with a Divine hand to lead us, the one chance gives a safer and a stronger case than ten thousand to one in our favour could offer us without that hand. Who would not, in the time of trouble, like to feel the leading of that hand.

FAMILY AFFLICTIONS.

Besides my personal afflictions we have had our share of family troubles. We know what it is to look into the flushed and feverish faces of sick children and upon the cold and pallid features of dead ones. We know just what it means to sit alone at the bedside of our sick, and watch in silence for the end that seemed coming nearer as the weary hours passed slowly on. To wait for daylight and the kind-hearted doctor, as one listens to the low moanings of helpless sufferers, is not a desirable task, but we have had to do it. When we were stationed at Listowel our eldest son came home from his work sick with typhoid fever. This dangerous disease was very prevalent in the community; people were dying on every side. Our boy was very low. As the fever was running its course the symptoms became very alarming. The people on the circuit were afraid to come to the house. For seven weeks not one person entered our house except the doctor and one neighbour woman; but with the blessing of God upon his efforts, Dr. Pattison brought our boy through. He lived and is alive yet. A word about the woman who did what others feared to do. She was an Englishwoman, only out a short time. She used to come in and help my wife every day, as she was not in good health at the time. When asked if she was not afraid of catching the fever, she would say: " I can't let any one suffer for want of help while I can help them, and I don't believe that any one dies any sooner for doing one's duty." We have often spoken of Mrs. Edmond Binning.

THREE TO CARE FOR.

The next winter after our boy was sick our eldest girl was taken down with the same fever. Again people were afraid to come to the house. My wife was sick and confined to the bed, too, and there was a baby about a month old to be cared for. Our friend Mrs. Binning was herself in poor health, but she did what she could, and between us we managed to go on in some way for three weeks, when I succeeded in getting a girl to help in the work. All this time I had my appointments to meet. With the help of Bro. James Vines and his brother Richard, two good local preachers, the work was fully done, and the circuit sustained no loss because of my home troubles. The next spring Mrs. Binning took diphtheria. My wife returned to her the kindness she had shown to us, in part and in kind.

A Dislocated Joint.

When we lived in Thornbury we kept a cow. My wife always made her own butter when she could. Like many other women, she is hard to please in that important part of table supplies, and like others also she is somewhat conceited about her own ability to make a good article. I have never disputed with her on that point, for I thought she was not very far astray in her ideas about the matter. Our cow was pasturing in a field a little distance from the house. One morning my wife took the pail as usual and went out to milk. In getting over some poles she stepped on one that rolled, and put her ankle out of joint. She was near the cow. After she met with the mishap she concluded that she would get the milk anyway. In going up to the cow she made another misstep, and

sprung the ankle to its place again. However, she
did the milking, after which she hobbled to the house
in some way. When I saw her face as she came in
I was frightened. She was as pale as a dead person
and nearly wild with pain. She did not walk a step
for over a month. I took her to see Dr. Maclean in
Meaford. He said the ankle had been out of joint,
but had sprung back by a sudden twist that had been
a terrible strain on the tendons. That ankle was weak
and troublesome for several years.

A Broken Bone.

I was away on a three weeks' round of quarterly
meetings. During the last week I was conducting a
camp-meeting at Melville, on the Orangeville Circuit.
There was a good work done at the meeting, but toward the last I became very uneasy about home. I
had heard nothing since I left, and I felt almost certain that something was wrong.

We closed the meeting about four in the afternoon. I
went to where my horse was and hitched up and started
for home. I drove twenty miles that evening. Next
morning I started and went twelve miles before breakfast. In fact, I went home just as fast as my horse
would take me. When I arrived and drove up to
the door I heard my wife moaning before I got out
of the buggy. I went in, and on inquiring what was
the matter I found that she had got her collar-bone
broken the week before. It happened in this way:
She was milking the cow at the door. Some boys
came along snapping a whip. The cow got scared and

made a sudden jump. The woman could not get out of the way soon enough. She fell over. The cow stepped on her and bruised her face and broke the collar-bone just at the top of the shoulder. Dr. Maclean was called at the time, did all that could be done, and left directions charging her not to use that arm and to keep perfectly quiet. She had gone to knitting and had got things displaced, and was afraid to call the doctor again because she had disobeyed him.

As soon as I found the condition of things I hurried up street for the doctor. He was away in the country. I went to a druggist and got the best liniment he could make. The shoulder, when I looked at it, was spotted purple and green. I applied the remedy and in twenty minutes she found relief, and went off to sleep, which she greatly needed, as she had but little since she was hurt. I never knew what were the ingredients of that liniment, but it was a first-class thing.

When I asked why no word was sent to me, the children said their mother would not allow them to send to let me know for fear it would disturb me and interfere with my work at the camp-meeting. I think that I have said enough for the present about doctors and doctoring.

CHAPTER XV.

REMEMBERED KINDNESS.

IT may be difficult to tell whether acts of kindness or deeds of injury imprint themselves more indelibly upon the memory, but it is not hard to settle the question as to which of the two should exert the greater influence on our actions. To cherish the remembrance of past injuries so as to influence our actions only tends to harden the heart and warp the character; so that in doing this we harm ourselves and only make matters worse. We thereby sustain a double injury—first, by the harmful act, and secondly, by remembering the act in such a way as to produce in us a sort of moral deformity. Thus we magnify into a life-long injury what should have been only a temporary grievance or a short-lived vexation. We may remember those who have wilfully and spitefully injured us as we would remember a rock that had once upset our boat—not with the intention of using dynamite, but with a desire to keep at a safe distance from it.

We must cherish feelings toward those who have injured us that will prompt us to help them if we can, and do them good when we can ; but that does not mean that we must hug them to our hearts. But the grateful remembrance of acts of kindness has a softening influence upon the heart, and it exerts an elevating tendency of character. There is nothing low or degrading in cherishing the remembrance of kindly deeds, and there is nothing in the acknowledging of them that is either dishonourable or humiliating ; but it is only doing sinple justice to the performers of kindly actions to let them know that the recipients of those kindnesses are neither forgetful nor ungrateful.

With these views and for these reasons I shall, in this chapter, speak of the many acts of kindness shown to me and mine during the thirty years since I entered the Christian ministry. Many of these acts were unexpected, and most of them were either entirely unmerited or only partially deserved.

As I have intimated elsewhere, when I went on the backwoods missions I had some means of my own, the results of hard work by myself and wife; but we also had a number of children to which three more were added within a few years after commencing our itinerant life. The country at the time was new, the people were mostly poor, and the Church members were few. Every family had their own difficulties to grapple with, and the minister had to take his full share of the burdens that always settle down on the shoulders of pioneers ; and the lengthened period that I had to face these difficulties makes my case an exceptional one.

Other men were sent into the new parts of the work.

They would be left there a few years, and then be brought out to the front. But for some 'reason I was kept there from first to last. There was not another instance in the Church that I belonged to where a man was kept on one District through twenty-two years of active service, and that District the hardest one in the Connexion, in more ways than one. If there was such another case, I never heard of it.

After our own means were gone, if it had not been for the kindness shown to us from time to time by church members and others, we should have suffered more than we did. I might almost as well undertake to number the hairs left on my head as to recount all the kindly deeds done to us. I shall have to content myself by giving a few details.

A Generous Irishman.

I use the term Irishman simply to indicate a man who came from Ireland. The man I speak of was a Protestant, an Orangeman, and a Methodist local preacher. At the time I speak of he resided in the township of Howick, and was a member of the Official Board on the Teeswater mission, on which I was stationed. His name was William Ekins.

When our first Quarterly Meeting came on he was present at the business meeting on Saturday. That was the year of the hard summer, that the older people still talk about in the back townships when the Government had to send provisions to hundreds of families to keep them from starvation. Not being a taxpayer, I was not in a position to ask for help in that way. The result was that we were one month without a bit of bread in the house. We had a very little johnny cake. But we had plenty of greens, consisting of cooked "cow cabbage." We also had a good supply of speckled trout, when we could catch them, and butter was to be had at reasonable figures.

Mr. Ekins came to our place for dinner. Two of our children were bad with cholera-infantum, induced, as was supposed, by the diet they were forced to live on. My friend brought with him one-half of a good sized veal, which he carried on horseback a long distance. He said when he came in with it, " I heard that you were trying to live on cattle feed, so I thought I would bring you a piece of one of them. I see that these little fellows of yours don't take to that sort of diet very readily."

On Monday morning, before he started, he said to me, " I do not see 'how you are to get along with all these children without milk. We have more cows than we need, and you may just as well have one of them as not; send the two boys home with me, and I will send a cow, and a boy to help drive it home, to-morrow." We took his offer without much pressing. The cow was brought and proved to be a good one. I offered to pay him for her, but he would take nothing, saying that when he gave a thing he never would take pay for it. We kept that cow for five or six years, and then she got poisoned in some way and died.

Our First Surprise Party.

We had been presented with donations at different places and in various ways. But the first real genuine "surprise party" that paid us a visit was in Meaford. We were living there, but my work was, at the time, on the District as Presiding Elder.

One evening I was sitting quietly by the stove planning a new round of quarterly meetings, when a rap came to the door. On opening it, in answer to the call, an old minister of the New Connexion Methodists came in. His name was Hamilton, and he lived only a few doors from where I did. The old man sat down, and made himself quite at home— a thing he had never done before. We sat and talked for an hour or more. At last a loud rap at the front door called me up again. As I was going to the door Mr. Hamilton said, very soberly, "Don't be frightened, Brother Hilts; I am sure no harm is intended." I could not understand what he meant until I opened the door and looked out. Then I began to see through the old man's little ruse. The yard was full of people. They made a simultaneous rush for the front and side doors, and in less than two minutes the house was full of as merry a talking, laughing and stamping multitude as ever carried their good nature and their baskets into a quiet, inoffensive man's dwelling. And for the next hour or two

It was hard to conjecture what they were about,
For upstairs, and downstairs, and indoor and out,
Their hands and their feet and their tongues were all going,
And one must be smart to know what they were doing.

But after awhile, when things quieted down,
They declared they had come from all parts of the town,
To present a small gift to the preacher and wife,
And to wish them success in the journey of life.

The gift was about forty dollars in cash, and any amount of good wishes, and some other things, all of which were highly appreciated, not more for the value of the gifts than for the generous, kindly spirit in which they were presented.

My friends in Meaford became very well posted in the matter of getting up these surprises to the ministers. I think I was subjected to four or five of them myself, but I managed to live through all of them, and never once said, "Don't do it again." I was present at one that was given to Brother Watts. He was taken completely by surprise. I never saw Watts so much confused before or since.

A Thoughtful Friend.

The question has sometimes been asked, "Does the Lord influence the kindly deeds of unconverted people?" I believe that He does. He tries to get men to do right: in doing so He touches the noblest impulses of the heart, and the loftiest faculties of the mind. He does not attempt to prompt a man to virtuous action by stimulating the lowest and meanest of his passions. These He holds in check while, through the potency of the Holy Spirit acting upon the higher nature of the man, God lifts him out of darkness into light, and places him on a higher plane of action than he occupied before. But where am I drifting to ?

At the commencement of my long affliction in Meaford, of which mention is made elsewhere, a little
occurrence took place which I will venture to relate.

I had only been on the circuit one month and no
returns had yet come in. Our supplies at the time
were very limited and my purse was nearly empty. I
had been worried some about the matter. One day
Mr. John Raymond called to see me. After sitting a
short time he got up to go. Then turning to me he
said :

"You are laid up. You have had no time to gather
supplies since Conference. Perhaps a little help now
would be worth as much to you as it would be at any
time in the year." With this he handed me a sum of
money. I would never have believed that the recep-
tion of a few dollars could make so sudden a change
in a person's feelings and prospects, if I had not experienced it. I received it, not only as a kind and
thoughtful act on the part of my friend, but I took
it as coming from the Lord. I looked upon it as a
pledge that, whether my sickness was of a short or
long duration, the supplies would be forthcoming.
And so it was. Though for five months, to a great extent, I was disabled, yet we were as fully and to all
appearance as cheerfully provided for as if I was doing all that needed to be done. Mr. Raymond was not
a professor of religion. His wife, however, was a
member of the Church.

A Pleasant Send-Off.

There is no time, it seems to me, when friends are more highly valued than when we are about to be separated from them. I found this to be the case when I was ordered by the Church authorities to leave Meaford.

I had lived in that beautiful town for seven years out of the last ten. According to the discipline and usage of the Church I could have stayed longer, but the Stationing Committee, listening to the few instead of the many, resolved to send me to another place. In doing this they acted in opposition to a petition bearing nearly three hundred signatures of members and adherents living on the circuit. But this is an unpleasant theme, and I do not like to dwell upon it.

When it was decided that I was to go away to another place, a meeting was called to be held in the church. This was largely attended by a mixed company, representing nearly every church in the town. After a number of short speeches from those who wished to speak, a purse containing sixty dollars was handed to me to pay, as they said, my moving expenses.

This was the third special favour bestowed on me by the friends in that community, during that year of heavy burdens and severe afflictions.

When I look back to that year, it appears to me like an April day, when sunshine and shadows chase each other over the fields. Sometimes the shadows deepened until the light seemed almost gone, and then the sunshine would make things bright and cheerful again. I should have said that the Conference met in Meaford that year, and the petition above referred to was presented by officials of the church in person. I may say, in respect to the town of Meaford, that if all gifts and donations were to be added to medical attendance, for which no charge was made, the sum total could not be less that $400.

What No One Expected.

When we went to Thornbury to live, the prospects were anything but encouraging. The church that I represented was weak in the village, and by no means strong in the country appointments. We went there as a sort of forlorn hope to try to rally a failing cause, but I was encouraged by the fact that there were a few grand men on the mission. When the Financial Committee met they promised me four hundred dollars and a house, the house-rent to be raised by a tea-meeting, and the surplus, if any, to be given as a donation. After the amount was voted, the next question was, Where is it to come from ? This was met by a proposal to see how much could be pledged there and then. In response to this John Loree put down $30 ; his brother William, $20 ; Dean Carscadden, $20 ; Peter Stoutenburgh, $20 ; James Maguire, $12 ; William Housten, $15 ; Jesse Gould, $15 ; Nelson Hurd, $12. When they added these sums together they found that they had almost three-fifths of the amount they needed, besides the grant from the Mission Fund. But these men made up nearly the whole male membership on the mission. But we were all encouraged to do the best we could. During the year we had two revivals. That was the first time in my ministry that I received all that was voted me. But that year I got every cent promised. To be sure it was a small salary on which to support a family of seven. But we managed to get through.

On Christmas Day they had their tea-meeting. They got it up on the old-fashioned plan of collecting provisions and cooking them, and then paying for the privilege of eating them. When it was over and we came to count results, between a surplus of edibles collected and not cooked and money on hand, it amounted to the nice sum of $130. This was $70 more than was needed to pay house-rent.

Who would not work, and suffer too, if need be, for such a people ? During my three years on that charge I did a good deal of hard work. But I was encouraged by much kindness shown me by the people. Brother Joseph Parkinson, who came to the mission during my second year, always seemed to know just what was needed and to bring it just when it was needed. Sister Wilson, of Heathcote, had a quiet and unpretentious way of showing kindness that was as amusing as it was thoughtful. She would never ask any questions, but watch her chance, and when no one was looking, slip a piece of meat, a roll of butter, a pound of yarn, or something else of use in a family under the seat of the buggy or cutter. For many years her house was the home of the preachers at the Heathcote appointment. I became so well acquainted

with that good sister's way of doing that I always
looked under the seat when I got home, if I had been
at her place. She is in glory now.

William James Kennedy and Joseph Bell, two young
men who were not then professors of religion, spent
one of the stormiest days of winter in gathering up
something for the preacher. They came to our house
in a blinding snowstorm, with a load of supplies, just
when we had cut the last loaf of bread and cooked
the last piece of meat. Mr. Adam Goodfellow and his
wife, although they were Presbyterians, showed me a
great deal of kindness. Mrs. B. J. Marsh used to come
and pay her dividend herself, if for any cause the
steward failed to call on her for it.

No one knows how to appreciate actions of this
kind better than· the itinerant in the new country,
where a little help at the right time does so much to
strengthen and encourage him in his work. By
dwelling so long on one circuit, I find that I am
using up my paper faster than I am exhausting my
subject. I fear I shall be obliged, for want of space, to
pass unmentioned very many kindly acts that would
be worthy of notice; but they are recorded on more
enduring pages than those of my little book.

It was while I was travelling the District that I
realized fully what Christian hospitality really means.
Five days out of six the year round, I was away from
my own home, and the most of this time I was dependent for entertainment for myself and horse upon the
members and friends of the Church; but in all the
homes I visited during these four years, I was not

once made to feel that I was not welcome. I think I realized a literal fulfilment of our Lord's promise of a hundred homes for one that is relinquished in His service. I never counted them, but I am confident that I had more than a hundred homes on the Huron District.

I will find room for the names of the more prominent owners of these homes, and I am sorry that I cannot make room for all. Commencing with Eramosa Circuit, the first name that occurs to me is Rev. F. M. Smith and family; then come J. Caspell, E. Loree, Wm. Hodgkinson, J. Copland, Geo. Copland, Bro. Ruddell, J. Leslie, Jno. Greasley, B. Rossel, two brothers Morris and old Father Scarrow.

Garafraxa Circuit—Morris Cook, W. Neal, Jas. Loree, Wm. Woods, Wm. Cotton, Jno. Cowan, H. Scarrow, Jno. Mitchel, Rev. R. L. Tindall, Mrs. D. Kyle, Mrs. Burns, W. Felker, J. Felker, A Felker, A. Ferrier, D. Ferrier, Jas. Kennedy and R. Eviligh.

Orangeville—James Johnston, Jas. Putellow, G. Moot, A. Hughson, Jas. Hughson, Wm. Hall, A. Wilcox, G. Wilcox, Rev. R. Large, M. Bacon, Wm. Bacon, Wm. Morris, Jas. McEcknie and Bro. Shields.

Horning's Mills—Mr. Silk, Wm. Blair, Thompson Brothers, Mrs. Watts, Mr. Hulbert, Bro. Scruten, John Silk, G. Broderick, Mr. Tupling and Mr. Siddell.

Creemore—Jno. Shields, Jas. Connor, Mr. Sinclair, Rev. W. M. Pomeroy, Mr. Casey, and others whose names I have forgotten.

Collingwood Circuit—Rev. J. F. Durkee, Jos. Parkinson, D. Carscadden, Jos. Conn, Jesse Gould, P. Stoutenburgh, Mr. Wagg, Wm. Housten, Wm. Kennedy, A. Goodfellow, Jno. Irwin, T. Carefoot, G. Wilson, R. Phillips, L. Prentice, J. Prentice, N. Devens, Jno. Conn, Mrs. Perrett.

Meaford South—R. Gilray, Jas. Thurston, Wm. Purdy, R. M'L. Purdy, Jas. Curry, R. Hopkins, Rev. C. Taylor, Rev. J. Foster, J. Cook, Geo. Reid and A. Gould.

Meaford North—Jos. Briggs, Wm. Raven, S. L. Wilcox, N. Lefler, S. Kirvin, E. Kerr, H. Kerr, Jas. Lemon, and Rev. R. Sanderson. My home being in Meaford, I did not require the hospitalities of the people in town; their kindness was shown in other ways.

Osprey Mission—Ben Smith, Mr. Ferguson, Mr. Gordon, Mr. Little, Jas. Alister, Rev. A. Cooper and Rev. T. Reid.

Mount Forest—Rev. R. Carson, Jno. Boos, Thos. Reid, A. Bissell, E. Boosley, T. Smith, Mrs. Buchan, Mr. Shilton, H. Bennett, Jno. Dixon, Jos. Dickson, Jno. Dickson and G. Stinson.

Listowel—Rev. John W. Moore, G. Maynard, Thos. Maynard, M. Tremain, H. Barber, Rev. Jas. Vines, R. Vines, H. Leopard, Wm. Kellington, Chas. Cousens, H. Cousens, C. Switzer, J. Rossell, D. Collins, C. Zeron.

Teeswater—Rev. W. F. Ferrier, P. Brown, G. Parr, R. Parr, Thos. Fairbairn, R. Dowse, R. Copland, R. Barber, Jas. Williamson, Wm. Cross, J. Snider, J. Gilroy, J. Crowsten, Jas. Crowsten, Wm. Bradley, G. McKibbon.

Invermay—J. W. Sanderson. J. W. Dunn, S. Cummer, J. Cummer, B. Talbot, Wm. Scarrow, Jas. Scarrow,

Wm. Carry, D. Clemens, Thos. Clemens, A. Clemens, S. Winch, S. Bricker, R. Zimmerman and Thos. Thompson.

Kincardine—Rev. G. Clark, E. Fisher, S. Fisher, Jas. Ballantine, R. Hunter, Henry Daniels, Thos. Robinson, A. Robinson, J. Browning, Jos. Shier, J. Shier, W. Arnold, Jno. Harrison, N. Pennell, Mr. Cole and Jno. Hodgins.

Hanover—Rev. J. Lynch, Wm. Martin, G. Harrison, J. W. Vickers, R. Reid, Mr. Rea, Mr. Rumley, U. Curtis, J. Hillis, Dr. Halstead, Sam. Hillis and J. Wilson.

This long list of names includes the families with whom I took up my abode more or less during my District work. When I commenced my term, the Rev. H. Dockham said to me, "If you try to play the pastor over all that large District, you will be played out before your four years are past." Although I visited many families not named here, I never felt that I was doing any more than the duties of the office demanded. I received many acts of kindness both from the people and ministerial brethren during these four years. These were crowned by the presentation of a " purse " at conference at the conclusion of the term.

Help When Needed.

In the town of Kincardine our circumstances at one time were very trying. I was lying entirely helpless. For four weeks I could not so much as feed myself or lift my head off the pillow, and the last one of our daughters lay in another room dying with consumption. She had been an invalid for nearly three years, and the end was now coming very near. I had, some time before, bought a little home, and had invested in it every dollar that I could muster. Now, when the extra expenses of sickness and death had to be met, we were very ill prepared to do so. When the people of the town learned of our sore affliction there seemed to be a disposition on the part of all classes, irrespective of creed or party, to render assistance.

The Presbyterians and Canada Methodists, following the examples of their respective ministers—the Rev. J. L. Murray and Rev. A. Andrews—came forward with their sympathy and help. Others, prompted by their own generous impulses, did their share in trying to lighten our heavy burdens. But I cannot speak of the many acts of kindness shown us by individuals for want of space.

Rev. Dr. Aylesworth, the presiding elder, came to the Quarterly Meeting, and when he saw how we were situated he of his own accord sent a short note to the *Canada Christian Advocate*, stating our case and asking the prayers of the Church. I suppose the praying was done, but that was not all that was done. A number of letters came to hand, containing sums ranging from one to fifteen dollars. One letter came from near Ottawa from a lady that I had never heard of. It contained a contribution of two sisters-in-law who saw the note in the paper. I am sorry that I cannot recall their names. Another letter came from a Sabbath-school in the township of Euphrasia, at a place where I formerly preached. The superintendent, Mr.

Milson, told the school about our trouble and took up
a collection amounting to thirteen dollars. From every
circuit on the Huron District, except two or three,
more or less money came, and also from people on
other Districts. One letter, containing a bill of paper
money, came from Eugenia Falls, from a sickly man
with a large family and not very much means. I
valued that contribution very highly, knowing as I did
the sacrifice that it required on the part of the generous donor to send even a small amount. I estimated
that gift not by the amount that it was worth to the
receiver, but by what I knew it cost the sender.

A Christmas Box.

At Christmas time one evening, while I was away
from home, two men came to our door and handed my
wife a letter. When I opened it I found that it contained a sum of money and a note asking me to accept
a "Christmas box" from a few of my friends in the
Presbyterian congregation worshipping in Knox's
Church, Kincardine. Two or three days after Christmas, as I was walking down the street, Mr. John Mc-
Leod, a merchant and a Presbyterian, called me into
his store and presented me with an overcoat worth
fourteen dollars.

Another Surprise.

Then in February of that same winter came the
greatest surprise of all. One day the Bruce *Reporter*
was left at our house. In glancing over it I saw a
notice to the effect that on a certain evening a lecture

would be given in the Town Hall, at which time the friends of Mr. Hilts would present him with an *address* and a *purse.* I could hardly believe my eyes, as that was the first intimation I received that anything of the kind was in contemplation. When I read the extract over to my wife, she said she had heard something about a surprise, but she knew but little about it. When the time came the Rev. William Henderson gave an interesting lecture on the Holy Land to a fair audience. Mr. Baird, then reeve, afterwards mayor, of the town, filled the chair. After the lecture a purse containing one hundred and sixty-eight dollars was presented to me by Mr. E. Leslie, who was a Canada Methodist; and Mr. Paul McInnis, a Presbyterian, read the following address :—

COMPLIMENTARY ADDRESS

Presented to Rev. J. H. Hilts by a number of Christian friends and well-wishers.

Rev. and Dear Sir,—It is with pleasure we embrace the present opportunity of expressing to you the high esteem in which you are held by ourselves and the community generally. You have been amongst us for a number of years, making your presence felt in a social, municipal and ministerial character, and in all these respects you have won the profound regard and confidence of your fellow-citizens of whatever party or creed. Your manly independence as a thinker and speaker, your fearless denunciation of popular wrongs, your kindly consideration and sympathy for those in distress, and your uniform readiness to rise above narrow sectarianism, and to assist your brethren of every denomination in the work of our common Lord, have greatly endeared you to Christians of every name and have secured for you a place in the hearts of the general public to which few can expect to attain. As a token of the estimation in which you are held, you will please accept this purse, which is the spontaneous gift of a number of your fellow-citizens who desire to make this public recognition of their sense of your personal worth, and which but very feebly expresses their admiration for your many excellences of head and heart. Signed on behalf of contributing friends.

PAUL MCINNIS.
EDWARD LESLIE.*

Kincardine, Feb. 13th, 1883.

It is not egotism that prompts me to insert this address. It is too late in life for me to be much affected by what people may think or say about me, so that I am not seeking for notoriety. I never was a hunter after popularity. But I feel that justice to others warrants the publication of the address in this chapter of remembered kindness.

The article, I am informed, was written by Rev. J. L. Murray, a Presbyterian minister, and the money was collected by men outside of my own denomination. The circumstance goes to show that our religion can carry people over the dividing lines of denominational differences and cause them to recognize a brother wherever they find a Christian.

* Mr. Leslie is now the Mayor.

A Birthday Present.

The day that I was sixty years old some of the members of the Ontario Conference of the late M. E. Church, along with other friends, presented me with a purse containing some $50, as a birthday gift. This was a very unexpected expression of brotherly kindness and Christian generosity, which afforded me much pleasure, and bound me still closer to my brethern of the Conference.

A Reluctant Removal.

In the spring of 1884 we left Kincardine and came to Streetsville. I very much regretted that I had to leave that town, where so many pleasant associations had been formed. But to all appearance my health was permanently broken up. My family thought that we could better our condition by making the change. When we came to this place we found ourselves once more among strangers. With the exception of two of our sons, who were employed here at the time, we only knew the Scruten family, with whom I had been acquainted at Horning's Mills, and Mrs. Dr. Thom, whom we had known as a young girl years ago in the township of Garafraxa.

In the fall of 1885 I had a very severe affliction, elsewhere spoken of. When I found myself compelled to give up, and take to my bed, I felt very much disheartened. I said to my wife, as she was fixing a place for me to lie down : "I am afraid that we are in for a hard time. The boys are gone and we are here among strangers. If we were in the back counties among our many friends, I would feel safer and better."

Her answer was, " We will not suffer here any more than we would anywhere else."

The boys had to leave to find employment, the business with which they had been connected having been discontinued. Well, it turned out as my wife said. When the doctor came to see me, after an examination he asked why he had not been called sooner.

I told him that I hesitated to send for him because I could not see how I was to pay him for his trouble. He said : " I am afraid you have put it off too long. But pay or no pay, I shall do the best I can for you." And he did as he said. Dr. Ockley is spoken of in another chapter.

After an absence from the prayer-meeting for ten weeks, the first time that I went I met with a great surprise. After the meeting was ended, the pastor, Rev. G. M. Brown, invited me to the platform, and after a few words of explanation, he handed me an envelope which, he said, contained some contributions by friends on the circuit to help us bear the financial part of our recent afflictions.

When I got home and opened the envelope, I found the amount in it to be $80. To this over $20 was added by individuals who came in person with their Christian, kindly help.

I have been told the wife of the pastor, with Mrs. J. Gradon, Mrs. Banin, and the junior minister, Rev. R. P. Bowles, had something to do with getting this timely help for us. Among those others may be named Mr. G. Anderson, Mr. A. Sibbald, Mr. Redman, Mr. Dracas, Mrs. Hardy, and Rev. J. A. Murray, of Streetsville, and Mr. Wm. Falconer, and Mr. and Mrs. H. Shaver, of Cooksville Circuit. Before passing on, it is only right to say that we have received many acts of kindness from Mrs. and Miss Franklin, also from Barber Brothers, of Toronto township.

OWEN SOUND CONFERENCE.

With one more instance I must close this chapter. The first Conference of the united Church that I attended was held in the town of Owen Sound in 1885. At that session I asked for permission to commute my claim on the Superannuation Fund. The reason that I wished to do so was because of the difficulty I found in meeting the requirements of the " Basis of Union " in the matter of "levelling up." I stated my case fully and without reserve to my brethren. The request was granted, but I was strongly advised not to commute.

As I went out on the street at the rising of Conference, I was accosted by the mayor of the town, Mr. Rutherford. He said :

I was pleased with your straightforward manner of presenting your case. What I want to know is this: Will you accept some help if it is offered by friends who would like to assist you ? "

I said to him, " I am not above receiving a favour when it is kindly offered, nor am I slow to confer a favour when in my power to do so."

I heard no more about it until the last day of Conference. Then I was told that some parties outside

wished to see me.   When I went out I met Mr. Rutherford, Mr. J. W. Vickers, from Durham, and Rev. J.
W. Sanderson. They handed me a roll of bills amounting to $60.

That met my pressing demands at the time, and
somehow, it seems to me that a blessing followed that
gift, as I have got along to the present without com-
muting, and with no very serious difficulty.

CHAPTER XVI.

LIFE ON THE RAIL.

IT is not the fence-rail, nor the bed-rail, nor the stair-rail that is the subject of this chapter, but I speak of a longer and stronger rail than any of these. It is the iron or steel rail on which the steam-horse draws his ponderous load. That load is sometimes dead and sometimes living freight. It is of the latter kind that I have a few thoughts to offer.

Dr. Thomas Dick said, some sixty years ago, "that the time would come when the inhabitants of a village could be carried over the hills and valleys at the rate of twenty miles an hour. But people called him daft; yet he was right after all, only his figures were far too low.

Shortly after the trains began to run on the Great Western Railway, a neighbour of mine, Jacob Kerr, of Caistor, went to Hamilton, and for the first time in his life saw a train in motion. When I asked him what it looked like, he said: "I can compare it to nothing that I have seen; but if you can imagine all the houses on one side of a village street to be chasing each other, about as fast as a horse can run, you will get an idea of what a train in motion is like."

Now every one is familiar with the sight of moving trains; even the cattle and horses in the fields have become so accustomed to the rattle of the cars and the screaming of the engines that they pay but little attention to them. In fact, their familiarity has brought contempt that has cost the life of many a farmer's horse or cow. Dr. Dick's prediction has become an everyday fact. There is not a day that passes, except the Sabbath, from the beginning of the year to the end of the year, that there are not people enough living in the cars to fill a large city. This is what I meant by "life on the rail."

I know of no situation in which a student of human nature has a better chance to gain an insight into the great variety there is in people's proclivities than is afforded in a railway train filled with passengers. There everybody is away from home, and yet everybody is trying to feel perfectly at home. There conventionalities are laid aside, and people indulge in a freedom of social intercourse that would not be tolerated in other places. The car is the greatest leveller that we find in modern society, unless it be a town or village fire. That brings people together in a way that is sometimes laughable.

In a town where I once lived one day about ten o'clock in the morning the fire-bell sent its warning peals ringing through the place until every home was visited by its echoes. The fire was in a large building on the principal street. In a few minutes hundreds of people were there—men, women and children. One man came running out of his shop and another from his store. One woman, who was putting clothes on the line, ran to the fire with a clothes-pin in her hand. Another woman was dusting the parlour when the bell rang, and she carried her broom with her. One came with a dish-cloth in her hand, and another, who was cutting meat for dinner, carried a large butcher knife with her to the fire. After the burn was over there was a good deal of merriment among the women about the hurried manner in which they had left their homes. At length the conclusion was reached that a fire was a good thing to bring people together, and let them see what their neighbours are doing. But after this digression I must return to "life on the rail."

The first subject of our studying of character shall be the officials called the conductors. These men are very important factors in making up the aggregate of a travelling company; and they present so many different types of manhood that it is not easy to believe them all to belong to the same fraternity, and were it not for their dress and duties, we should take them for entirely opposite classes of persons. One is all kindness and good-nature; ready to give assistance in every way in his power. The smallest child is treated with as much courtesy as the strongest man; and the oldest and plainest lady receives as much con-sideration as the prettiest and sprightliest woman on

22

the train, at the hands of this gentlemanly official. This man has everybody for his friend, and travellers like to go on his train, and will do so when they can. Then there is another conductor who is the very reverse of this. He feels his importance, and he makes other people feel it too. His face is never very pleasant to look at, but it can get up a scowl at a minute's notice if some luckless passenger happens to say or do anything that is not provided for in the rules of service. He is the one that every man hopes will be on some other train than the one he is going on. A third conductor comes in between these two, and has some of the habits of both. When he is in good humour, he is all that is nice ; he is then as sweet as honey, and pliable as the down on the chin of green sixteen. But when he is a little out of tune, he is as snarly and crabbed as a Scotch terrier with a chestnut burr in his ear. This is the man of whom people will say, as they go into the car: "Well, I do hope the conductor is in sunshine to-day." There are other varieties and modifications, but these are the leading samples that have come under my notice during the years that I have more or less studied "life on the rail."

Our next subject for contemplation will be found among the passengers, and here an almost endless variety presents itself to our view. All kinds of people in all sorts of dress, and representing every class of society, are here thrown into each other's company without any regard to social standing or political and religious differences. Here wealth and poverty meet on the same level. Innocence and guilt are in the same

range.   Modesty and impudence are face to face.
Pollution and purity look through the same window.
Pride and humility sit in the same seat.   And age and
childhood drink out of the same cup.

But let us take a little while to study individual
cases.   See that young man just coming into the car.
The one with a small satchel in one hand, and a little
cane in the other.   See his nice little moustache, and
how tightly his clothes fit him, and his hair is parted
in the middle like his mother's.   I don't think he has
any sisters.   He is what was called a dandy in my
young days.   I believe he is called a " dude " now.
He is by no means a dangerous person.   He thinks
too much of himself to run any great personal risk, and
he has too high an opinion of his own worth to do
anything that is really low, vulgar, or mean.   He is
quite harmless, in fact ; he is useful in a certain way :
he is to young ladies what a tin rattle is to children,
viz., a source of amusement.

But look toward the other end of the car.   There is
a man of an entirely different make-up from the "dude."
I refer to that big, red-faced man who is filling one
seat with his immense person and another with his
personal effects.   He thinks a good deal of himself.
But he is not much troubled about what other people
think of him.   It makes but little difference to him if
half a dozen women are standing for want of room to
sit down.   He does not think of moving his traps
until the conductor gently reminds him that one
sitting is all that he has paid for, and that three
sittings in a crowded car is a little too much of a

gratuity to one passenger. See with what an injured air he moves his property, and looks daggers at the two ladies who take the released seat. Do you ask who is he? I cannot tell you. But if I were going to define him, I should say that he is a sort of compromise between a beer barrel and a travelling cigar shop.

But, see, there is another character that is worth a passing thought. It is that little man near the middle of the car. He is just now talking to the big man with a bald head and sandy whiskers. He likes to talk with men larger than himself. He feels a sort of security in their presence. Look sharply at him. You can see conceit in his very looks and hear it in every tone of his voice. I dare say that he is now telling the big man of some feat of activity or strength in which either himself or some of his friends have acted a leading part. Deeds of daring and acts of prowess are among everyday occurrences in his active and venturesome life. And yet, perhaps, if the truth were known, this same little man never scared anybody very much, and never hurt anyone worse than he could do by bragging over them. But the train stops, and the little man goes out. Soon the conductor calls out "all aboard," and we are on the move once more.

Short as our stop has been, it has given time for a new passenger to come into the car. This time it is a woman—a modest, timid, trembling, self-depreciating little woman. She comes in as if she was not sure that she had a right there, although she has bought and paid for a ticket which she still holds in her hand.

See how wistfully she looks over the seats as if hoping
to find an empty seat, and yet fearing to do so. There
is only one vacant sitting, the other end being taken
up by a big boy, who looks as if he were in strange
surroundings. "Is this seat engaged, please?" The
question is put in a voice soft and musical as a lute.
"No-'m, unless you have pre-empted it." "I—I have
not done anything to it," she says in a frightened way.
"Well—well nobody says you have. Sit down if you
want to," answers the youngster. The crimson
deepens on her face as she timidly drops into one
corner of the seat, giving a look of grateful acknow-
ledgement to the boy who had been so kind as not to
contest her right to a small part of the space that she
has paid full price for. Whatever that little woman
may do in other things, I do not think she will be a
success as a traveller.

But here we are at another station, and a number
go out. Among them is the big man who occupied
the two seats. Now let us watch those who come in.
Ah! Yes, there he is; I have been expecting him for
some time, and here he is at last. I mean the "swell."
See with what self-importance he strides up the aisle.
He is looking for a chance for two seats, facing each
other, so that he can sit himself down in one of them
and throw his morocco-covered feet on the cushion of
the other.

Now he is seated, take a close look at him. He is
a strange compound. It would be difficult to de-
termine whether a feeling of contempt for ordinary
humanity, a desire to display his mock jewellery, an

inordinate love for self, or the hope that a good dinner is awaiting him at home, is just now predominating in that man's thoughts and feelings.

He is of a class who are not of much use in the world's activities, and yet he would be missed if he were gone. He furnishes a complete contrast with the modest little woman mentioned above. He is convenient to tailors, shoemakers and jewellers to exhibit their wares upon, and in him we can see how much puffing up humanity can bear without an explosion.

But here comes another subject for our gallery of pictures representing "life on the rail." See that good-sized, elderly lady just coming into the car. That spruce-looking young man who carries her valise is likely her son, and he appreciates the relation. If I am not mistaken, we have here a family premier, a home secretary and finance minister all in one. She is just the kind of woman that a man could trust to manage his home, guard his interest, rule his household and handle his money—such a one as any man might be proud to call his wife, and one that any child ought to be glad to own for a mother. But we must not dwell too long in this lady's company, however pleasant it might be to do so.

We find in the other end of the car another woman who is sufficiently characteristic to be worthy of a little attention. See that big, old, grey-haired lady sitting in the corner of the car just opposite the stove. She is a vain old dame, or I am no judge. Notice how she has her hair frizzed and banged. Look at the gay colours on her costly headgear. See how she fairly glitters with cheap decorations of various kinds. She is whimsical, too, as well as vain, and fastidious as well as whimsical. And if we may judge by the scowl that is sometimes on her brow, she has a bad temper and sharp tongue. We will not be much astray if we write "vixen" upon her forehead, and dismiss her as a second edition of "Mrs. Caudle," the renowned subject of the "Caudle Curtain Lectures" that were on the market some years ago.

We will get one more picture illustrating "life on the rail" and then turn to some incidents in connection with the same theme. In selecting a subject for our last picture I find two claimants, and I hardly know which to take. There is that fidgety old man down near the door, and that blonde coquette sitting under the centre lamp and just now dividing her smiles among three young men who are playing around her like so many little satellites. On the whole I think the old man's claims are the strongest, and besides, he is not so often seen as the other, so that we had better take him while we have a chance. This little man differs in many ways from the one we met with a while ago. That one was comparatively young ; this one is old. That one had confidence in himself, and was satisfied with things generally. This one has no confidence in anybody, and is not satisfied with anything. He is continually fidgeting about something or other. The train is going too slow and will be behind time for the stage, or it is going too fast and will be at the next station before the track is cleared for it, or it will jump off the rails and run down an embankment and do nobody knows what. And so this little man goes on all the time. But here is the station and we are freed from the little annoyance of the fidgety old man. He went out of the car expressing the opinion that the screeching of the engines, the ringing of bells, the rattling of the train and hard-heartedness of the officials, all taken together, make life on the rail so very uncomfortable that it is but little better than martyrdom, especially to nervous old men and women.

INCIDENTS OF TRAVEL.

I was once going on the evening train from Palmerston to Kincardine. At the Listowel station a wedding party came aboard. They were going to Ethel. They were mostly young people, but they made things in general pretty lively while we were favoured with their company. Two of the young men seemed to act as sort of scapegoats for the crowd, as everything was charged to them. One of the young women seemed to enjoy a monopoly of the fun, as a word or two from her would start the giggle and "ha ha" among her companions at any time she chose to utter it.

The spirit of song, too, appeared to have boarded the train with them. The whole distance was whiled away by them either in singing or laughing at the jokes of the lady spoken of. When the train stopped at the station and they got off, I could not help serious thoughts and feelings, and I did offer a silent prayer for them, that the burdens of life might sit lightly upon their shoulders, that the cares and anxieties of life might not weigh too heavily upon their hearts,

and that the snares and pitfalls along the path of life
might never entangle their feet or do them harm.

A Cranky Old Woman.

The train from Toronto to Hamilton was about
ready to start, when a fine-looking young couple came
in, and took a seat near the end of the car, and only
two seats from where I was sitting. I soon decided
in my own mind that they were emigrants, that they
were English, and that they belonged to the working-
classes. Just then an old woman with a basket on
her arm came in and sat on the wood-box, the car
being crowded. It was not long before she drew the
young woman into answering questions about herself
and husband. Where I sat I could not help hearing
what was passing between them. I soon learned that
the man was a farm labourer and the woman had
been a domestic servant; that they had been married
one day, and had started for this country the next;
that they had left all their relatives behind them;
that they expected to find an old acquaintance in
Hamilton; that they had come here to make a home
for themselves, and that the woman was a good deal
lonesome and a little homesick.

When the old body had got all the information she
could, she said to the young woman, "O! I am so
sorry that you have come to this country. I am from
Scotland, and I am going back there just as soon as I
can get money enough to take me there. This is a
bad country to live in, and it is almost out of the
question for old country people to live here at all,

because the natives are such rogues and liars that you cannot trust them without being cheated, nor believe them without being deceived."

The other woman by this time was crying, and nearly broken-hearted. Then I spoke to her and said,

"My good woman, you must not believe what that old lady is telling you. I have been in this country a great deal longer than she has, and I know what she is saying is not true. There are sharpers here the same as there are in all countries; but the great mass of the people, both natives and others, are the very reverse of what she represents them to be.

"I could give you the names of hundreds of families who came from the old country as you have done, and they are comfortable, and contented and happy in good homes of their own. Health, industry, sobriety and economy under the Divine guidance are sure to bring success in this land."

She looked up and said, " We have health, industry, sobriety and confidence in God; we must learn economy by practice."

I said to her, "Go ahead with a clear conscience and a resolute will, and may the Lord bless you, and guide you in the way to competence."

The old woman was just levelling her artillery at me, when an old man in a seat behind me called out to me, "I say, stranger, I move that the daft auld body be sent to bedlam, for she does na ken what she is crackin' about. Auld Scotland haes nae need o' the

likes o' her. She is ower fond o' the barley bree to be
o' ony use in ony land."

The old lady subsided and the young one dried her
tears.

A Medley of Song.

One evening I was on a train from Guelph to
Palmerston. The train went very slow and it was
long behind time. The night was very dark. There
was a good deal of jerking and jolting as though the
engine was trying to play "balky-horse." It would
stop, and then start with a sudden spring that made
everything jar. Many of the passengers became very
restless, and some of them impatient. One gentleman
was pointed out to me as Senator Plumb, who had an
engagement to deliver a political speech in some one
of the villages ahead of us. He seemed to accept the
situation as cheerfully as a man who had lots of poetry
in his composition could be expected to do.

One lady attracted some attention by her lamenta-
tions about the baby that she knew was crying for her
at home. An old couple who were on their way
to visit the family of a married daughter, became
quite uneasy at last when they found they could not
reach their destination before bed-time.

Just as everybody began to feel discontented a
couple of young men in one end of the car started to
sing,—

> " We won't go home till morning,
> Till daylight does appear."

The effect seemed to be almost magical.   In a moment some boys in the other end of the car commenced at the top of their voices to sing,

"There's one more river to cross."

They would say at every second verse,

"One more station to pass,"

and then laugh over their success in making the change.

Two young ladies near the middle of the car began to sing, in a clear, sweet tone the

"Sweet by and bye."

The mingling of the voices, and the blending of the different tunes, along with the great diversity of sentiment, made the performance one of more than ordinary attractiveness.   As the train drove into the station at the end of the trip, I could not help wishing that on the morning of the resurrection, and after the last river is crossed, these singers may all find a home in "the sweet by and bye."

CHAPTER XVII.

CHANGE AND PROGRESS.

WHEN we compare the present with the past, we see that wonderful changes have been effected in this country during the term of one lifetime. Some of these changes imply real progress, and some of them, perhaps do not. We must not forget that there may be much change, with but little progress.

I can well remember when things in this country were very different from what they are at the present time. The condition of the country, the state of society, the position of education, and the influence of the churches have all assumed widely different aspects since the days of my boyhood. Then the country was very largely in an unreclaimed state. Much of the soil was still covered with primeval forests. Society was honest and industrious, but unpolished. Education was in a crude and inefficient condition, the schools being the merest apologies for institutions of learning as compared with our present school system. The Church was less deficient in zeal than it was in means and appliances.

THINGS HAVE CHANGED.

The yelping of the Indian dog, and the war-whoop of his master have died away in the distance, and in their stead is heard the hum of the threshing-machine, the rattle of the railway train, the whistle of the steam engine, and the ringing of the school-bells. The tall forest trees have given place to the orchard trees. The log hut or slab shanty has been succeeded by the more elegant frame or brick, or stone dwelling. The cow-path has grown into a turnpike. The clanking of the logging chain has been exchanged for the tinkling of sleigh-bells, and the old ox-cart has its successor in the fine carriage.

Society has changed, too, as much as the country has improved. The people of the past generation had very different ideas respecting many things from what we have. And their surroundings in early life differed from those of the youth of the present day ; but they made the best use of the few advantages they had. To say that they were weaker than their descendants, either mentally or physically, would be to say what is the very reverse of what is true. To admit, however, that for want of proper training and culture, they were less able to show what was in them, than their grandchildren are, is only granting what cannot be disputed. But if some of those sturdy men who cleared up the land in our front townships, could visit the scenes of their old-time toils, and see some of their great-grandsons trying to handle an axe or a hand-pry, they would be as much amused as we would be to see a boy start off to mill, with a bag thrown over a horse's back, having a bushel of wheat in one end of it, and a big stone in the other end to make it balance.

If some of the old dames who helped to make the homes of our country, and who were so handy with the wheel and distaff, the rolling-pin, and the knitting-needles, could revisit the room-of-all-work, where her house-wifely skill won its former triumphs, and catch some of her great-granddaughters trying to darn little Bessie's hose, or to patch Willie's coat, she would be likely to take the work into her own hands, and say, "Law sakes, child, what do you know about mending children's fixings? Let me do this, and you go and pound some kind of tune, like "Auld Lang Syne,' or 'Bonnie Over the Rhine,' out of the pianner."

Let it be understood that I am presenting the extremes. Some of the grandmas were as much at home in the parlour as they were in the kitchen. And some of the granddaughters are as much at home in the kitchen as they are in the parlour. These old people did their work, and did it well according to their opportunities and the means at their disposal. Well will it be for us, who have inherited the fruits of their honest toil, if we are as true and faithful in our day and generation as they were in theirs.

But there have been great changes, too, in educational matters during the last fifty years. In fact, the schools at the time of my boyhood were very rudimental in their modes of instruction, and extremely limited in the range of subjects taught in them. Very many of the teachers of those days attempted nothing more than the fundamental branches of common school education. And a man that could read pretty well and do ordinary sums in arithmetic, as well as write a fair hand and spell most of the words correctly, was looked upon at that time as being a fair scholar.

But how different it is now, when our boys and girls are ready for the high school at twelve or thirteen. At sixteen they are fit for college, and many of them are graduates at twenty-one or two.

But, it may be asked, is our system, with all its excellences, the best that could be adopted ? Is there not too much drawing the youth of our country away from the common walks of life, and towards the colleges and the professions ? Will not the various industries and interests of the country be made to suffer by so many of the young being encouraged in the belief that toil is degrading, and that a labouring man is inferior to a professional man ?

Would it not be better to make our schools to so far harmonize with the real and actual wants of the people, as to be their educator in the ordinary affairs of everyday life, instead of absorbing so much of the time of thousands of children on subjects that are of little or no use to them after they leave the common school ? Better to train the children to be active workers in the great national hive, than to merely fit them to fastidiously sip the honey that other toilers have gathered.

The professions are already overcrowded, and every year adds to the difficulty. It has been truly said, in regard to these professions, " There is plenty of room at the top." But it is also true, that the ascent is so steep, and the way so full of anxious aspirants, that very few have the ability and energy to rush up the steep acclivity, press through the motley gathering that intercepts his way, and reach the top. Are there not men in the professions who rank as third or fourth class there, who would have made first-class farmers and mechanics? I do not mean by this that farmers and mechanics need less brain, or less force of character, than the doctor, or lawyer, or clergyman. But a different combination of faculties is all that makes a successful man in one calling out of an individual who would be a complete failure in another.

But I am told that a classical education does not disqualify a man for work. That may be true. But does it qualify him for work in the ordinary affairs of life? I am now bordering on to seventy years of age, and I have never seen a B.A., or an M.D., or lawyer, comfortably and contentedly or successfully shoving the plane or holding the plough. The time that should have been spent in learning how to do these things was given to other things that are of but little practical benefit in these callings. True, there are some highly educated women who are good housekeepers; but they can adapt themselves to surrounding circumstances better and more readily than men can do.

Our school system seems to take it for granted that

23

every child is a universal genius; and it seems to over-look the fact that success in one thing does not guarantee success in everything. The system, as yet, is not sufficiently elastic to adjust itself to the various demands of the great variety of minds, for the cultivation and development of which it ought to provide.

In the churches, too, we find change and progress. Not that they are more earnest and zealous. Not that they have more of love for God and humanity. Not that the members are more spiritual, nor that the services are more punctually attended. In none of these things can the churches of to-day claim to be much in advance of what they were half a century ago. The difference is found in clearer conceptions of the demands of the world upon the Church, in a fuller recognition of the claims of missionary effort, in a stronger feeling of unity among Christians, in a closer application of Bible precepts to the practices of every-day life, in a keener sense of individual obligation, and in embracing a wider range of subjects, and in laying broader plans for carrying out the Divine injunction to Christianize the world.

The results of these changes are found in the great increase in the contributions to the various institutions of the Church, in the advancements of the cause of temperance, and in the expansion of missionary operations.

There have also been great changes in the habits and methods of domestic life. Machinery now does most of the heavy work at which our fathers found their hardest toil. Both out door and in the house the

burden of life's toils is made light by the substitution
of the mechanical contrivances for the exercise of bone
and muscle. Men do not now need the napkin to wipe
the sweat from the brow, so much as they need the oil-
can to grease the machinery. Everywhere is heard the
hum of whirling wheels and revolving pulleys. From
the kitchen, where the cook handles the egg-beater,
to the barnyard, where the men drive the steam-
thresher, the heaviest work is done by some sort of an
unconscious servant in the shape of a machine.

An Old Homestead.

Not many months ago I visited an old homestead.
In a field near the house were a number of men working at wheat harvesting. The present owner was
sitting quite comfortably on the seat of one of those
machines called a harvester, driving a fine horse team
around the field, cutting as good a crop of fall wheat
as any man could expect to reap. The men were
binding and "shocking up" what the machine cut
down. There were four men at one dollar and seventy-
five cents a day, which, with the wages of the teamster
and horses, along with the use of the harvester, I
estimated at twelve dollars a day. They expected to
cut ten acres that day. Now, that would be one
dollar and twenty cents an acre for harvesting. Allowing fifteen dollars for hauling into the barn and
threshing, and five dollars for contingencies, would bring
the outlay up to thirty-two dollars, after the wheat
was grown, to make it ready for market. There would
not be less than two hundred bushels, which, at eighty

cents per bushel, would be one hundred and sixty dollars for the field of wheat.

But while I was making these calculations it occurred to me that, long years ago, I saw other harvest hands going over the same piece of ground. The father of the present proprietor was swinging a grain cradle as but few men could do it. His oldest son and a neighbour were raking and binding. The field was very "stumpy" then. Fifteen bushels to the acre would be the highest yield. The wheat was hauled into the old log barn on a "woodshod" sled. It was trodden out on the floor with oxen, or threshed out with a "flail," and cleaned out of the chaff with an indescribable instrument called a "fan." What was not needed for bread and seed was carried with an ox team over twenty-five miles, and sold for seventy cents a bushel, and mostly store pay at that.

I knew that man for a number of years, and I never heard him complain of hard times. I never knew him to be without money in his pocket, nor without a slice of bread and butter for a hungry traveller, or an unfortunate neighbour. He and his thrifty wife practised that kind of domestic economy that gauges its wants by the possibilities of supply, and keeps its outlay within the limits of its income. And they had many neighbours who were like them in these things.

These are the kind of people who have left us the fruits of their honest toil. Let us, who have entered into their labours, follow more closely their example in needful industry and self-denial. Then there would be less complaining about hard times, which mostly come in on the line of our extravagances.

BACK COUNTRY TOWNS.

Before closing this chapter, I wish to say a few words about the lively towns that have sprung up in the territory where my ministerial life has been passed.

When I commenced my itinerant life, in 1856, Orangeville was a small village, so was Meaford, and Owen Sound, and Kincardine. Now they are towns. Next came up the villages of Mount Forest, Listowel, and Walkerton. These are all towns now. Later still came Wingham, Shelburne, and Palmerston. I travelled over the sites of these long before they were thought of as places for towns. Durham, Paisley, Port Elgin, Arthur, Fergus, Elora, Teeswater, Thornbury, Tiverton, Priceville, Chatsworth, Flesherton, Eugenia, Southampton, Tara, Hanover, Clifford, Harriston, Chesley, Mildmay, Bervie, Ripley, Singhampton, Heathcote, Kimberley, Ethel, Bluevale, Brussels, and last, but not least, Clarkesburgh. These are all places of more or less importance, and some of them are rapidly growing into the dimensions of towns.

There are two or three other subjects that I intended to notice; but the space at my disposal is filled up.

CONCLUSION.

I always feel a sort of sadness come over me when I am parting with friends. So now, kind readers, I experience regretful emotions at taking leave of you. With many of you I am personally acquainted. I have sat at your tables, I have slept in your beds, I have warmed myself at your firesides and in many ways I have shared your hospitalities.

For some of you I visited your sick, buried your dead, baptized your children, and married your sons or daughters.

With some of you I have prayed and wept, as you knelt in humble penitence at the feet of the Crucified One; and when you found the joys of salvation I rejoiced with you.

With others of you I have not the pleasure of an acquaintance; but I trust that you are not unfriendly either to myself or my little book.

I have given you facts in as pleasing a manner as I could, without extravagant colouring. I have tried to tell you the truth in describing these experiences. In doing this, I have used the language of the home circle as it is spoken by the working people of our own country.

If I have succeeded in meeting your expectations, I shall rejoice; but if I have failed to do so, I shall regret very much that my ability in this has not equalled my desire and intention. The disappointment will be more keenly felt by the writer than it can be by the reader.

And now, wishing every one of my readers a prosperous and contented life, and a home at last in the bright beyond, I must reluctantly say good-bye.